CRANBERRY QUEEN

CRANBERRY QUEEN

Kathleen DeMarco

talk miramax books

NEW YORK

For my mother,
Lucy Falciani DeMarco

CRANBERRY QUEEN

ONE

Today

He—the Monster—is now dating someone whose name begins with "L."
I think her name is Lola or maybe, possibly Lolita. (Tiptoeing off the
tongue. How lovely. Lovely Lola Lolita.) The Monster, everyone says,
is much better now. He doesn't drink (I'm not around) and he doesn't
smoke (I'm not around) and he doesn't stay out all night and ring
"L's" doorbell at four thirty in the morning (drunk and smoky). He's
older, wiser, and unwilling to go backward into that great abyss that
reads me.

But I'm better now too. (It's taken three years, three months, and five
days to recover from "I didn't sleep here last night," which really meant
"I didn't sleep at my apartment last night because I picked someone up
from a Knicks game with my friend Freddy since, frankly, I didn't want
to be with you anymore and couldn't figure out a way to tell you.") But I
am a much improved, much more emotionally mature, much more serene
person now. (This according to Mom, Dad, therapist Barbara, friends

1

Wiley and Betsy, brother-who's-bored-with-this Ben, boss Darius, and colleagues Peter and Serena.)

I work for (drumroll) *that* Internet company. I can't tell you much more than this because it would go against Darius's strict confidentiality policies. I could be killed or, worse, sent to obedience school for intransigent dot-com employees who don't understand *how everyone in the world is waiting to destroy us.*

(Okay. I just checked the manual. I am allowed to say I work in marketing and that I work with very bright and very able young men and women. Our job is to convince the rest of the world that we are, and our company is, the brightest and ablest. Because we are one of the few companies to actually earn a profit, people believe us, making my division seem very effective.)

It is a very good company. I have the kind of stock options people dream about, and my 401(k) is bursting with money (or so they tell me). My parents are healthy, my brother is getting married, and my best friend, Wiley, is getting engaged. The astrological planets are all in alignment, courtesy of my Aunt Margaret, who, besides being an astrologer, is a psychic, a chef, and one of those people who can predict any future occurrence in your life, even, say, the day you'll cross a crooked bridge or the night you'll meet the man of your dreams, and you will believe her wholeheartedly, because that's how much you trust her.

According to Aunt Margaret, I'm set to have the best three years of my life.

This is especially fortuitous, because I have the biggest day of my life tomorrow. Tomorrow, I go to a wedding where the Monster will be. With L. And I have summoned up all of my astrological and emotional and physical strength to attend this wedding of my incourteous friends, Maria and Michael, who have invited the Monster, feeling it better to propel me headfirst into Engaging in Life, Part Two, by Getting Rid of the Past. (People do this because they think it is helpful. It's not about you, they say. And it never was, they continue. Frankly, they say, this behavior of yours is not becoming. It is in utter contrast to you, the Cybermarketer of the Tri-State Region. You are a beautiful and smart and successful woman, and you must must must get over this addiction. "It's like *heroin!*" shrieks Maria. "Lick your wounds and move on!" admonishes Michael.)

Tomorrow, I will embody what it means to be aging gracefully. I will be the Perfect Single Guest. I will be the Katharine Hepburn (at thirty-three, not eighty) of the wedding. I am going alone. And I am not allowing myself *one second* of self-deprecation. Not one second. Affirmations and visuals. I am Elizabeth Bennett in *Pride and Prejudice*. I am Bette Davis in *All About Eve*. I am anyone, anyone at all, but me, Diana Moore, brown of hair, nine of shoe, and wide of thigh.

Tomorrow

I am home. Home home, in Princeton, New Jersey, not New York, New York.

There's been an accident. A truck, a big huge Mack truck the size of a Trump building (but gray, not gold), hiding cases and cases of brown-bottled beer, has made a wrong move on a small road in the southern part of New Jersey, Route 206. Route 206 has only two lanes, which makes no sense in this overpopulated state, but presumably someone in power believes that restricting the road to only two lanes forestalls the advent of a further population explosion.

Presumably these same people have not realized that a two-lane system clogs cars, frustrates drivers, and imperils a family of three (Mom, Dad, Ben) driving to a dinner deep in Southern New Jersey. These same people have not seen any logic to expanding a roadway so that a bleary, sweaty, fleshy man, vodka steaming from his pores, angry at the Range Rover sputtering in front of him, angry that the man with the ponytail driving the

4

Range Rover *has* a Range Rover, angry at himself for not picking up Willy, his eleven-year-old son, from his mother's today because he went to the bar Fredo's instead, angry angry angry—so fuck it, fuck it all, he thought, I'm going to fucking pass this fucking asswipe Range Rover asshole, I don't care *who's* coming down the other side, I don't care if the President and his fucking Secret Service guys are barreling down this shitty road, fuck it all, I have the bigger car, I don't need a Range Rover, I have this, my TRUCK, my beautiful big motherfucking TRUCK, and goddamn it, what was up with the blonde at the bar?

My mother. My father. My brother. The truck driver is fine, scarred on his forehead, repentant (of course), his anger supplanted by dread and nerves. He wishes (while in his sister's Plymouth Horizon, as they drive from the police station later that night) that *he* were the dead one, because he's sure that the survivors of the family whom he hit are going to sue him for millions, sue the beer distributor for millions, and he might as well shoot himself in the head; fuck it, he wishes he were the one who got hit by someone drunk. He turns to the backseat and sees an empty beer bottle. He sees himself cracking it against his head, the bottle breaking in his hand, brown glass mixing with flesh and dark blood. Later, after he's in his bed, he remembers this straggling beer bottle and wonders why he didn't do just that.

And now I'm at home. Aunt Margaret and a cousin we call Uncle John are there, as are family friends and priests and doctors and people I don't know, bustling around in the kitchen. They leave me alone, which is good, I think, because I don't know what I'm supposed to do. But maybe it is bad. Maybe it is all going to fall apart. I think about yesterday, when I said that today, which was then tomorrow, would be the biggest day of my life. The wedding of Michael and Maria must be occurring right this second. Or maybe seconds ago. They stood and got married. Monster and L were there. Other friends. Parents. Dancing, drinking, and filet and cake and bright flowers against white tablecloths. Mom had called me today before I left, and had said, "You're *you*. You're a wonderful person, a *good* person. Come off it, Diana. You're still pretty. You're *so* pretty. Have patience, Diana. I know it's hard." My eyes had grown wet, and I had looked up toward a light while I replied (embarrassed at my need for self-validation), "I'll be okay." "Love you, Diana." "Love you, Mom." Click.

That was going to be the biggest day of my life.

"Diana, sweetheart, the doctor's here. He thinks you should maybe take something, a pill or something; it'll help you sleep."

I stand, smile, no tears yet for me, the heretofore ceaseless crying machine. I take the pills from Doctor Metrovich, our family's doctor since I was a child.

"This'll help, eh, child, this'll help. Here's a couple." He hands over the tablets. I swallow them, no water. He looks at me, a ruddy face, deep wrinkles etched in red skin, black hair slicked back, thick aviator glasses with a brown tint, and kind, very kind dark eyes, all composed in an expression of selfless sympathy.

"You—you'll . . ." He stops, words failing him, and instead grabs me by the arm with very strong fingers and pulls me close. A hug that I feel, I feel completely. I concentrate on the strength of his fingers, the deep pull of the flesh from his wrist to his elbow, his shirt sleeve, his smell, everything. This is living, I think. This is the touch of the living. Everything I know is now changed. The people are here, they are moving, the air is the same, it is exactly the same, but everything has changed; everything from this moment on has changed irrevocably, and I know that my "recovery"—if any, and right now that is very doubtful— my *recovery* will take mountains of days and months and years; it will take so long that already I feel hopelessness deadening my senses, as if a lumbering giant moving under the earth has shot his massive arm through the ground and has hurled me up up up in the air, me as weightless and flimsy as a piece of silver tinsel, and I am lost forever, and I don't even care.

TWO

The Day Before the Funerals

My brother's fiancée, Laura, smashes cake pans and measuring cups together. No one does anything about it; Laura's older sister, Dawn, stands with me, in the kitchen, watching as Laura bangs and bangs the baking instruments against one another. The clanging is terrific and awful, entirely appropriate, one half of my mind thinks; if only I were to feel a thing, I'd feel battered and whisked and cooked. Laura's curly red hair swings in the back as she throws more and more utensils together. "We talked about a house." "I've got to get to work." "We bought Springsteen tickets, we have plans to go to Seattle and then to New York; we *just bought the tickets!*" Everything is muddled, and then everything is silent. Dawn looks at me, almost as if she wants me to calm Laura and ease Laura's pain, but of course, then she remembers that I am the quintessential victim, the sudden orphan, the beloved (if spoiled, Dawn thinks), attractive (if getting older, Dawn thinks), self-obsessed (she lives in New York in the *Village,* Dawn thinks) woman who has lost her entire immediate family. Pity like a dishrag, I feel; pity she extends, like using a dirty dishrag to dry yet again dirty plates, and I just stand there, in my kitchen, wishing Laura would bang some pans again.

It is this acceptance of a state of utter passivity that befuddles me. One week ago, I was passive in life, and everyone tacitly accepted it but loathed me for it. Now I am supposed to do nothing, and everyone thinks it's fine, appropriate, and anything else would be strange.

Strange, I think, is your parents and your brother dead. Strange is being in their home, listening for my father to reach the kitchen chair slightly panting, pull it far back, and sit with *Barron's* in front of him, mentally calculating his stock riches. It was astonishing my entire life, watching him do numbers in his head. Like Dustin Hoffman in *Rain Man* he was, from his earliest childhood. His father, my grandfather, would make him stand on a porch when he was about five, in front of his friends. "Six hundred thirty divided by twenty-seven." "Twenty-three point three three," said my dad, and the men would harumph and smoke cigars and then tease my dad for being so smart. My grandfather would tell him to go inside and eat a cookie; he had earned it.

I have no ability with numbers. My brother had inherited that trait, although he hadn't used it. My brother, Ben, could do anything, but mostly he could make people laugh. Peter Pan even at thirty-six, he was the kind of person of whom six hundred different people would claim, "He's my best friend in the whole world." His willingness to tease and be teased, his ability to be warm and embracing of even the most insipid people (I think of his next-door neighbor Monica) was extraordinary. I don't have that trait, either; when confronted with horribly stupid people—"aggressively stupid," I tell my friends—I am terse and mean and throw the fact that they are slow and moronic into their faces like gravel. Ben and Laura had met fairly recently, and he had told me during a recent trip to New York that he had never thought, ever, that at thirty-six he could fall so hard.

Laura finally stops clanging the pots. I have done nothing but stand there in the kitchen. Dawn has stopped attempting to silence her sibling and has instead gone outside to tsk-tsk with the neighbors. Laura turns and looks at me.

"We had Springsteen tickets." I nod.

"I was supposed to be at a wedding," I say. Nothing means anything; the words fall and disappear, like snow on a black highway.

"I don't know what to do," she says. My eyes open wider. She is beautiful, Laura, in her grief—she is beautiful without her grief, too, which obviously would be a better situation for her, but I think how much Ben would fall even more in love with her if he were here as he should be.

Later, as I "take a spin"—my dad's language for driving around the neighborhood—I look at the streets where I grew up, where I rode my bike home from swim-team practice, where I ran around the football field for field-hockey practice, where I went to church with my mother, where I went to elementary school and middle school. I force myself to think of my mother, and I hear her say "I'll be pushing up daisies" as I think of long car rides, just the two of us, heading to visit one of her four brothers. This was my favorite time with her, although I remember it only in the abstract (which is better, I think), since instead I am given, like the best steaming breakfast brought to me on a platter, a sense of belonging, belonging to someone, my mother, my mother, Rose Pallitta Moore, my mother with whom I spoke almost every day, my mother "I'm sensitive too!" "Woowhee, he's a good-looking man," "My little girl, my little girl," "You just go in there and say in no uncertain terms you're doing that job!" "Be patient, Diana, be patient," "Turn to God," and "I love you, Diana, it'll all be all right."

My mother, who is dead.

The Morning of the Funerals

It's summer, June, the month of weddings and, for me, the month of funerals. I am a celebrity, kind of, a celebrity turned inside out. No one wants to talk to me—or rather, no one knows what to say to me, but they all want to see me, touch me; I am the deformed creature at the zoo. "How's she doing?" I hear, and "Who's staying with her?" and "Dammit, we're all just tiptoeing around her when what she needs is someone to talk to her and ask her what she wants!" (This from Aunt Margaret, who in a second, I know, will be in here bringing me tea.)

I am in the living room, an elegant place, tasteful furniture and well-placed books, clean windows looking out onto a landscaped lawn (my mother had a knack for choosing colors and cultivating plants, a genetic trait, she claimed, owing to her Italian ancestry; only last year she had spent thousands of dollars installing an irrigation system with subtle evening lights highlighting our home). A portrait of my father hangs over the fireplace; a stunning portrait of my mother, in her wedding gown, adorns a side wall ("It hung in Bachrach's for years!" she'd tell people, only halfway embarrassed). Pictures of my brother and me, and my brother and Laura, and a picture of me with the Monster cut out displayed around the room. Food is abundant; everyone brings something home-cooked or store-bought that seems home-cooked, and even though appetite is something I don't recognize as a component in my body, I will have enough food (if I stay here) for the next five years. I want to laugh, I realize, because no one is coming in here to talk to me—they're just milling about outside the room, as if I were in a coma.

Maybe I am in a coma.

Maybe it's me who isn't talking or moving. I cry at night, I cry looking at the ceiling, at the overhead lights, I cry in the morning, in the shower, I cry looking into the refrigerator and getting into my bed. I cry myself awake in the middle of the night, and I cry and cry alone in my old bedroom, so that it seems like the insides of my stomach are touching, that I am one great vise clamp, closed tight. I don't know why in front of people I have been so seemingly composed. I don't want to eat, and I don't want to talk, and I don't want to cry anymore, but it is truly the one response I understand, the one I cling to. Therapists have been called; my therapist, Barbara, rings every night. But what is there to say, to do? Unless I too get abruptly killed, or I abruptly kill myself, I am destined to be here for the rest of my time on earth without the people closest to me, the people with whom I had a perfect intimacy, a lifetime of threads sewn into me and into them, torn apart and gone.

"Diana?" I turn. It is my best friend, Wiley. She is blond with clear green eyes, willowy and strong.

"Hey," I say. "Anything new?" I grin; it's a stupid thing to say, but I want to smile at her and act like this is all a joke.

"Story has it that you're onstage today," she begins, the wry tone of her voice in contrast to the gravity on her pale face. "Thought you might benefit from my theatrical training. Deep breaths, lots of deep breaths, and lots of wine. Cigarettes, too, for me, but I'm thinking that may not be the answer—"

"A coughing fit on the altar, probably not a good thing. But you know, I could do it. It'll be the one time in my life no one will say anything. You know what? Give me a cigarette. Right now. I'm going to start. I *want* lung cancer."

"Yeah, me too." She laughs with me. "You know, why stop there? Lung cancer takes too long. How 'bout finding some of that infected meat from England? Mad-cow disease? You'll be gone quick—it'll eat through your brain in no time."

"Pretty. Me on the altar smoking, or me with my brain devoured." I pause and then say something I know will provoke Wiley. "How sad. My mom and dad want me on an altar, and they have to go get killed for me to get there."

Wiley winces. No wonder I have no boyfriend; I say awful things. I think awful things. I'm trying for that gallows humor, and instead I'm churlish and unfunny.

"Sorry," I say. "I can bypass cigarettes and go straight for heroin."

"*That* I can help you with." Then she reaches out and takes my hand, dry and flaking, and I think of my mom yet again ("Did you see that cream I left out for you? The one by the sink? Take it with you—you've got to put on cream every night, Diana; it doesn't have to be expensive. Ann Talese uses Vaseline. You have to stop wasting money").

"Diana." Wiley interrupts my train of thought. "You don't have to speak today unless you want to. Everyone would understand."

I listen, knowing this was coming. "Yeah, I got it," I say. Of course I have to speak. Otherwise I'm failing even at this. Failing at Funerals, see it in your Life Syllabus under Sudden Orphan Syndrome. I stop and stare off through the living-room window. As usual, I am taking this to an extreme. I can feel it climbing over me, the gushing, limitless sensibility of a small child. Oversensitive, melodramatic—I yearn to be one of those adults who are always composed, who can accept this inconceivable tragedy and still remain reserved and gracious. I bet British people could do this; I bet they could be courteous and appropriate. "Oh, Aunt Beatrix," British Diana would say, even though I have no Aunt Beatrix; "So good of you to come, really. What's that? Oh, no, I'll be fine, really, you are so kind."

Instead I see American Diana, spitting out words like watermelon seeds. "My parents and brother died in a car crash," I'll say. "A drunk driver." Oh oh, my inquisitioners will stammer, I'm so sorry.

The Funerals

The church is covered, practically wallpapered, with flowers. People stream down the aisles, down the pews. I notice that not everyone is wearing dark clothes. Nor am I, which is ironic, given that almost every day in New York I wear black. I'm grateful for the kids—my cousin Jennifer's little children, Mairead and Elise; my mother's cleaning woman's three children, Matthew, Patrick, and Lisa. With the children, the bright flowers, the church's white walls, and the sporadic flashes of colorful clothing, and with all the people swarming in, around the caskets, shaking my hand, kissing my cheek, looking for meaning in my eyes when I'm just so tired and so transplanted and so deeply angry to be here at all—I'm furious, furious that this church is so shockingly, unacceptably alive.

I stand at the altar. I look out, the sea of people in front, expectant. What will she say, the Orphan? I take a breath. "Well, here I am on this altar at last, and my parents aren't here to see it. Figures," I begin feebly, and I can see at once that the audience is uncomfortable. I see everyone I know, and I see the boxes, the caskets, the flowers, and I have to speak.

"I can't say I had the best family in the world, although I think I did, but I haven't had another one, so I can't compare. As many of you may know, I'm a fan of facts, of reality." This isn't true; I lie all the time, but in some ways, my lies come from this same thirst for grounded reality. What surprises me more is that I sound so clear, so normal. Am I at a wedding or at a funeral for three people? I continue. "So I can't say things I don't know for sure to be true. That means, however, I can say my father was brilliant; that my brother was charismatic and my mother was ferociously loving." I pause. "*Was.* How did that happen? How has this all happened?" Careful, Diana, don't go ad-libbing; you know what you're going to say. But my mouth opens, and more words fly out. "I'm glad you're all here—except for you, Winston McHugh, because I haven't forgotten you saying you wouldn't go to the prom with me." Laughs, finally, but I should be talking about *them,* not *me.* "I'm glad you're here, but I wish you weren't. I wish you were back at your homes and that you, Ann, were planning to see my mom for coffee at six a.m. tomorrow, way before my dad wakes up, and I wish that you, Stephanie, could yell at my dad tomorrow afternoon for not finishing his zoning resolutions earlier, and I wish so much, Laura, that you and Ben were in the car, headed to Springsteen tonight. I can't encapsulate a life, three lives, up here. I can't tie up their spirits inside of me, either, even though that's the poetic thing to say. My mother and father, my brother, they're all I *have*—they're everything—and I hate the man who killed them; and I know that's wrong to say here on the altar, in front of God and you all, but you have to know what I'm feeling, that I don't know what to do with all of you, and I don't know how not to call home and talk to my mother. I don't know how to do that, and if I could kill, if I could kill the driver of that truck, and he would live only so that I could kill him again and again and again, that may help, it may help, it may . . ."

Silence, no laughter. I have gone crazy. No one will fault me for it. I can't even remember what I was just saying. I look away from the church pews filled with people to the back of the church. A handsome older man stands alone against the wall, a full head of dark hair, a dark suit. He nods at me. I don't recognize him.

"I'm sorry. Thank you for coming, and thank you all for helping me. My mother would be very grateful." I'm shaking. I grab one wrist with the other hand to stop the pulses. I sit down by myself, head down; I don't want to look at anyone. More people talk, music plays, and finally, the funeral procession. I don't want to go to the cemetery. I want to go back to New York.

Twelve Days Later

This is the worst. Yesterday was the worst. I can't believe I'm still taking showers, that I'm still putting on deodorant. I can't believe my self goes through these motions, these rituals, and I have no history anymore, no antecedents, nothing.

And then I think, we're all alone, right. In the grand expanse of the universe, of time, we're all by ourselves, and our one life on earth is just part of the never ending ribbon of life, blah blah blah.

Winston McHugh told me after the funeral that he had never realized I had invited him to the prom. He's a landscape artist now, a gardener. He has no hair.

Thirty-one Days Later

Today, when I was out running, I saw a bird. A strange fat bird with a crimson head and a reptilian tail.

I cry while I'm running. It's early—I don't sleep, so I'm out, sportswatch on, running along Battery Park on the southwestern edge of Manhattan. It is late July, and even at around five a.m., the air is thick with New York smells, Hudson River smells, and the smell of low gray clouds retaining yesterday's heat. There are homeless people asleep on the benches, and they are covered in layers of green fatigues.

No one else is running. I reflect, tears falling yet again, that just a couple of months ago, pre-accident, in April or May, this kind of serene (if heavy) atmosphere would have been the perfect operatic backdrop to my oh-so-tragic rejection by the Monster. Today, of course, it is just a sky.

My parents. My parents! Never? Never . . . nev-er nev-er, this is my pace as I run, and I say this opposite-of-affirmation as I run: "Ac-cept-It-Di-a-na-Your-Pa-rents-Are-Dead." I think of myself as a boxing bag, a woman shrunk to the size of a soft football, who is hit and hit again by an evil but invisible force. I cannot take the hint; each time, I swing back to face my nemesis, and each time he batters me, harder and harder. "Do-Not-Be-A-Ba-by. Think-of-Ho-lo-caust. Think-of-Ar-men-i-a. Think-of-Peo-ple-Worse-Than-You." I haven't spoken to Laura since the week after the funeral. She had gone on a cooking spree after Ben's death; her town in Southern New Jersey was overflowing with apple turnovers, brisket of beef, and risotto with mushrooms.

I don't believe this is my life. I was a chosen child; I was pretty and resourceful and sweet. My mother and I talked on the telephone every day. And now it has been thirty-one days. I am alone. I am a-lone. I-Am-A-lone.

Some of my friends have been constant visitors; some have not measured up. Wiley calls every day; she and her boyfriend, Christopher, invite me over to their place for dinner two or three times a week. (When I was lamenting the loss of my ex-boyfriend, the Monster, I was not considered good dinner company. I was told it was unbecoming for me to be so disappointed. Everyone but me seemed to know that he would not meet my expectations. "You knew too," they'd tell me, "if you really thought about it." "Let's just say he was a car," Christopher would tell me, "the most amazing car in the world. But even if that were true—and it *isn't*—imagine that the car has no brakes. You can't have a car with no brakes!" And then, of course, the most infuriating response, actually a non-response. *"I'm sorry you feel that way."* To hear that feels the same as if you opened up the most elaborately wrapped Christmas present and discovered it was filled with mud. I want to tell people who have grieving friends, grieving for any reason—death, heartbreak, or just a bad day: Do not under any circumstances say, "I'm sorry you feel that way," unless you want them to be more unhappy than when they began the conversation.)

Still, no one tells me this anymore. Now I can do anything. I could slander my friends. I could have threesomes on Broadway. I could squander my inheritance on Ecstasy and a Porsche and a "look how cool and profound I am" trip to Thailand. No one would dare say a word; I am blameless.

My mother, on the other hand, would never permit me to act so indulgently, so frivolously. She would say, loudly, "What are you trying to prove?" and (in her favorite expletive) "Cheese and crackers! This isn't the way I raised you! You're a better person that that! Talk to God, Diana, or go get help. But you're not a shallow person, Diana; this isn't you."

My days are spent almost entirely in my apartment. Work gave me a leave of absence. But I am rich now; money is not a problem, nor should it be in my lifetime, provided I don't act foolishly. The phone rings, and I don't answer it. I lie in bed, sometimes in a retching position, wailing. Why do people let me cry like this? Why doesn't someone out there notice my situation and rush to soothe me? My mother would; if she saw me in such pain, she would make me poached eggs, she would make me feel better, she would tell me how worthwhile I am.

Yet to others, my tragedy is hovering halfway in their minds between "current" and "old." I am like the filing on the desk that hasn't found its way to the cabinet although it is already tucked away safely in a manila folder. So I run—my only activity, and one that I feel is ordained by the Greater Influence, by God Him- or Herself, especially when I spot, on three consecutive days, my Magic Bird.

I am the only person to see this bird. I have never seen anything like this animal before. It wobbles on small burnt-orange splayed feet, and its blazing red head and neck protrude from a bulbous green-brown body. But the true mark of distinction is its tail. A flat, reptilian plank matted down in bright green feathers. It is a special bird, it is a unique bird, it is only for me.

I am sure if another runner were to appear, God would whisk the bird from the park and place him in another part of the globe to be of some emotional succor to some other sobbing jogger. God is sending this bird to me to tell me that everything will be all right. Everything will become normal; my life will be normal, and the acrid, overwhelming pain of three deaths will close itself up, sealing the poison inside, safely away from the rest of me.

I do not stop crying, but I do keep an image in my mind's eye of the bird waddling around the green expanse, on the section of the park that affords a clear image of the Statue of Liberty.

Forty Days Later

It is August. I am invited to Martha's Vineyard for the week with Michael and Maria, one of many invitations I have refused this summer. I have returned to work; I pretend to everyone that I am okay, the Super Recoverer, and then, at night, I am infuriated that everyone believes me. Are they dumb? Or do they just not care? Are they just too wrapped up in their own lives to pay much attention to me, the neediest one of all?

At work today, I saw an older man, handsome with thick dark hair, walk swiftly through the office. I recognized him immediately as the man who stood in the back of the church at the funeral. A stalker, I am sure. I follow him. He darts down a different hallway. I assume the Charlie's Angel pose in the hall, my back flush against the wall, my hands clasped together, ready, with no gun but the strongest of intentions. The man emerges, does not see me, and keeps walking. Eventually he knocks and enters (at the same time—clearly a man of little patience) the office of my boss, Darius Peretti.

I sneak down (as much as one ever sneaks when she walks upright and turns down the hallway nearest her boss) and stand outside the tinted windows of Darius's office. Darius is a pompous little man who wears tight pants and fancy, shined shoes. He is alarmingly sweet when you first meet him, and his clear dulcet voice emphasizes this impression of docility, of integrity. But this is all a front; he is a liar, a manipulator, an unimaginative man. He would be horrified to discover that the high impression he has of himself is not shared by all those in his environs. If he heard the stories, he would be crushed.

I stand outside his door, waiting to pounce on the stranger, but am interrupted. Peter Culling, my colleague, walks by and raises an eyebrow.

"Don't tell me," he says, noting my arms in their "Fire Away!" position even as I slowly retract them to my side to be Normal Diana again. "I don't want to know. I'll tell them I never saw you."

"I'm, uh, practicing," I say, and wait for Peter's rejoinder. He's one of the wittier men on the staff—wire glasses, wiry, always wearing old corduroy sports jackets, even during August in New York City.

"I can just imagine," he rolls his tongue. He too is affected by my status as Tragic Professional, and he won't go as far as he would like—or I would like, for that matter. "Try taking five more, or five less, of whatever it is they're giving you." He begins to walk away. "Bye, *Sabrina.*"

I stand outside now, and more people pass. I realize I have to move, so I go back to my desk. Later on, when Darius comes by in his "Hello, Beautiful!" moment, I ask him who the gentleman was.

Darius gives me his best quizzical look and says, "Who? I didn't have any meetings today."

"You did," I say. "I saw him. A tall guy, thick hair, older . . ." Darius shakes his head.

"Nope. I'm telling you, nobody. Maybe you just—" I have no idea how he's going to finish. Maybe I just—invented a person? Maybe I just—take too many pain relievers? Maybe I shouldn't be walking down the hall when I should be figuring out the best print campaign for the new partnership agreement?

Darius turns around. In front of all the cubicles, he *claps*. I'm not kidding—he claps for our attention, just like someone saying, "Chop chop!" Serena Beach, my other teammate in marketing, looks at me. She weighs about six pounds, most of it in her head. I flinch. I don't usually like Serena, because she sucks up to Darius, but it's possible during my absence she's discovered his idiocy. Darius, meanwhile, is announcing that Bob Petkowski, his boss's boss's boss, is coming to the office next week.

"Everyone must dress appropriately, be appropriate, and you must seem busy; you must appear like you are working on the most passionate project of your life."

I check out Serena again, but she's staring at Darius. I guess I'm wrong about her.

Bob Petkowski can fire Darius if he wants. This is what we are not supposed to acknowledge. Instead we are to suffer under Darius as if he were our king and we his loyal subjects. From where I stand today, Darius's concerns seem comical, blustery. Not that I'm above this, but when your mom and dad and brother are dead, it does make you wonder about people like Darius—people who, as T.S. Eliot said, spend their days wriggling on the head of a pin—constantly worrying for the day when Bob Petkowski flicks him carelessly off his perch, as if Darius were no more significant than a dust mite.

The Day Bob Came to the Office

My lethargy is rife. I do nothing. (Diana Embellishment again. Actually I do two things. Three. I run. I eat. And I go to work. Anyway.) It still feels like an extended state of somnolence—possibly awake, possibly asleep, and none of it matters. The phone rings, the cell phone vibrates. My friends, the crows. I wait a day and then alert one of the people in the watchful group that I'm alive and haven't killed myself, and the crows go away. I take this to mean that none of them really cares. I'm an actor pretending to be grieved and strong, and even though I think I'm incredibly transparent, everyone goes along with it. "Wake up!" I admonish myself. "They care about you, but you're not their *family,* they haven't said you're more important to them than anyone else. They think you're terrific and had a horrible tragedy happen to you, but *you're just not that special to them.*" If I'm really in a self-destructive mood, I recite the clichés people have told me, as if they're giving me a suit of armor piece by piece. "One day at a time," I say. "Time heals," I repeat. But instead of pieces of protective metal, each aphorism feels like a flap of wet paper stuck to my skin.

I go to my therapist's office. She is Earth Woman mixed with Joni Mitchell, and she is *über* cool. What I liked—and like—about her is that she never did that dig-deep-and-find-it's-all-your-parents'-fault routine, even when they weren't dead. Now, she doesn't shy away from their very human-ness even though they're no longer flesh and blood. She isn't afraid to say, "That's your dad, what do you expect?" or "That must be your mother talking." Today, I spend the session talking about the Monster. I make up what he's doing and how relieved he is to be away from me, especially in light of the accident; how he's blissful with L and thinks of me in random, infrequent pulses—like when you suddenly wake up with a crick in your neck that you've had before but not in a while.

"I'm sure it goes like this," I tell Barbara. "'Diana,' he thinks, 'nice girl, glad she's gone.'" Barbara, to her great credit, grimaces—she's way too smart not to know my games.

"Stop it!" she says. "I can't take this!" *It's about time,* I think.

(This is not to say, by the way, that I don't believe the Monster is not, in fact, blissfully happy with L and similarly happy, when he thinks of it at all, not to be with me. That is an absolute. I see them sleeping next to each other, her with long blond hair and even, thin thighs; he witty and happy and relaxed and confident. I've never seen her, but I know she isn't needy, she isn't bereaved, she isn't wacko. Probably she's a publicist.)

"See you next Thursday," Barbara says. "It's okay for you to think about things other than your family—you can't stop what you're thinking. You've got to be gentle with yourself. Promise me you'll try to be gentle." I give her the thumbs-up sign as I exit.

On the street, I check my watch. I'm late. In the old days, Darius would glare at me. Now, I'm innocent of every charge, and it fortifies

Darius's idea of himself as Sympathetic Guy if he doesn't hassle me.

I reach the glass door of the vast hallway that is all of our offices and realize immediately that something is different. Phones are ringing off the hook. I walk by Serena, who's wearing her *glasses* for God's sake, which she never does. No one looks up. I am sure I'm in the wrong department, but no, this is the place. *Ring ring!*

Peter too seems very serious. He waves me off when I stop by the cubicle.

"Jesus, Diana," he begins, then stops himself. He's whispering.

"What's with the phones?" I ask, suddenly whispering too. Peter smirks.

"You'll never believe this one." He motions me to come closer. I do but am interrupted by a man, a short, Humpty Dumpty-like man with smart, small eyes and a long forehead barely covered by dark hair.

"Who are you?" Humpty asks.

"Diana Moore." I answer. "Who are you?" This is unlike me, but grief has handed me a new script, and I'm uninhibited in ways I'd never before explored. I really don't care what Humpty thinks of me.

"What's your position?"

"Marketing Manager."

"Like it?"

"Like what?"

"Your job."

"Uh, yeah. Yes. I love my job. I love it more when my colleagues aren't acting so *serious,* but—" Humpty looks at me, raises his eyebrows, nods his head.

"Continue," he says.

I wonder briefly if I should quiz him, but right behind Humpty is Peter, who is grinning so widely I suddenly feel a bolt of energy. Truth is, I'm feeling a glimmer, a taste, the beginning sensation of engagement, of dialogue, and even though it isn't my nature, or at least my nature of late, I leap onto the back of this bullet-like force and hold on tightly.

"Continue with what?" I ask.

"I want to know about your job."

"I want to know about *your* job," I say. Humpty's lips stretch—it may be a smile, it may be a frown.

"I'm new here, never been here before, and want someone to tell me what a typical day is like."

"Haven't you seen Darius?" I ask. He flinches, although it is a small enough movement that I'm not sure.

"I'd rather hear from someone like you."

"Someone like me." I repeat.

"Yes. Tell me if you like it here. Is this division productive? What would you do to change it?" I can tell that Peter is listening to every word, but given that the phone is ringing every three seconds, no one has a chance to eavesdrop.

"I'll tell you one thing. The phones never ring like this. They must be broken." I turn to Peter. "How long has it been like this? Has anyone called maintenance?" Peter has the strangest look on his face, and color rushes to his thin cheeks. He blows out air then suddenly, abruptly, laughs.

"What?" I say. It is now a full roar. I turn around. Behind Humpty is Darius. His face is the color of death.

"You think the phones are broken?" asks Humpty.

"They must be." I look around for someone to confirm this. But everyone seems to have no voice. "This has never happened before." Silence. And then a sound from Darius like none I have ever heard—a grumph, harumph, *kk-k-grymphhgrrmph*. Humpty turns to him.

"Are you okay?"

"Sure, Bob. No problem." Darius coughs. Then, recovering, he grabs me by my elbow. "Bob Petkowski, this is Diana Moore. The one I was telling you about."

He's *touching* me. Darius has never touched me before, and I do not enjoy it. It feels like my mother pinching my flesh between wrist and elbow, when I was a child and had done something dreadful but she hadn't wanted others to see her angry. Darius as my mother? I pull my elbow away from him in a pronounced gesture. I extend my hand to Bob.

"Hello."

"Hello," Humpty/Bob says. "Okay. All right. You've been helpful, little lady." *Little lady?* Did he just say *little lady?*

Bob turns to Darius. "I've got a meeting, but we'll need to talk later. I'll call around three." Bob shakes Darius's hand and then returns to me. "Good to meet you. And thanks. Thanks a lot." Bob walks out, agile for a man of his girth. Before Bob has pushed through the glass doors, Darius whirls around toward me.

"Get into my office! Now!" He sounds like the principal. Still, I take a step. Then I turn toward Peter.

"Pete, can you—"

"Now!" barks Darius. I stop, my heels melting into the floor. Darius continues. "I said in my office, Diana. Which part of that don't you understand?"

"Why are you acting like this?" I answer.

He sputters, literally. Spit spurts from his mouth as he formulates words to lacerate me.

"Do you under—do you get it? Do you?" He gropes for words, his carefully pomaded hair quivering. "Insubordination? Fucking insubordination, that's what it is. I could fire you right now. I should. I should. I should just fire you, or else I could take all of our marketing plans and all of our press releases and light them on fire. Light the match. That's what you just did. Do you understand what you just did?" He's not breathing. "It was critical that we appeared a productive organization for Bob Petkowski. And you saunter in here, forty-seven minutes late, and say the phones *are broken*?"

Darius no longer looks like death. He looks rancid, splotched, a red apple with deep brown dents. For a moment, I am quiet. Inside, though, I feel a tree growing, a small tree, young, healthy, a tree just beginning to appreciate air and sun.

"Oh, my," I begin. I look to Peter, who shakes his head. Serena's big head stays perched above her cubicle wall, as do many of my other colleagues'. This is the kind of drama that will be replayed during company picnics and weekend retreats.

"Oh, my," I continue. "You paid someone or did something to make the phones ring so Bob would think you, we, were busy."

"You say that like it's a bad thing," Peter speaks from his cubicle. I look over. He grins. But then I turn back to Darius, who stands there, looking straight at me. I speak.

"You really thought—you thought that would make a difference?"

Darius's eyes pop; his neck veins pulse underneath his thin red skin. "It was critical for Bob Petkowski to understand the scope of our work, and you have no right, no *right* to tell me anything. You don't know how important it is that appearances are maintained, that—"

"Darius, you can stop. I quit." *What?* I can't quit, I suddenly remember. I need this job. I need a place to go every day. I look at Peter.

"Aw, Diana, you can't leave," Peter says, and it is just at that moment that I realize I can do just that; I *can* leave. I am stringless, obligationless.

"What?" It is Darius now. "You're going to leave because I'm reprimanding you?" I suppose it doesn't look good for the Tragic Orphan to leave the company, especially after a dramatic public encounter with her boss.

"No. I'm leaving because—" I walk to my desk. There is a picture of my parents, a fake waterbug that my friend Betsy gave me, and a copy of my all-time favorite play, *Angels in America, Parts One and Two.* I gather everything into my arms, pull my handbag over my shoulder, and reach in to shut off the computer.

"Diana, listen," begins Darius.

"Diana, come on!" says Peter, slightly annoyed. "You just can't do this."

I look around the office. The drama is not quite over. I notice all the minutiae, the computer cords, the paper clips—my mind spins into work mode, remembering the client I was supposed to call about advertising rates.

"Diana, if you want to be a player, you're going to have to absorb some body blows. You can't just quit." It scares me how well I know Darius's face. Now he's shifting into Darius the Manager, which to him means he has to take care of me. "Where are you going to go? C'mon. Take off your bag, go back to your desk. No one wants you to leave."

"I want to leave," I say, and can't stop myself from thinking that, even now, when Darius is backpedaling, he can't just say "I'm sorry." Not that that would make a difference. Suddenly I'm resolved. I push my bag up on my shoulder. "I want to leave."

"What, you suddenly—"

"I can't." I search for the words that will make the difference, make him understand how I'm apart from this world, how my tragedy has pushed me onto a raft where I can't impute significance to daily workday politics. "It—*this,*" I gesture around. "This just doesn't matter."

And then I turn, and I walk. When the Monster cheated on me, when he told me he had slept at an expendable girl's apartment, I knew I was supposed to slap him across the face and say something succinct that would affect him for the rest of his life, something like "She's a beautiful girl, Hubbell" ("She's a beautiful girl, Monster?") or "You should have seen the guy I picked up at Blockbuster!" Instead I stayed there with him for the next thirty or so hours, crying, holding onto a wraith of past moments, watching as it disintegrated into little silver particles blinking in front of my wet eyes.

But today, here, I am different. Today, now, I am leaving, moving, people staring after me. I stride confidently, yet I have no idea what is propelling me out the door. The old Diana would stop, overjoyed that the people with whom she had worked had expressed a desire to have her around them, to keep her in their midst. That would be a home run for the old Diana Moore. But today, right now, there is a new force in me. Perhaps it is that tree that I felt suddenly burst from inside, perhaps it is just a subconscious need to rid myself of old structures, or perhaps it is just some serendipitous combination of whimsy and impulse and courage and resignation.

Whatever it is, the result is the same. I quit, and I leave, and then I am gone.

THREE

Just When It Can't Get Worse

Say what you want about January, it is September that is truly the month of rebirth. Or maybe it's only that way in New York City. In New York in September, people dash about with suntans and reserve energy and Palm Pilots bursting with new information—they are ready to attack the world, exhibit force and wisdom and summer-like serenity. I think this is because, in September, you can take the best of summer and spring and late winter and mix it all up like a pile of gold and red and orange leaves, so that come Labor Day, you're protected and ready, the best of all possible worlds.

Except for me.

I had been out of work for two weeks. My theory about the crows proved accurate. No one asked, I told no one. Everyone believed I was still gainfully employed at the Internet gargantuan. My apartment was under water—well, not actually water but a sea of clothes and newspapers and Pop-Tart wrappers. Mail, bills, and sympathy cards coated the kitchen floor; I slept on top of my bed and spent hours looking at the paint chipping off my ceiling. One time, after I'd been running, I lay clenched on the bed, staring upward. I have a skylight, and it was ten a.m. and sunny, so the light was yellow and potent. I had no idea emotional pain could wrack one's stomach, one's internal organs, like this. I had had no warning that this pain was so pervasive, that the absence of my father and brother and mother could even *occur,* let alone be maintained. When I left work for the last time, I reached for my cell phone to call my mother. I was on the street, outside the building, and still exhilarated by my performance. I had to call Mom. She would be so proud—she always feared I was not assertive enough. ("Do you want to go to assertiveness classes, Diana? I read about some in Philadelphia. You have to just say, 'I'm not going to accept that behavior. That is *unacceptable.'*")

It is by far the strangest component of death. You grow up in a love-filled home, you emerge headstrong and shy at the same time, you fumble through this place of Responsibility and Obligation and Ambition as if you were in a dark room, hitting big blocks of furniture as you grope around, and with time and phone calls and experience, you end up as an adult who has a loving relationship with her family but is also, at the same time, independent. Your communication is mostly through telephone calls, but the connection is potent and alive.

The point is, you learn to operate every day in your adulthood without the constant presence of your parents, of your family. This is deemed good, appropriate. The converse is that when they're gone, when they've been killed instantly by a drunk driver on a two-lane road in Southern New Jersey, you think that because you're just traipsing around New York City in an ordinary way, as you did before they died, you're just a phone call away from reassurance and admonishment and love. So when you quit your job and walk on the street, and you pick up your cell to call your mother and *she's dead and she will always be dead,* the inside is blown out. Your mind and your heart are blasted as if by a cannon and what remains is the flesh covering the skeleton of a thirty-three-year-old woman in New York, hair blowing in the gusts of devastation, and your eyes blink and your fingers clench and your shoulders hunch and a man on the street, a random limo driver, sees the shape and hears the moans and says, "Hey— you okay? Need some help?" and you just keep moving, keep moaning, wondering, wishing, hoping that you'll be flung around in the air like a tiny, blinking ember of a vanquished flame.

But everything is the same. *Everything is the same.* Your apartment. Your stairs. Your body. Your face. Your phone lines. Your clothing. Your mail. Everything is the same. No wonder people turn to religion. An answer from up above, from up in space with the dying embers—that would be the only recourse, even when the answers aren't satisfying, even when the "Turn to God" messages sound as probable and effective as Suzanne Somers's Thigh Master.

I wonder how long I can stay like this. I wonder if I can keep up the subterfuge. And then I remember that it is all a construct of my imagination; no one else considers this a subterfuge, no one else knows what I'm doing, and no one else cares.

I make a decision to do something. To be active. To do. I stand, I put on clothes, I find a twenty-dollar bill, and I head out onto the street.

I shall go to a movie.

Waugh in Love

I'm early, sunglassed, and carrying a book. *A Handful of Dust* by Evelyn Waugh, a recommendation from someone some time ago. I buy a large combo popcorn and soda. After I take a seat, I read. Brenda and Tony and Brenda's lover. Are people like this, I wonder, unfeeling, untouched by emotion, able to fling off marital vows and sleep with another and wish—ache, actually—for the cuckolded spouse *not* to take everything so to heart? Where is the line to be drawn—where, when do the boundaries appear separating hypersensitivity from appropriate sensitivity from insensitivit—

"Excuse me."

I look up. It's him. The dark-haired man. The one from the funeral. The one from the office.

"Yes?" I ask, as if I don't recognize him. I am surprisingly calm. He'll tell me soon enough who he is. Up close, he looks very distinguished, clean-shaven, handsome, tall, and casually, if fastidiously, dressed. I look at the ceiling, then at him again, then the chair. Is he going to talk?

"Yes?" I ask again, unsure what to do.

"Is this seat taken?" he asks. No. The seat isn't taken. In fact, most of the seats in the theater aren't taken. In fact, as it is obvious to anyone, anywhere, this seat is not taken. *Who* is this?

"No," I answer. "Of course not."

"Terrific!" The man sits down. I look at him in a dart-like fashion and then around the room, searching for anyone who may be watching, who may be in on this joke. Nothing. I don't have time for this, I think.

"Who are you?" I ask.

"Sam," he says, a nice smile on his face. He's about fifty.

"Sam, I'm Diana."

"I know."

"I know you know." Comedy Hour. I'm not pleased. "Why do you know me?"

Other people come into the theater, and it doesn't seem quite as strange that Sam is sitting next to me anymore.

"We met a long time ago," he says. "Have you read much Waugh?" He pronounces Waugh like "Waw."

"That's how you say it?"

"Waw. Like awe," Sam says. "Want to hear a great story? John Wayne is cast in one of those big religious movies, a tiny part, his first role, I think maybe he plays a centurion or something, and the director, William Wyler, tells him after a take that he needs to show more awe. John Wayne says, 'Oh, I got it, I know what you mean.' The scene goes up again, cameras are ready. Wyler says, 'Action!' John Wayne, with all equanimity, says, 'Aw, surely this is the Son of God!'"

Sam laughs, and I do too. But then I remember he is a stranger.

"Who are you?"

"I told you. Sam." He moves in his seat, and suddenly I feel his arm inadvertently pressed against mine for a moment. I freeze. And then I look over and I see his thighs. Strong male thighs. I suddenly remember how long it has been since I've been close to a man—close, shoulders touching, the length of the body, the span of the back. Visceral, painful, I shudder. I realize I am nauseous. I shake my head, a flinch. Sam notices.

"Are you all right?" he asks.

"Yes." I'm angry now. "And I want to know who you are. I think you're following me."

Sam's face wrinkles. But then his face breaks into a different expression, one of aloof warmth. He smiles. "Yes," he says. I look at him—*what?*

"Yes. I am following you," he says.

"Well, thank you for admitting it," I say. "Why are you—"

I stop, panicked. The Monster is in this theater. He is there in front of me.

"Diana?" asks Sam.

"I have to go." I stand and begin to push my way through the row. "Excuse me, but I have to go." I rush to the back of the theater, and only then do I allow myself to turn around again. My heart pounds. At the last second before the lights fade to black, I see the Monster turn around, and I realize I am wrong. It isn't him. I am ridiculous yet again.

The theater is crowded now; the previews have begun. I consider for a moment attempting to find Sam, to grill him about his motives. But then I decide otherwise and walk out of the theater. Outside, the light hurts my eyes.

Days and Nights

It is very bad right now. It is overwhelmingly, impossibly bad. I do not know how this will end. I do not see the pathway I should take. "And to dust you shall return" is part of the Church's teachings, and as I look at my arms, my legs, my flesh, I consider this eventual disintegration of skin and bone, and think that for me the process has already begun. I can feel the flakes fall from my emotional skeleton; ashes falling from my desiccated soul. Surely this cannot go on. Surely there will be something, someone.

Surely.

The Intervention

Serena Beach, my big-headed ex-colleague, has told Wiley, who has told Betsy, who has told my Aunt Margaret, who has told Uncle John, who has told my therapist, Barbara (ignoring multiple therapist-discretion rules, but Uncle John doesn't care about such things), that I have not been at work for over four weeks. This is a signal, a flag, a reason for an emotional flare. It is the new millennium; therefore, there is one optimum recourse. The Intervention.

I read a short story once about whole potatoes in a shoebox, left to grow wild. The ensuing tendrils seeped through the crevice at the bottom of the closet door and encompassed the room, the inhabitant, the reader. I have no potatoes, but a month's sediment of New York City dust and hair and crumbs and papers seems to be every bit as menacing. The bathroom tile lies broken on the hair-matted floor; crumbs from foods half-eaten a month ago are felt under bare feet; dead plants drape starved brown leaves against dirty clay pots. On the other hand, I have paid the rent on time, and this is key. If my rent is paid, if I take a shower, if I dress, then I am sane and viable. It's a fact.

Yet the intervention is arranged. One afternoon, in my apartment, on top of my bed, staring at the skylight, I hear feet clomp up the stairs. I hear them come closer. Then the knocking on the door. "Diana! Diana!" I recognize Wiley, I recognize Betsy, I recognize Aunt Margaret. "Please open the door."

I stand, walk to the door, swing it open, and, with a big smile, say, "Welcome!"

Aghast. Mouths agape. Hanging open. I think it might smell in here.

The four of them step in. I try to watch their faces for anger, but all of them seem impassive.

"Oh, Diana," says Aunt Margaret. "Oh, Diana, I am so sorry." She goes to hug me, but I pull away. I want to be courted, I want to be wooed, I will not collapse crying at the first "Oh, Diana."

"Jeez, Petunia," says Betsy. "Jeez oh man, I would've come; you know that. This place reeks." She is my athlete friend, pretty and healthy like the women from the U.S. soccer team. I see she is calculating how to couch her direct and blunt words, but she can't. It isn't possible. Wiley paces the room; she runs her fingers through her hair. Uncle John has gone into cleanup mode and is picking up papers, finding trash bags.

"I don't have any food to offer you," I start, "but I do have some vodka. I know it's a bit early, but seeing that you've all taken the day off for me, maybe we should sit back, have a drink."

I do not know where this voice comes from. She is nasty and sarcastic and rude, and I would smack her if I could.

Wiley has gone into my bathroom—a terrifying safari through broken tile and filthy towels—to grab a brush. She sits behind me, and I make no fuss as she pulls the brush through my knotted hair.

Uncle John marches from small room to small room until he decides to open the windows and let in the air. Betsy stacks papers on top of each other to give herself a place to sit; she is the one friend who lives always in the style to which I am currently accustomed.

As Wiley pulls the brush gently through my uncombed hair, I realize she's trembling.

"I am so mad at you," she whispers, but she isn't, not really. "I, you, I should've come sooner. I knew it, I knew you were doing this, but I just, I just—" She pulls the brush through harder as she is distracted by what she is trying to say.

"Easy," I say. "No need for additional pain."

"You're not funny," she tells me as she lays the brush down. She looks to her left, spots something. She turns back to me, raises an eyebrow. Then she reaches out, over to the offending area, where she pries a book from the top of a bowl of old cereal, a book now stuck to the rim by old milk.

"Diana," she starts, "what do you want us to do?"

"I'm fine," I say.

"Oh yeah, you're fine; you're fine just like people in a coma are fine." This from Betsy. "You should have called us."

"Betsy," says Aunt Margaret, "I really don't think that's why we're here."

"I just don't get it," Betsy says. "We're your friends."

I don't know what to say. I love all of these people, and they are, now, my closest family. But I wanted them to come here; I wanted them to pay attention.

"Diana," starts Wiley, "we can figure something out. We can figure a way to make it better, to make it, this, better. You can't live like this. And you've got to, we've got to, find a way to make you tell us when you need us."

44

"Don't do that, Wiley; just don't do that."

"Do what?"

"Don't patronize me. You are all feeling guilty, so deal with it but please realize it isn't my fault." I have gone from sarcasm to vitriol in less than sixty seconds. Someone should sponsor me for NASCAR.

"You know, Diana, you know—I can't tell you—this, this fucked up behavior . . . couldn't you have just said something? Couldn't you have just said it?"

I can see the words clog in her throat—a traffic jam of sympathy and wrath. I need to trust her, she thinks; I need to trust that she'll be there for me when I need it.

"Yo, pal," says Betsy, "I mean, come on. This looks like my place." She's right. It does.

"Yours is worse."

"Quit it, Diana," Betsy replies. "This is serious." I look around. Now the gravity of her quest, of their collective quest, settles in their mien.

"We're here for a reason," says Uncle John. "Everyone here loves you and cares for you. We know you've undergone, you're still undergoing, something very terrible." Uncle John stops. He's a successful investment banker on Wall Street but is also the kind of man who makes time to take his grandchildren to FAO Schwarz whenever they ask.

"It is what it is, Diana. It is what it is." Uncle John speaks solidly but with empathy; he is trying very hard. "You can't take your flags down now. This is the battlefield of life, the battle of everyone's life, and you've been dealt a hand more difficult than most, no kidding, no kidding at all—but you're a strong young woman, and you cannot, I will not, none of us will permit you to live like this."

I sit back. I have split into two so that Diana One lies listening obediently, while Diana Two watches from above, seeing from on high all the people crowded in the tiny room, shuffling, expounding, advising, intervening.

"We will help you," Uncle John is saying, "and if you can't do it yourself right now, it's okay. But from now on, we will help you. You want to live with us, any of us, fine."

"Well, I really don't have room—" says Betsy.

My uncle silences her. "I didn't mean it literally," says my uncle. "You communicate, you tell us what is necessary, and we'll abide by it."

Aunt Margaret, so far quiet, steps toward me. She is a beautiful, large-eyed woman, thin and boned, her skeleton, I think, like that of a long fish—white, tiny, slender bones attached to each other in a kind of fish lace. She wears swishing silks with bold colors, and I think again that she is the coolest aunt anyone ever had.

"Why don't I move in here for a while, Diana? I could do that."

"You don't have to."

"I know, but I want to. Or else I could find a place near here. People need habits, and we need to get you into a new habit. I don't care what it is: cookies at midnight, walks at dawn, massages, books, movies, whatever. Wiley's right. We can figure this out. But you need to get help. I've been thinking and thinking, and—"

Uncle John interrupts her. "Tomorrow morning, you're going here." He rips out a piece of paper from his datebook. "I've made the arrangements. They're expecting you."

The card: DEPRESSION MANAGEMENT, Dr. Elliott Sinofsky, Director, 850 Park Avenue.

"I have a therapist," I offer.

"Maybe it's time for a change," Wiley responds.

"What's the matter with you?" I ask. She won't answer. "Come on—what's the matter?"

Wiley takes a breath. She is typically so reserved that I am actually excited for her response. Wiley's one of those people who despise manipulative behavior; to Wiley, the psychology that makes some of us restrict words or alter our behavior just so it will provoke a response in another person is abhorrent. It isn't that she thinks everything has to be explained; it's just that to willfully lie to get the other person to answer what the first person should have just asked for directly—that's like throwing acid in Wiley's face. I know this, and I *still* do it. Why is my need any less imperative than hers?

"No. No way. I won't go there. Stop switching the subject. You make me want to hit you." She almost grins, which for the first time sparks a genuine smile in me.

"Please, that's what I need. A good punch in the face."

"We could arrange that," says Aunt Margaret. "My neighbor's son is a prizefighter, I think, over in Queens. He's very good."

"Wouldn't that be cheaper than Dr. Sinofsky?"

"Diana," Uncle John growls, "you know that money isn't a problem."

I look around at everyone, and something inside of me relents. They have come. I should be embarrassed by my manipulative behavior, but I am not. Just like a pregnant woman should be able to eat what she wants for the first time in her life, a grieving woman should be able to push and pull the people closest to her, just to give her that little confirmation she needs that they care, that they really care.

"Okay," I say, examining the card, "I'll go." I stop. "What else?" I ask.

"You'll really go?" asks Aunt Margaret. I nod. Scout's honor. But Wiley knows me best.

"Don't pull any of your shit!" she says.

I roll my eyes. "Okay, Adolf."

Betsy stands. "I'm going for a run." I consider this and realize it may be my exit strategy.

"Can I come?" I ask. Betsy looks at me strangely.

"No, you can't. Of course you can; what's wrong with you?"

I'm tempted to respond with something sarcastic, but the snarliness has left me, and I'm back to being Diana again.

"Why don't you two go," says Aunt Margaret. "We'll stay here and clean up a bit."

"You don't have to do that—"

"Would you please let us?" asks Wiley. "Please?"

I look at Uncle John. "You're going to clean?"

"What makes you think I can't? You think I don't know how?"

"I didn't say that," I reply, "but now that you mention it—" Uncle John swats me in the head with the roll of newspaper he's holding, and then he pulls me in for a hug.

"I love you, kid; you know that," he says, and I know it's true.

"We all do, Diana," says Aunt Margaret. "We'll figure something out; you won't have to do this alone."

"But you've got to let us," begins Wiley. "You've got to—"

"I got it," I say. "Don't worry."

The Pheasant

Betsy and I run the exact same way, which means we don't speak to each other, we just run. It's late, almost dark, and we reach the expanse of green in front of (and across the river from) the Statue of Liberty. I feel strong and pleased that Betsy is with me. I'm not vulnerable this evening.

Our pace stays sharp and consistent. When we turn around at the halfway mark, Betsy looks around.

"What?" I say, my first question of the run.

"Nothing," she answers. "Just looking for the pheasant."

I freeze, as if all the noise of the river and the boats and the Wall Street brokers and the ferry drivers is swallowed up by my crashing fear.

"Pheasant?" I say calmly, still running alongside Betsy, step for step. "What does it look like?"

"A pheasant—you've never seen a pheasant? It's like a turkey, fat; you know, actually like a hen but with colors."

"A hen," I say. I think of my Magic Bird. "Would you say," I begin to Betsy, "that a pheasant has, say, a *reptilian* tail?"

Betsy smirks. "A pheasant has a green, flat tail, if that's what you're asking."

I am embarrassed. I am Embarrassment. Look me up, read about me, color me red.

It is no wonder, no surprise, that I have grown into one of those women who are delusional, frantic, undeserving. My Magic Bird is a pheasant.

Exodus

The next morning, I wake up and do not stop moving until I am out the door. I shower, moisturize, wash and dry my hair, pull on the last pair of clean everything, and leave the apartment, locking the door, putting the key in a bag that contains Altoids, *Brideshead Revisited,* Pop-Tarts, sunglasses, wallet, two pens, a brush, and one set of running clothes. I'm down the steps, out the door, and as I walk, I am determined not to let any thoughts escape the steel vault of my brain—at least it is a steel vault this morning, I hope. (Usually it is a vault made of standing slices of Swiss cheese.)

I go to a garage on the West Side Highway. I keep my car there, an old Volvo, 1990, about eight million miles on it. It used to be green, but it is definitively gray now. I pay the parking-lot attendant, put the car in reverse (it is a stick shift), then into first gear, and then I drive. I drive down the West Side Highway to Canal Street, to the Holland Tunnel, to the New Jersey Turnpike, heading south.

I don't think I want to go to Princeton, but maybe. Maybe I'll go to Florida. Maybe Cape May. Maybe Rehoboth Beach or St. Michael's or Savannah or Charleston. No, I won't go to Florida. I was there in February with my parents, and I don't want to go there again. Besides, there is too much construction.

These are the jolts of thoughts I'm allowing to bang against my skull; then I force them back into the vault. I want french fries. Is there a map? Do I have exact change? The clock is wrong. How long will it be before Maryland? I would like to go to Italy. My mother wanted to go to Italy. I want to be a different person. Who is Sam? Did I invent Sam? I want to drive somewhere, south; I want to go somewhere and find people who know me, although I know no one in the South—except for the Monster's friends in Atlanta whom I haven't seen since the '96 Olympics and I kind of think they've forgotten me and would rather, anyway, spend time with him and his charming wonderful beautiful makes-him-so-happy girlfriend, Lolita Lola. *Back!* I order my brain. *Put that one back in the vault! Put it back and squash it with something, a file cabinet or an old creepy blanket.*

I turn off at Exit Nine. New Brunswick. A river—the Camden? the Roanoke? (*no, idiot, that's in Virginia*)—streams underneath the overpass. I go onto Route One, South. No reason.

But Route One isn't working either. It is lined, at first, with green lawns and trees, buffeting the entrance to either Johnson & Johnson's massive headquarters or the campus for Cook College's agriculture school. Then the road bequeaths strip malls and Taco Bells and just too many traffic lights. This is not what I want, although I have no idea what I want. I take the next exit, Finnegan's Lane, I think.

Then I'm on a mishmash of roads, Routes 518 and 522 and 527 and 547 and 539; I have no idea where I am. If you grow up in Princeton, all you learn is how to get to New York City. (A friend with whom I grew up used to say, "New York City, *gulp,* it's the center of the *universe;* I mean, you can fly to both Moscow and Paris from there!") Maybe, if your parents wanted some cultural diversion, you'll know how to get to Philadelphia, and maybe on a true "road" trip, you'll go the long way, via Lambertville and New Hope and Bucks County, past streams and green trees and chic, artistic boutiques and picturesque bridges, to see the "country."

But Princeton, to many of the families who live there, is simply *not* New Jersey. It is Princeton, a place unto itself. Moreover, this sentiment is never voiced—a true Princetonian would never need to note its distinctiveness. Like Caroline Kennedy or President George H. Bush, the need to assert one's dignity or otherwise account for one's subtlety and innate aplomb is nonsensical, a ballet dancer pirouetting in a swamp.

In any event, the Princeton I grew up in is pristine, classic, a university town above all else, nothing garish or loud, neither in architecture nor inhabitants. I am not ashamed to declare that I do not have a problem with this. I don't like garish things, I don't like loud architecture, I don't like pushy, aggressive, to-argue-about-everything-is-to-be-truly-enlightened people. Give me reserve, give me respectful hesitation, give me grace any day of the week.

But now I am driving in what looks to be Iowa. (I have never been to Iowa, but I know it looks like this.) It can't be New Jersey. This is land, real land, green and outstretched, a verdant expanse as long as a Caribbean beach, bordered not by an ocean but by tall, multicolored, autumn-painted, red, gold, and green trees. It is early, before noon, and the sky is completely blue, with no clouds—the kind of blue that poets would say is the color of robins' eggs, or bluejays' breasts, or, as I would say, the blue of childhood, the blue as bright and empty and untainted as a child's mind, without any splotch of heartbreak and orphans and sudden death.

I feel like Alice, tumbling down a rabbit hole in a fantasy place labeled the Garden State. I grew up in New Jersey; I've been to rural places (in Maine, not New Jersey, but how different could it be?), yet this is very strange. I stop the car and get out. I am on the side of the road near a farm of some sort, a farm where there are rows and rows of small bushes about five feet high, planted equidistant in what looks to be sand. I step over the guardrail and look around. There is no one, absolutely no one, on the road. I step to the bush. I see a cluster of small clumps, dried clumps, of . . . berries. Blueberries, I realize. This is where they come from; this is how they grow. For some reason, I thought they grew only in Maine. I get a glimpse of class warfare over blueberries; Maine blueberries are wild, not cultivated. Maine blueberries reek intrinsically of estates and reserve; New Jersey blueberries by definition must reek of noxious gases and neon. Could there be some association between big-haired Jersey girls and these small, dried berries I hold in my hand? I look down the rows of bushes. No. I answer my question. No one who knew what I was holding, what I was seeing, would ever make that connection. This is a foreign land; this is a strange place. This is *New Jersey?*

I get back into my car. I am now on Route 563. New Jersey Route 563. I can't be far from Princeton. New Jersey isn't Texas; there are only sixty miles from Philadelphia to the ocean. The other thought forming is that I can't be far from the Route of Death, Route 206. *Two-O-Six. Back!* I say again. *Back in the vault!* Laura lived in Southern New Jersey. My parents and brother were headed there, to a place called Berlin. Or was it Egg Harbor? Hammonton? I force myself to banish that thought. Right now, there is no past, no history. Right now, I am only Diana Moore, fleeing New York City and a Depression Professional named Elliott. I am allowed to do this. I am an Adult, a Survivor, a Driver, a Person on a Trip. Surely this is enough for one person.

As I think, I drive, and I realize I am no closer to civilization than before. I am in Pennsylvania. I am in Delaware. I am in Kansas. In New York, Wiley is furious, Aunt Margaret is pained by my willful abandonment of her, of all of them. I will be the next person who dies, maybe I'll be raped and killed by a driver of a truck the size of Manhattan.

A lake appears. I drive slowly so I can see it. Small, blue-green, surrounded by sand mixed with brown *somethings*. I stare at it from the driver's-side window. Maybe there are many lakes, maybe there are homes here in Kansas alongside lakes, maybe—

OH MY GOD OH MY GOD OH MY GOD!

Marlboro Girl

I stand on the brake. I stand on the brake, and my car skids across the lane, crashing into the guardrail on the other side. I see it. The motorcycle.

I see a bright green motorcycle with thick tires lying on its side, the tires still spinning, steam rising. On the pavement—the black pavement, surrounded only by green pine (*I think they're pine*) trees on one side and a lake on the other, an old Volvo turned the wrong direction on one side of the road and a green motorcycle lying on the ground on the other—I see a body, a housecoat—*a housecoat of green and blue*—legs splayed, splayed on the ground, slippers, could they be *slippers,* pointing sideways, OH MY GOD. I have killed. I have become Oedipus. (Makes no sense, but I need the feeling of tragedy.) I am wreaking revenge on the gods. I have killed this person in a housecoat and brown slippers driving a green motorcycle.

I have slid to the passenger side of the car. When I try to open the door, it seems to be melted into the guardrail. I move to the left and push myself out of the driver's side. Steam seeps out from underneath the hood. I am bleeding somewhere, but I don't feel anything. Why are there no cars no police no ambulance no sirens? I haven't been in the car that long—are there no people in this strange, beautiful, silent place?

Housecoat moves. Maybe it's the wind, yet there is no wind. (Maybe I am in New Jersey after all.) One of the splayed legs moves, one on top of the other. A cough. A definite cough. I hear it. Alive. Life life life life, THANK YOU GOD THANK YOU GOD, it's moving, it's moving. Will the motorcycle blow up in a burst of flames, and will we both be engulfed and will no one ever know? An old lady sits up. *An old lady on a motorcycle?* White hair straight and cropped, her eyes open, she is alive, but she isn't standing; I've paralyzed her, she can't walk, she will never walk.

"Oh," I say weakly, "oh my God, I am so sorry I am so—"

An engine roars behind me. I turn. Another green motorcycle careens toward me, stopping at the last possible second. The rider dismounts; it is all happening so fast, I'm not sure exactly what "it" is. Tan fingers yank the helmet off a head. Long hair spills out, a sheet of gold. "It" is a beautiful woman.

"What the—" She jumps off her bike and runs to the old woman on the ground. "Rosie, are you okay?"

"I'm fine, I'm fine," says the older woman, now sitting up. "Calm down; really, I'm okay."

"Are you out of your fucking mind?" Me: she's talking, yelling, screaming at me. I hit an old woman wearing slippers on a motorcycle. An old woman named Rosie. The woman yelling at me has large brown eyes. Straight nose. "Are you out of your *fucking mind*?" Muscular arms, thin, striking. She looks like the partner to the Marlboro Man. She isn't young, she isn't old. She's probably my age. "Are you deaf?

You almost killed my grandmother, you fucking lunatic!" She's the Marlboro Girl; she should mate with the Marlboro Man and have little Marlboro kids. I watch her clap her hands, right in front of my nose. "Hey! I'm talking to you!" She spins around and strides toward my car, checks out the license plate and returns, hair waving out from behind her, silhouetted by the sun. "New York," she says contemptuously. "What a surprise."

I see Rosie on the ground, her arms clasped to her knees. I see the lake behind Marlboro Girl, gleaming, the blue deep and clear and rippling, trees along the perimeter, trees as far as I can see. The motorcycle lies on its side. I've hit a person, a *person.* I breathe hard, fast, and I cry, helplessly, a torrent through which random thoughts slice with the clarity of diamonds.

"Sweetheart," says Rosie. "It was our fault. My fault."

"Martyr syndrome again. C'mon, Rosie. She blindsided you; it isn't like there are a million cars on this road. What is the matter with you?"

I understand her language, but I cannot respond; I do not know how to pull from my feeble brain an explicable response.

"Can you speak? Are you mute? Hand signals, something? C'mon, you almost killed my grandmother; do you get it? I said, what is the matter with you?"

I hear that derisive voice in my head tell me to stop crying like a baby and speak up, take responsibility, *answer* her.

"Take a breath, slow, slow, take a breath, stop crying; I'm okay, see I'm okay," Rosie speaks softly to me, but I hear her voice snap when she speaks to Marlboro. "Be nice," she says sharply.

Marlboro whirls back around, ready to light into me. But then she pauses, appraising me, and instead of yelling, she lets out a booming laugh. All the venom she just spurted out seems to have evaporated, the mean words now floating over the lake like a balloon lost by a child.

"What is it?" the old woman, Rosie, asks Marlboro.

"Her," she answers, pointing to me. "What a mess."

FOUR

Paradise

"You're bleeding." Marlboro kneels down next to Rosie and looks closely at Rosie's knee. I do too and see that the skin has broken right underneath her right knee, and it is bleeding, as if Rosie were a little girl who had just fallen off her bike.

"Oh, this isn't anything," says Rosie.

"I'm so sorry." My first words since the accident are evanescent, water bubbles about to break.

"She speaks!" Marlboro exclaims.

"I'm okay," says Rosie. "Really."

"You're bleeding too," says Marlboro Girl, now looking straight at me. "On your forehead." She taps her own forehead, above her right eye. I do the same, and when I bring my fingers in front of my eyes, I see the blood. "Do you always go after elderly women on motorcycles? Rosie isn't as young as she looks."

"I—I wasn't paying attention," I say.

"Well, that's clear as day," says Marlboro.

"Sweetheart," says Rosie, "what's your name?"

They're both looking at me. We sit in the middle of the road. I have a brief moment of orientation—the three of us and our respective vehicles, an awkward blot staining a black stretch of highway.

"You do have a name," asks Marlboro, "don't you?"

"Yes," I respond. "I have a na—I mean, it's Diana. I'm Diana."

"I'm Louisa," says Marlboro. She extends her hand. I take it, shake it, and then, Princeton manners kicking in, turn to Rosie with my arm outstretched.

"I'm Diana," I repeat.

"Yes," says Rosie, "I heard you. It's only my knee that's bleeding. My ears are fine."

"Right," I say.

"At least you've stopped crying; you should get that checked, that crying thing," says Louisa. "You know, Diana is one of my favorite names. Artemis, you know, the Greek goddess, the moon, all that, I love mythology; I read them all the time as a kid. Hey, maybe that's my problem?" She looks at Rosie.

"That's the least of your problems," smiles Rosie.

"Thank you, Grandmother, nothing like insinuating to Diana that I have a lot of problems." She turns to me. "She lies. I am one of those perfect people you meet once in a lifetime." She grins at Rosie. "Aren't I?"

Rosie shakes her head, not answering her. Instead she says, "Help me up, dear, would you?" as she lifts her arm for Louisa to take. Louisa stands, brushes off her jeans, and gently pulls Rosie to her feet. Rosie stands right next to where I still sit on the blacktop, the hem of her housecoat skimming my hair. Close up, I see the blood from her skinned knee drizzling down her leg, and I notice that Rosie's skin has that stone-white hue of the elderly. Then Rosie wobbles slightly, her feet shifting to assume balance, and I wait to see if she will fall to the ground, this time dead as a doornail.

She doesn't.

Louisa picks up Rosie's bike and stands it on its kickstand. She taps the front tire with her boot, and then the back tire.

"It's all right," she says, bending to examine the fender more closely. "Good thing you were going slowly."

A butterfly flits by. White wings.

"Where are we?" I ask, squinting as I look over at the lake.

"Where do you think you are?" asks Louisa.

"I don't know," I say.

"You don't know?" asks Rosie. "Where are you going, dear?"

"Yeah," continues Louisa. "How did you find our paradise?"

"Oh," I start, flummoxed. *Answer them,* I yell at myself, *say something.* "I got lost," I reply.

The noise of an approaching motor causes us all to turn our heads. A pickup truck drives in the distance, heading in our direction.

"Hey!" Louisa rushes into the road and lies down on the center lane, arms outstretched, legs outstretched, like a snow angel on the blacktop.

"Come and get me!" yells Louisa from her prone position. "Goodbye, cruel world." I stare at the tips of Louisa's boots—they are pointed straight to the sky.

My mouth opens to say "Hey!" and "Come back here!" but I don't know which phrase to choose, and instead an image floods my mind, a picture of a beer truck heading for my father's Mercedes, speeding up when it should slow down, my father flinching, his mind racing with the need to get out of the truck's way but trapped by a guardrail on one side and a car on the other. I leap into the road and yank Louisa's arm.

"Get up!" I shriek. "Get up now!" I jerk her arm. She doesn't respond.

The pickup truck bears down on us. "A truck's coming, come on!" Louisa shuts her eyes, pulls her arm away from me. I gape at her, serene on the blacktop, and then turn to look up at the truck, which is going even faster. I spin around to Rosie who sits on the guardrail. She stares back at me puzzled, as if I'm a tricky math problem she's been asked to solve.

"C'mon!" I pull Louisa's arm as hard as I can, and she rolls out of the truck's path. Just as she moves, the pickup truck screeches to a halt right in front of us. The driver steps out, a man with aviator sunglasses and a sprawling Afro.

"What the hell happened here?" he asks as he takes off his sunglasses. His face is broad, creased and brown, friendly.

"Hello, Carlos," says Rosie calmly. "I thought it was you."

"Ow!" Louisa explodes. "What are you, out on leave? Forget your lithium?"

"I thought—" My explanation crumbles in the light of my glaring stupidity. "I thought you were going to get killed."

"Oh, really," she retorts. "I was going to get killed."

"I said, what the hell happened here?" asks Carlos, inspecting my car and Rosie's bike.

"It was nothing," Rosie says.

"We're okay," says Louisa.

"I hit her with my car," I say.

Silence. Carlos purses his lips, swivels his head as he considers the motorcycle, the steaming car. "All right," says Carlos. "We'll get this figured out." He looks out to the lake and then returns his gaze to the three of us. "Give me a second." He walks back to his truck.

Louisa looks at me, her mouth in a straight line, her eyes afire. "Nutcase," she says.

"You come with me," Carlos speaks to Rosie as he returns. "Mickey'll come back with the boys for the cycle and the car." He then turns and looks directly at me, and I see that his brown eyes are kind but uncomprehending. I feel my knees tremble, knocking against one another. The lake shines under the sun, and the wind blows slightly near my skull. My head hurts, a pain from the inside, a clanging, a pounding, the worst orchestra in the world.

Carlos walks Rosie to the cab of the pickup truck and helps her get inside. Louisa and I are left staring at each other. She rubs her right shoulder with her left arm.

"You pulled so fucking hard," she says.

"I didn't mean to hurt you," I say, squinting. The sun is behind her, illuminating her skin, the color of her eyes. Her hair blows slightly out behind her shoulders. She should be a model, and this should be a photo shoot.

"Are you all right?" Louisa asks.

"Yeah," I answer.

"I don't think so," she says. "Like I said, you're a mess."

She's wrong. I'm a disaster area. She should call the federal government and have them issue a warning.

"You coming?" Carlos calls to me, but I watch Louisa as she puts on her helmet, jumps onto her motorcycle, and rides off into the distance. I turn the other way. My smashed car gleams in the sunlight, marring the vision of the serene lake behind it. My feet feel glued to the road.

"Is my car okay here?" I ask.

"Yeah," says Carlos. "Mickey's on his way. Come on." Carlos stretches out his thick, muscled arm.

I walk toward the truck. *Mickey's on his way.* That explains everything. Mickey's on his way, and Carlos is taking Rosie and me away from the scene of the accident, and Louisa is already on her way on her motorcycle, and I don't even know where I am. New Jersey? I've heard about a wilderness in New Jersey, pinelands, *the* Pinelands I think they're called; I've driven through them on my way to the shore. They looked like trees along a highway.

The butterfly flutters past, its white wings flashing, sprinting toward the lake. I look up and see another one, orange-and-black wings, alighting for an instant on a tuft of green spindly weeds, until it flies away in front of me, until it goes out of sight. I check my watch. I am far away from everything I know, the Fates have (finally) intervened and thrown me here, and it is only one in the afternoon. My body feels funny, and I think I isolate a strain of recklessness amidst the familiar stupor. This is paradise, they said, and I am here, stuck here, and Louisa said she was perfect and that I was a mess, and she certainly looks perfect and I certainly am a mess, so maybe, just maybe, this is where I'm supposed to be.

Resting

The window is down on the passenger side of Carlos's pickup truck. As he drives down the solitary road, I stare out at the trees flashing by and try to envision where I am.

"You and Louisa out racing?" I hear Carlos ask Rosie, who sits wedged in between us in the front seat.

"No," Rosie answers, "not racing. Just riding."

"That something you should be doing?" Carlos asks.

"Yes," Rosie replies.

"You sure?" Carlos persists.

"Yes," she repeats, "I'm sure as I can be sure of anything that it's okay for me to ride around here next to my granddaughter."

"Yeah, but—" Carlos begins anew.

"Stop it," Rosie interrupts. "Case closed."

I bring my head back inside the truck just as Carlos grumbles, "Louisa should know better. But she probably—"

"Stop, Carlos." I hear an edge to Rosie's voice. "Just stop."

"You here for the celebration?" Carlos asks me.

"Celebration?" I reply.

"There's a big party tomorrow night, dear," says Rosie. "You have excellent timing."

"People plan for months; it's a little town, but it's our biggest event," Carlos says. "Maybe you've heard of it?"

I shake my head. Carlos grins at me. "Well, it's probably nothing like the city, but everyone here looks forward to it for months. This is the best time of year down here; the fall, can't beat it. Alice's been cooking up a storm." He stops. "So what happened out there?"

My impulse is to say that there was a drunk driver and now I'm an orphan. "I was staring at the lake and looked up and saw this motorcycle in front of me, and I turned the wheel and thought that—" I hesitate. "I thought I had killed Rosie when I saw the motorcycle lying on its side."

"Take something tougher than that car to kill me," responds Rosie after a moment.

"It's a Volvo," I say, and wonder why I'm instinctively defending my car as a killing machine. "I mean," I stammer. "You know what I mean."

"She shouldn't be out there, anyway," says Carlos.

"Carlos," Rosie answers him.

"We've tried a million times, my wife and me, to get her to stop riding around like that. But no, she don't listen. Rosie doesn't listen to anyone; she just gives you that smile and nods like she's paying attention, and then she's back again doing whatever she wants, not worrying at all about anything. And when Louisa's here, she gets more crazy, not less." Carlos clutches the steering wheel a bit harder as he talks.

"When you get old, everyone wants to protect you," Rosie says to me.

"They don't remember that if you managed to get this old, you've probably figured out how to protect yourself."

Carlos turns into a driveway. We've reached a smattering of homes. Carlos parks next to a narrow three-story home that is painted bright cornflower blue. On the other side of the same driveway is a similar-style house, this one painted blazing yellow. Across the street is a larger house with a wide porch. It is painted vivid pink. I saw something like this in Taos once—a row of homes, all brightly colored, against a stark, treeless horizon. Here, against thick green and orange and red trees, the effect is similarly cheerful, similarly embracing.

Louisa stands near a garage in the back of the house, her motorcycle standing beside her.

"'Bout time," she says. "The newspapers and TV reporters have been calling. They'll be here any second."

"Rosie!" A tall man emerges from a screen door on the side of the blue house. He has a shock of white hair, and his cheeks are red. He wears a blue flannel shirt.

"I'm fine, Gabe," Rosie speaks as she steps out of the truck. "Just a scratch," she says, "that's all."

Gabe takes Rosie's arm. Rosie turns to me. "This is Diana," she begins. I extend my hand. Gabe ignores me and starts walking to the house with Rosie. "Don't worry, honey," Rosie tells me as she passes by. "He's not a big talker." They go inside the house. Behind me, I hear Carlos speak to Louisa.

"I'm heading out to the fields," he says. "I'll see you later, right?"

"Yeah," Louisa answers. "I don't know what time, but I'll find you."

"Bye," he calls to me. "Don't go staring out at any more lakes."

"I won't," I say as I watch him drive away.

"So," says Louisa. I stare back at her. "You up for a picnic?" Louisa asks me.

"What?"

"A picnic. You know, some food, some wine, a pretty place, all that."

"I know what a picnic is," I answer, confused. "But I have to deal with my car." I stop. "Don't I?"

"Mickey's got that under control."

"Who's Mickey?"

"The mechanic. I bet he's already taken your car to his shop."

"How did he even know?"

"Carlos probably radioed him from his truck when you weren't looking."

I look around again. "Do you always ask strangers to picnics?" I ask.

"Only if they've hit my grandmother on her motorcycle."

"Yes, right." I pause for a second and then continue. "What if they've hit you, too?"

"Those people get a full-course dinner," she answers. "Maybe tomorrow you can try for that, if your car's ready." She turns to go indoors. I stand there, perplexed.

"Tomorrow?"

"I think you wrecked your radiator. This isn't New York, you know. Plus, Mickey's busy with the harvest. And there's the celebration tomorrow night." She pauses. "But guess what? We even have phones here. Shocking, I know. You can call whomever you need to and tell them you're stranded." She opens the screen door and steps inside. "Listen, you're stuck here, and I'm hungry. Rosie would get mad if I didn't take you along. Come inside." The door slams behind her.

Quiet. I look at my watch again. It is now one thirty-two in the afternoon. I lean against the house, facing the road. I can hear myself breathe. I clutch my arms around my chest. I close my eyes.

70

"Hey!" Louisa sticks her head out of the open screen door. I open my eyes and blink in the light.

"What are you doing?" she asks.

"Resting," I say.

"You know what they say," she answers as she holds open the door for me. "You can rest when you're dead."

That word again. I suddenly see my mother's and father's and brother's caskets. But for this moment, the drape of dread and loss lifts just a bit. As I walk inside to Rosie's house, I am strangely placated by the idea that Mom and Dad and Ben are merely resting, awash in pleasant dreams, and that when they wake, I will be there waiting, with a newly fixed Volvo and a group of brand-new friends.

The Adventurer

The first room I enter is the kitchen. There is a large oval wooden table dead center, surrounded by an old-fashioned gas stove and an even older-fashioned refrigerator. Louisa opens the refrigerator door using the large silver handle. Inside is a gallon of milk, a bottle of Absolut, and two limes, cut open and dried out.

"Cold as Christmas," Louisa says. "I think it's even better than the new ones. We have one of those, too, down in the basement. Don't want you to think we're in the Dark Ages. I know what you must think. I've lived in the city. I hate that New York attitude. I left to get away from that." Louisa pulls out the top drawer near the sink. She pushes things around until she finds a pack of cigarettes. She takes one and lights it. "Want one?" I shake my head. "So, okay?"

"Okay what?" I ask.

"No attitude."

"Oh." I answer. "Sure. No attitude."

"So where do you live?" She speaks from behind me.

"The Village." I've turned around, facing her. She lounges against the counter. I see that above the sink, on the windowsill, are fresh flowers, asters, and I notice that the kitchen is spotless.

"Where?"

"West. The West Village."

She grins. "Now I can start figuring you out. You can tell a lot about a person from where they live in New York." She stops. "They're in there," Louisa says, as she motions to the room through the doorway with her cigarette. "I'll be in in a second. Want anything to drink?"

"No," I say. "I'm okay." She looks me up and down, like a bouncer does when he doesn't want to let you into the club.

"No, Diana. Actually, you're not. You're really not."

I am not used to someone being so direct with me. In New York, Wiley would tell me that I looked fine, maybe a little tired. Aunt Margaret would serve me tea. Here, I'm presented with Louisa's words flying at me like baseballs from a pitching machine, and I keep getting whacked because I'm too slow to catch any of them.

I walk through the archway into the living room. Immediately I'm struck with its warmth. The couches are deep and big and seem as if they will be soft; the coffee table is worn enough so you can rest your feet on it, and the afternoon light shines through the big windows framed by long white panels of curtains. A round area rug covers the floor, on top of which a big, beautiful golden retriever flaps its tail. Fresh cut flowers, white and yellow and red and gold, bloom in vases set around the room. Rosie is sitting on the couch, a glass in front of her on the coffee table.

"Hello, dear," she says. "Come in, please. Did Louisa get you a drink?" Rosie asks.

"She asked, but I said no."

"Now that's just nonsense," Rosie says. "Louisa! Bring Diana a drink, after her afternoon." The dog has walked over to sit near my chair. I lean down to pet its thick orange-yellow hair.

"Gwen," Rosie says. "Her name is Gwen."

"She's beautiful," I say, which is true.

"She's my equilibrium," says Rosie. "Things go wacky, I look at Gwen, she wags her tail, I'm fine."

Louisa walks in, hands me a glass. "Here," she says.

"Thanks." I take the glass from her and lift it to my lips, swallowing a large gulp.

And then—I spit it on the floor. I feel my cheeks heat up; I imagine them growing blush red and watch the liquid seep onto the carpet.

"Surprise," says Louisa. "A little vodka to calm the nerves."

I have now hit Rosie with my car, yanked Louisa across the road, and spat vodka on their carpet. If I had taken the cigarette Louisa had offered, no doubt I would have burned down the house.

"Sorry," I say, mortified.

"No problem," says Louisa. "Guess I could've warned you." She sinks into the couch next to Rosie.

"Dear?" asks Rosie.

"Yes?" I say.

"Is there someone you want to call?"

"Yes," I say, images of Wiley and Aunt Margaret and Uncle John running about in my skull, all with differing expressions of concern.

"The phone's in the kitchen," says Rosie. "On the counter." She looks at me, as does Louisa. I want to formulate an answer to their unasked queries, and I want it to be perfect, unassailable.

"I'm on my way to visit my parents," I tell them. "They're in South Carolina." When I hear the words hit the air, I flinch. This is not a perfect answer—this is preposterous; this is an outright lie.

74

"I love South Carolina," Rosie says, a broad smile sweeping across her face. "Charleston has to be one of my favorite cities. I was there once, right before a hurricane hit; can't remember the name of it, but the sky was dark gray, and the winds swirled everything around. Gabe lost his favorite hat, I remember, but oh, what a place." She drinks from her glass. "Do they live there?" Rosie asks.

"Who?"

"Your parents," she answers, a curious look on her face.

"Oh. Right." *But they're dead. My parents are dead.* "They're there now, until they go to Florida for the winter. They also have a place in the Vineyard." I realize what I'm doing. I am appropriating Wiley's life. These are her parents, wonderful people; I've known them for twenty years. I realize I can keep up this subterfuge, even if it feels like I'm submerged in a lake holding the raft above my head.

"Let's go." Louisa motions back to the kitchen. "We have a picnic to get to." I stand up, too quickly, for my knees give way and I stumble. I grip the back of the couch to regain my balance.

"Louisa," says Rosie, "she's too shaken up to go on a picnic. I have something here; I'm sure I do." Rosie moves to stand.

"Don't bother," Louisa tells her. "You have nothing. I ate the last piece of roast this morning. You have limes. That's all."

"I'm fine," I say, "and I'm really not hungry."

"When did you eat last?" asks Louisa.

"This morning."

"What did you eat?"

"Why?"

"I want to know."

"I had, I had, actually," *why does this sound so foolish; it is a perfectly normal breakfast food,* "I had some Pop-Tarts."

"Oh." Louisa nods. "Look, just come on. Wash your face, call your parents, and let's go."

"Don't we need to call the police?" I ask. "There was an accident."

Louisa smiles. So does Rosie.

"Good idea," says Rosie. A moment passes. "Gabe? Gabe, are you out there?" Rosie yells. Gabe ducks under the doorway and comes in from the porch.

"Gabe, you know that I was in an accident today and that this young lady hit my bike, not on purpose, of course?" Rosie says.

"Yep," says Gabe.

"You okay with that?" asks Rosie.

"Yep," Gabe answers.

"You're the police?" I ask, wishing I hadn't come in *right* on cue.

"Yep," he says. "Is that it?"

"Yes, Sweetie," says Rosie. "Just wanted to make Diana feel more comfortable." Gabe walks back outside, the aluminum door slamming behind him.

"Satisfied?" asks Louisa.

I look at her, I look at Rosie, and I consider myself, stranded here with strangers. Diana Moore, orphan. Diana Moore, dumped girlfriend. Diana Moore, lunatic in need of a Depression Professional Named Elliott.

But here? Here everything is different. Here I can be Diana Moore, a blank slate. Here, maybe, I can be someone else, someone new and different.

Diana Moore, *adventurer.*

Calling Home

Louisa follows me into the kitchen. "Listen, if you want me to drive you somewhere, I can. Philadelphia isn't that far, about an hour. Maybe you can take a plane?"

"Take a plane where?" *I have no place to go.*

Louisa's eyes widen. "To South Carolina, isn't that what you said?"

"Right," I say, remembering. "South Carolina. No," I murmur. "That's not necessary."

"What?" Louisa turns to me. "I can't hear you."

"I think . . ." I stop. "Remind me where we are."

"New Jersey." Louisa shakes her head. "What is it with you? Seriously. Is there something wrong?"

"It's been sort of a tumultuous day."

"I know," Louisa retorts. "I was there." She hands me the cordless phone. "Tell your parents you're going to have a spectacular afternoon." I watch Louisa leave the room, and then I stare at the telephone hanging in my hand, heavy like a free weight.

I don't know why, but I dial my parents' number in Princeton.

Since June, the house has stayed exactly as it was, the same elegant home in the same elegant setting, all the bills paid by someone, Uncle John maybe, everyone in Princeton waiting for me to do something. At least that's what it felt like, a collection of expectations steeping inside of me whenever I reached within five miles of the place. But I was not ready to "clean up," to "pack everything away," to "start anew." Not because of nostalgia or bereavement but because I was too tired to even contemplate what it meant to pack up the house. I used to picture myself there, in the basement going through old clothes, in the attic boxing up broken toys, but I couldn't actually go there and do it. The task seemed—and seems— insurmountable. I have no desire to climb Mount Everest. I don't want to swim the English Channel. And I don't want to go to Princeton and close my home.

The phone rings. An answering machine picks up. My mother's voice. "You have reached the Moores. Please leave a message." I had been adamant about not removing the tape. Aunt Margaret had backed me up when people protested—they had told her it wasn't right, it was eerie, I had to accept things, move on with my life. "She's keeping that message if she wants to keep it," Aunt Margaret had told them, and I knew it took all her self-restraint to keep from adding "you impudent horse's ass."

I hear the beep. And—God forgive me—I speak. "Hey, Mom, Dad, it's Diana calling. I'm going to be late. I got in an accident; don't worry, really, don't worry. I'm fine, just my car's a bit hurt. I'll see you in a couple of days after it's fixed. Love you, bye."

And then, as cleanly as the stem of a crystal glass cleaves from its base,

I break. Clicking the phone off, I stumble toward the screen door. I clutch my arms around my waist, trembling. *Do not do this, Diana,* I tell myself. *Do not cry, not here, not now.* I shut my eyes, my lids clinched together in a tight wet grip.

"Hey!" Louisa's behind me. "Everything okay?" I wipe my eyes with my shirtsleeve, a gesture I know she sees, but when I turn around she doesn't flinch, even though I'm certain it must be obvious I've had a breakdown of some sort.

"Yes," I say, "everything's fine." Louisa examines me for a long moment but stays silent. Then she turns around, picks up a backpack she's laid on a kitchen chair, and hands it to me.

"For supplies," she tells me. I take it. "C'mon." She pushes ahead of me and goes out the door. I follow her.

Outside, I'm struck by the intense afternoon sunlight. I take a deep breath and look around from the top of the outside steps. The day is perfect, cloudless, beaming. The idea of a city seems foreign here—it is a place where the sound of one solitary car devours the silence in a way that sixteen fire trucks and a car alarm can't manage to do in New York.

"Your chariot awaits," I hear Louisa say, and I take my first step, wiping my eyes one more time, blacking out the sun for only a brief second.

Millie's

Outside, Louisa holds up a green motorcycle. I look toward the garage at the back of the house and see, through the open door, about seven similar motorcycles stacked neatly against one another.

"All yours?" I ask Louisa.

"Ours. Rosie's and mine."

"Right," I continue. "How old is she?"

"Seventy-six," says Louisa. "Doesn't look it, does she?" She holds two helmets, one of which she hands to me when I reach the bottom step. "You've ridden before?"

"Yes," I say. A complete lie.

"Don't worry too much. These aren't really motorcycles anyway: They're dirt bikes. We need them in this place. Wait'll you see the land around here—it's mostly sand, like the beach. We're near the shore here."

The shore. Another memory. Here in this wilderness, it seems as if my memories are lined up, like matches in a matchbox, and any random word can tear one of them out, strike it, and out it flames. The shore community of Avalon, New Jersey, is about fifteen minutes north of Cape May, and it's where my parents really had their summer house, not in South Carolina. It is one of my favorite places on earth, and as I grew older, I was happy that people had an incorrect picture of what the Jersey shore meant so that my little spit of land stayed private.

My dad and I went to see movies at the one movie theater in adjacent Stone Harbor. My mom and I went shopping, walking or buying ice-cream cones. My brother and I partied at Fred's, a no-frills bar with live bands, and once or twice we lost our ride and ended up walking part of the three miles to our home in Avalon, late night, until someone picked us up so we could continue drinking at the rambling old bar, the Princeton. Romantic walks on the beach with old boyfriends, and wonderful evenings where someone else grilled fish and handed me drinks, saying, "Just think of this as your own private paradise."

I look around where I stand. Outside, fresh air. This wilderness. Louisa calls it a paradise. Maybe I've just come full circle.

I put on my helmet. The visor flaps down in front of my eyes; my hair is smashed against it, and I can barely see. I get on the bike behind Louisa, wrap my hands around her waist. She turns the key, revs the engine, and we go.

I feel the power of the engine immediately. We go out the driveway and onto a blacktopped road; she injects more gas into the machine, the motor roars, and my excitement builds. We're riding into the great unknown, and I'll accept whatever comes.

Except for what happens.

Which is that we stop.

We have driven approximately one thirty-second of a mile. I have been on the bike for exactly five-point-two seconds. We could have walked this distance in less than a minute.

"Why—" I begin.

"A little at a time. I've seen how you freak out with moving vehicles."

"But this seems—"

But Louisa has already jumped off the bike, removed her helmet, nudged the kickstand so the bike rests on the dirt, and is headed into a building directly in front of us. I think of what Betsy would say, "Yo, crazy-lady. Probably shouldn't have wasted the gas." Yet I don't say a word.

The building is an old-fashioned home with a wooden porch. When I push through the front door, I see it is a general store, and I feel a bit like one of the archaeologists who discovered King Tut. There is nothing inauthentic about this place. It is the genuine article, a store with a push-button cash register that propels a giant "2" or "9" up into a glass rectangle, a place to buy Quaker oatmeal and Nestlé Quik and Bumble Bee tuna, as well as WD-40, ballpoint pens, tampons, garbage bags, tablecloths, and herbal tea. There is a grill and a milkshake machine and a wide-smiling old woman behind the counter. Louisa has just kissed her on the cheek.

"Louisa," the old woman greets her, "we were just talking about you."

"Sssh," Louisa says, pointing to me. "Look, Millie. I've got a visitor. This is my new friend, Diana." I wave from the corner. Millie's chubby, bright-eyed, and quite old. But her voice is strong.

"You're the one who hit Rosie, right?" She looks at me for confirmation. I imagine the old telephone game of youth and see all these adults sitting cross-legged whispering accounts of my accident from ear to ear.

"Told you news travels fast." Louisa lounges against the counter.

"Um, yeah, yes," I stammer, "but I didn't mean to."

"Well, of course," Millie smiles. "Who means to hit anybody! Well, Anthony Hamilton tried to plow down Mark Smith's fence, but Mark deserved it, if you ask me, but no one *tries* to hit anyone, even people from New York." Millie speaks loudly, as if I can't hear. I look at the wall behind

Millie—for sale is a book about the Jersey Devil, subtitled *Mrs. Leeds's Unfortunate 13th Child.*

"Millie, nice people live in New York. I lived in New York, remember?" Louisa's defending me.

"I didn't say anything about not-nice people living there. I don't know a thing about it. Never been there. My daughter, Michelle, you remember her, she's been there, and her husband's from near there, someplace, what's the name? I'll think of it in a second; give me a second, it'll come. What's that place again, Mason?" Millie yells to the back of her store. A man's voice bellows back.

"Rye."

"Right." She looks at us. "Rye."

"Mason's here?" Louisa asks.

"Where he always is, back there, thinking he's going to fix that oven for the first time since 1969."

"Mason—" Louisa calls, singsong. "Mason, guess who?"

"I bet he's looking in the mirror right this second." Millie talks as she stacks dollar bills in the same direction. "Bet you ten to one he comes out here with his hair combed, what little is left. He's got a thing for Louisa, he does, but I don't mind; she can have him if she wants."

"Be careful what you wish for," Louisa tells Millie. "Mason's a catch." I notice tables in the back and a chalkboard that lists "Philadelphia Cheesesteak" and "Malted Milkshakes." Then, in a minute, a big man lumbers out from the back. He's easily Millie's age—which I'm putting somewhere near eighty. His flannel shirt is striped with black grease stains, but his hair is freshly combed. We can all tell "freshly," because of the grease stain on his forehead, near where he must have pushed the comb.

"Hello, Louisa," says Mason.

"Hey, handsome," she responds. "This is Diana."

"Did a number on your car," he tells me. I'm in a 1950s TV show, and Ozzie and Harriet are on the way to tell me to be more careful. "Mickey was sayin' it's a good thing you got yourself a Volvo. I don't like buyin' foreign myself, but I tell you this, it works out for young ladies like yourself so you don't end up wrapped around a tree."

"Get that look off your face, Diana," Louisa tells me. "There's a lot of good in a place where people notice what goes on. Can't get that kind of attention in New York."

"New York City." Mason's eyebrows rise; he says the words as if he's saying *West Nile virus* or *E. coli bacteria*.

"Mason, don't start," Millie interrupts.

"I'm not sayin' anythin'! I'm just speaking three words: 'New' 'York' 'City.' No crime about that, is there? Just why," he says, looking at me, "would a pretty girl like you want to live in that godforsaken place?" Mason rubs his eyes, getting more grease on his face. Louisa grins at Mason.

"What are you lookin' at?" he asks.

"I know you're looking worse than Mickey does," says Louisa. "Go look at the mirror." Mason walks over to an old mirror hanging on one of the wooden columns. He grimaces.

"Why don't you tell me I've got grease all over my face?"

Millie hands him a paper towel. "I thought you wanted it that way."

"As if I care what I look like at my age."

Louisa walks over to Mason and examines him in the mirror. "I liked the grease. Made you look like Clint Eastwood."

From my perspective, it seems like Mason blushes, and I take a deep inward breath when I acknowledge the kind of effect Louisa has on men, even married men old enough to be her grandfather.

"I didn't mean to get you upset," Millie says to me by the counter, "about mentioning the accident and all. Carlos said you were terribly upset, and really, you shouldn't worry; Rosie's tough as nails. Tough as nails."

"Oh gosh, no, I'm not upset," I say. "I deserve it."

"Oh gosh, no, but we've forgiven you," mocks Louisa, who's eavesdropping. She ducks down another aisle. I look around the store. In front of Millie, under the glass cabinet, is a panoply of penny candies: the red gummy bears, the red and black string licorice, Mary Janes and caramels with the white center.

"Which do you like?" Louisa stands beside me.

"Whatever you want," I say. "That's fine."

"You know what that means, Millie," Louisa says. "Bag 'em up." Louisa moves again, somewhere else in the store, and now I'm alone with Millie.

"Well, you picked a good day to hit Rosie, I'll tell you that. This celebration we have, it's getting bigger all the time. Tomorrow night, everyone's going a little wild, happens every year. In a good way, I mean. Anyways, this is the perfect time of year to come, when everything's as pretty as it can be; you'll see what I mean soon. Louisa's showing you around, right?"

"Yes," I reply. Everything feels strange: my feet, standing here on this wood floor; my arms, feeling detached from my shoulders. I stare at my fingers, moving them apart and back together. This is the sensation of benumbed misery flowing like my blood through every part of my body. I hear Millie speak, but her voice blends into the air of the room, and it too, like my limbs, seems detached. I force myself to pay attention.

"She's got some other friends coming, I think. She'll say she's here to be with Rosie, but you ask me, she has some *ulterior motives.*" Millie winks at me as she enunciates the last two words. "Know what I'm saying?"

"No," I respond.

"What?" asks Louisa, who has surfaced behind me. "What are you saying about me, Millie?"

"Nothing bad," Millie answers. "Now don't get mad, honey. I'm just saying you've been pretty excited about your friends coming." She pauses. "Especially that nice young man."

I watch Louisa beam one of her model-perfect smiles at Millie, but there's a frozen quality to the placement of her lips, and her eyes have turned frigid, inscrutable.

"I'm excited every time I visit you," Louisa answers evenly. "You and Mason are just so exciting." Despite my solipsism, I hear Louisa's voice grow pointed, and I turn. She faces me. "What's the matter?" she asks sharply.

"Just thinking," I say, as she lays out a paper tablecloth and a loaf of homemade bread and peanut butter and a wedge of cheese and some Carr's crackers on the counter, then walks toward the back, to a place I can't see. Millie rings everything on the cash register.

I dig into my pocket and pull out some money. "How much do we owe you?"

"Oh, no you don't," says Millie. "Louisa's got a charge here, like everybody else. Makes things easier to just send one bill at the end of the month." Millie writes out the total on a little slip of yellow paper, the cashier pads they used to have at drive-in restaurants. Louisa returns with three bottles of wine. Millie adds the cost to the yellow slip of paper and hands it to Louisa, who signs it.

"Can we borrow the corkscrew?" Louisa asks at the same time she reaches for it behind the counter, where it lies near the cash register. But as she gropes for it, it clatters to the ground below.

"Oh, just a second," says Millie as she bends over to pick it up. "Do my old bones good to try to touch the floor."

Louisa looks at me. Then she reaches above the counter to where the cigarettes are and grabs a pack of Marlboro Lights. She pushes it into the pocket of her blue windbreaker just as Millie climbs up the counter holding the corkscrew. Millie's face is flushed.

"Not what I used to be, no question about that," Millie says as she breathes heavily and throws the corkscrew into the bag.

"Thanks, Millie, my all-time favorite person in this place, you know you are." Louisa leans over the counter and gives Millie a kiss on the cheek. "C'mon," she motions to me. "Say goodbye to Millie. My goodness, don't they teach you to be polite in *Manhattan*?"

I'm stupefied.

"Diana, earth to Diana," says Louisa.

"Bye, Millie." I know I sound wooden.

"Bye, Mason!" Louisa yells.

"Don't go driving like a maniac," Mason hollers.

I follow Louisa out the door.

"Here," Lousia says, as she motions for me to unzip the backpack she handed to me at Rosie's. I push it toward her, the limpest of gestures. She takes it and stuffs the groceries inside. Then she folds the paper bags neatly, shoving them inside as well.

"Too heavy?" she asks. I lift it and shake my head. "Good," she answers. "We're not going far." She jumps onto the cycle. I stand there, the backpack in my hand, my helmet still hooked onto the handlebars. "It's picnic time, remember? What're you waiting for? Directions?" She takes a breath, then points to the backpack. "Put that on first, then the helmet," she instructs.

"Why'd you do that?" I ask. It makes no sense.

"What?" She stares at me, then shakes her head. She pulls her helmet off and looks me straight in the eye. "If I don't pay for the cigarettes, I don't feel as guilty smoking them." I don't move. "C'mon!" She's exasperated. "It's better for Millie and Mason, too; they won't feel guilty about selling them to me. It's only four dollars. What are you, a saint?"

And then, as if she's reading my mind, Louisa grins at me. "You want me to go back inside and pay for them?" She leaps off the cycle. Everything she does is fast, thoughts to action in a nanosecond. "Will this make you feel better?" She's almost up the steps.

"Wait," I say, because I feel that cloak of mediocrity sweep over me, the one that signals to others that I am unimaginative and scared of risks. "Let's just go," I say.

Louisa turns and comes back to the bike. She pulls her helmet on in a second and waits for me to do the same.

"You sure?" she asks me.

"Yes," I answer.

"It really isn't a big deal," she tells me. "I even think they know. Trust me."

I pull my helmet down and barely have time to snap closed the strap before Louisa's kick-starting the cycle and revving the engine. I hold on tightly as we soar out of the dirt driveway back onto the highway. Judgments, confusion, grief—they fly out of my mind like the sand under the cycle's wheels.

And in their place, something new, something exquisite.

I'm flying, flying down a black highway where we are the only occupants, the only people partaking of this space in time, drenched in blue skies and green trees on either side of the road, alone and free and fast, very very fast, and I'm not scared, not at all; I'm breathing, I'm exhilarated, I'm like the wind and the sun and the speed of the air, and I don't know at all where I am or who I'm with or what's about to happen, and none of that matters, because I am flying, *flying,* and it is, for this very brief moment, perfect.

Big Bog

Louisa drives for what seems to be a long time, but I have lost all sense of context. Still, my sense of euphoria lasts—nothing intrudes upon the momentum of this feeling. My sense of hearing is dulled by the wind and, in my mind, the force of my bliss. There is no need to hear—one needs only sight (for the sky! the trees!), touch (the wind! the machine!), and smell (fresh, bountiful, ubiquitous pine scent!). Such is the delight of a motorcycle ride in the wilderness of New Jersey.

Louisa turns off the blacktop highway and onto a dirt road, a trail hooded with trees and branches. We ride on sand, thick white sand spotted with pinecones. Louisa takes a sharp turn. I clutch her waist tighter, she revs the motor one more time, and we soar into a clearing where she abruptly clutches the brakes so that we both jerk from the seat when the bike comes to a stop.

Louisa hops off, removes her helmet, and puts on her sunglasses in one motion. I am slower, but I, too, eventually dismount and gingerly remove the helmet. I turn toward Louisa. She stands in front of a stunning sight: a lake, a blue pool of water, blue and green actually, sapphire and emerald, teal and jade, clear and clean and slightly bubbling from a scant gulp of moving air. I look around her to the right. There is a mountain of red dirt, about ten feet high, thick and solid and immense, a glacier constructed of sifted red clay and white sand and some ordinary brown dirt. The pool is carved out of this, this sifted earthen mixture, and I am drawn again to the scope of this body of water, almost a perfect circle, surrounded by pine trees.

"It's called Big Bog," says Louisa. "Dug out to be a cranberry bog but never cultivated. They filled it with water from the aquifer and never drained it. Now it's just for us." Louisa kneels to the ground and drags her hand in the water.

Cranberries. They cure urinary tract infections. Alicia Thomas, one of my college roommates, bought cases of Ocean Spray Cranberry Juice Cocktail for this very reason.

"This is cranberry country, blueberry too." Louisa speaks while I stare. This sight is extraordinary, and I want to absorb it all. I don't care about Louisa and her mercurial ways. I don't feel a modicum of concern for Wiley and Aunt Margaret, who are probably frantic by now. At this moment, I am the island that reputedly cannot be, the person who needs no one and has no earthly concerns, who can survive merely by gaping at nature's wonder hidden deep inside the country's most densely populated state.

"You have the strangest habit of going off, you know," says Louisa. "I mean, everyone goes off into their own little world, but you're a professional." Louisa has removed the tablecloth from the backpack and spread it on the red dirt banks of this lake. It is paper and it is white, and it flaps around on the edges like flattened birds' feathers. I like it better when Louisa doesn't speak. "You want some cheese?" She's spread some

Brie on a cracker and holds it up to me. I shake my head. I wish she'd stop talking. I want to stare. I didn't know that I needed to get out of the city so much.

"You have to talk to me," Louisa says. "Otherwise I'm going to have to do something outrageous."

"What can you steal here?" The words fly out before I have a chance to trap them. But Louisa isn't perturbed. She grins.

"I don't know," she says, looking around. "I'd steal the whole kit and caboodle if it was possible. Wouldn't you?" I do what she does, turning slowly around, soaking in more of the beauty, mentally recording how the autumn light burnishes everything, gilding the treetops and the red dirt, turning it precious. "Put it right in my pocket and take it with me wherever I go. I try to do that anyway up here." She taps her head near her temple. "Things get bad, I get depressed, I try to think of being out here."

"Does it work?" I suddenly have a mental image of two knights in armor fighting, one using a shield etched with caskets, the other engraved with pine trees.

"Depends on what I'm upset about. Sometimes I come out here and just cry." Louisa is behind me. When I turn around to look at her, I see she lounges on one elbow, one leg outstretched. Her manner is languid, confident. I can't imagine her crying, ever.

"So what is this place?"

"The pinebarons."

"The what?"

"It's called the Pine Barrens."

"Oh." So this is the place. The wilderness of New Jersey, the Pine-lands, Pine Barrens. One and the same.

Louisa grins at me. "Never heard of them, right? Don't take this the wrong way—I was a New Yorker once—but New Yorkers always think

New Jersey is all *Sopranos*-land, that and toxic-waste dumps." She gestures around. "This is our little secret."

I sit next to Louisa on the ground. "I don't blame you for keeping this a secret. It's incredible." I hesitate and, after a moment, admit the truth. "I have heard of the Pine Barrens. I just—I even have driven through them." I look around. "But it didn't look like this."

"Don't tell me. You saw some signs as you cruised by on the Atlantic City Expressway, the parkway?" While Louisa speaks, she smiles.

"Yes." I nod.

"That's like saying you know New York if you drive up the FDR. Not even close." She takes a deep breath, and I think she wants me to infer that the air she's inhaling is special, pristine, unlike the rest of New Jersey. She continues. "Behind those trees—for acres, for miles—are all the crops, all the reason New Jersey's called the Garden State. Again, New Yorkers don't know this—don't get mad; I told you, I lived there. I used to get mad, but now I just remind myself how ignorant people are."

"Thank you," I respond.

"Not you," she says. "Not necessarily."

I ignore her. "I don't see any crops."

"They're here, I'm telling you, behind all these trees. That's where cranberries and blueberries and tomatoes and peaches and cucumbers and string beans and soybeans and all kinds of things are planted and cultivated and harvested. Go fifty miles in any direction. You'll find them."

I remember the dried blueberries I held in my hand before I hit Rosie, before I met Louisa. I think of my Dad eating peaches. I watch Mom cut a cucumber, and I remember the Monster using the food processor Ben bought me for Christmas. (Slices of green pepper are still on the ceiling.)

"You ever hear of 'Pineys'?" she asks me.

"Nope."

"Rosie, Gabe, Millie, Mason—all of them. They're called Pineys."

"You're a Piney?"

"No," she says, for the first time looking away from me. "Not me."

"Why not?"

"I'm not from here," she tells me. "I'm an interloper. My grandparents are here, but I grew up outside Philadelphia. Bryn Mawr."

I'm pushed off balance, as if I've been teetering on a balance beam I didn't know was beneath me. My college boyfriend (the one who got away, stupid me) was from Bryn Mawr, a stately place of rolling lawns, stone mansions, and cricket clubs. In the pedigree of United States towns, Bryn Mawr and Princeton are first cousins. They thrive on the lineage of their inhabitants and the classic structures of their edifices; the Pine Barrens, on the contrary, seems to thrive on its natural glory.

"My mom never came back here after she left for college." Louisa stares up at the sky as she speaks. "She met my dad her first week of school, and they married before she was twenty." She turns toward me, grinning. "If you ever meet her, don't tell her that I told you she never graduated from Vassar. She likes to pretend she did." Louisa lies back onto her elbows. "I came here every summer, spent it with Rosie and Gabe. Mom wasn't a big fan—she tried to get me to go to some camp—but Dad insisted that I come here instead. He loves it down here; he'd move in a second if Mom would let him."

"Not a bad idea," I murmur, thinking I could move here. Maybe this is where I could hide.

"Where are you from?" Louisa asks me.

"Me?" I hesitate.

"Connecticut? You look like you're from Connecticut."

"No." I shake my head. *Why do I want to say Katmandu?* "I'm from Princeton. Princeton, New Jersey."

"You got to be kidding me," Louisa laughs, her booming laugh from earlier, a laugh that encompasses my grief and my fear, and I feel suddenly like Louisa has seen right through me, that with her laugh she's x-rayed me and found the sharp-edged pain that keeps my insides permanently bleeding.

"You're too much, Miss Diana." Louisa picks up a bottle of wine. "You're too much." She digs in the bag for the corkscrew. "You show up, out of nowhere, poof! Like the John Malkovich movie where people fall onto the turnpike, only you crash smack into Rosie, and then you start sobbing and then you pull me so hard my arm almost comes off and—anyway—" She plunges the corkscrew into the top of the wine bottle and continues, "It seems as if you've got a lot of stuff going on in that little head of yours."

She stops. I wait for her to say that she knows everything, that somehow she's read my mind, that she knows about the tragedy, that she knows everything there is to know about Diana Moore and wants me to go away and leave her family alone, car or no car.

But instead, Louisa motions to the water. "Pretty, isn't it?"

I nod. "Yes," I tell her. "It's amazing." I look around again, soaking in every detail of Big Bog, the blue water, the mound of reddish dirt, the golden sunlight from above, the vanguard of spectacular autumn-flecked trees around the perimeter of the bog, the sky, the blue-golden streaked-with-clouds sky. I cannot believe I didn't know this existed in my own state.

"Princeton's a nice place." She turns to look at me. "Class of 1988."

"You're kidding," I say.

"Nope," she tells me. "I hold the distinction of being their least-achieved graduate."

"I went to Harvard," I tell her. "Same year."

94

"And here we are," she says.

"Here we are," I repeat. Louisa takes a deep breath and sits down on the bank of Big Bog. I follow her lead. We are both cross-legged, separated by about a foot, as we stare at the sun setting over this most silence-provoking place on earth. It is precisely at that moment that I hold what I've been wanting—serenity. It will disappear in the time it takes me to rub my fingers together. But for right now, I have what I want.

Starlight

Today (rather, tonight) I savor the magnificent numbing provoked by enough glasses, enough *bottles* of good red wine. It is as if I've had a massage on the inside, the liquid curling and furling its way through my system, and I'm peaceful, relaxed—until I look up above the water and see that the memories of my family have transformed themselves into a visceral presence. I see them breathing; I see them alive.

Mom smiles at me; she loves me, I know. My father wants me to be happy, but he's still analyzing a *Racing Form*: the horses, the bloodlines, the results from the most recent races. It matters not to me, in my wine-imbued haze, that he is hovering above the blue-green water of Big Bog, looking at the *Racing Form,* his bulk standing straight, his glasses on, writing notations on the side of the newspaper, as if to bet tomorrow. Ben is there too; he, no surprise, is dancing. Jumping up and down, my barrel-chested brother dances. (Yes, he is hovering over Big Bog too, and yes, it would look ridiculous—if you were *sober*—to hover over a lake and dance, but I am not sober, so for me, it is okay.)

But then I realize Ben dances as if he's with Laura. That is why he looks so happy, and I am smacked by pain. I cannot gaze any longer at this chimera; I know I will crumble. So on earth, in *reality,* next to Louisa, I take another gulp from the wine bottle. Then I turn in another direction. And there in front of me is my mom again, in a slightly different outfit, her hair styled slightly differently, smiling at me. But the pain wallops me again, and I cannot bear to look at my mother, my father, or my brother, alive and defined and hovering on top of a body of water in New Jersey. It is too much.

"You sure you want more?" Louisa nudges me with a wine bottle. I nod. She pours the last drops into a paper cup. I sip from it, savoring the flavor, remembering how long it has been since I drank anything. In New York, many people had suggested, only half-jokingly, a jaunt through the city's pubs; alcohol, they said, would be my foil to grief. At the time, I had pictured the alcohol igniting my misery, like brandy in a cooking skillet. I was wrong. Alcohol has only exacerbated the erratic quality of grief. Perceptible thrumming erupting into a shotgun-like blast of pain—that's grief without alcohol. Grief with alcohol is the thrumming interrupted by an Uzi.

Still, tonight, five months later, I am with this stranger-friend Louisa, and I continue to drink. Next to me, Louisa lies on her back, staring at the sky. She seems remarkably sober. "Can you believe this?" she asks me. "Can you believe this sky?"

"Sure," I answer. "A sky is a sky is a sky." This is inaccurate, because what I look at right now is one of the most magnificent skies I've ever seen.

"You don't know how lucky you are."

"No, I don't," I answer. She doesn't know how lucky I am either.

"Wait till you see the whole thing," Louisa continues.

"I've already seen it, and I like it."

"No, you haven't seen anything yet, not anything."

"Okay," I answer. "I trust you."

"You shouldn't," she answers, not missing a beat.

"Oh," I respond. "Really?"

"Really," she answers. "I'm a fuckup."

I look at her, model-perfect while she says she's a fuckup. This is either (a) not true, but I'm going to have to listen to her presumed travails just so I can reassure her she's fine or (b) true, which will make her all the more alluring to everyone, including me, because it is always so damned fascinating when someone with Louisa's gifts is truly a fuckup. That's why an Angelina Jolie is always going to win over a Winona Ryder. Fuckups are more interesting.

But. Maybe, maybe Boring Girl from Princeton with a Triple Tragedy might qualify as interesting too. Maybe.

"Hello? Diana?" Louisa's sitting up now. "I'm not kidding. I'm a huge fuckup."

"I got it," I say.

"That's why this is so important," she gestures around the area. "This is like the most pure place on the earth—it is the purest place on earth—and I can't mess it up anymore. I can't."

"I'm sure it isn't that bad."

"You have no idea," Louisa says. "You have no idea." She stands, puts her hands in her pockets, and begins to walk to the bank of the bog. I stay where I am, watching her walk away. I am tired, I realize, tired and drunk.

Louisa walks back toward me. "Rosie has cancer."

This is not what I expected. "What did you say?"

"Cancer," she repeats.

"I'm so sorry," I say. Louisa sits down. "How serious?" I see Rosie's blue eyes, the crinkling of skin, her expression as she watches Gwen and drinks her vodka.

"She's in remission," Louisa starts, and I breathe easier. "But it's been scary."

"What kind?" I concentrate on sounding rational, clear-headed.

"Breast, twice," she says. "Two bouts of chemo. Not a pretty sight. One day, about a year ago, we were at Millie's, and her legs buckled, and she fell to the floor. Scariest thing in my life. Her eyes filled with tears—it killed me. Really. I thought I was going to lose it, but I held onto her and put her in a chair. Millie helped me. It was awful."

"That is awful." I repeat Louisa's words, because I cannot, in my present state, offer new ones.

"But she's better. I'm heading out after the harvest. I've been here for about a month. Rosie has Gabe; she doesn't need me. She's much healthier now. Besides—" Louisa sits up. I stay lying on my back. My eyelids grow heavy. "I think I'm going to have an escort out of this place."

She says "escort" with a lilt, and my sodden brain realizes I am supposed to react. "Cool," I say, like I'm fifteen.

"His name is Jack. He's coming tonight." Louisa stops. "I haven't seen him for seven years." As she talks, I look at the stars. I tap her on the knee.

"Hey," I say. "Look up." She does. "Now make a wish."

Louisa glares at me. "I'm saying something important."

"I know," I insist. "So make a wish." Sober or not, I'm a very superstitious person. I should know better; I must have wished seven trillion times that the Monster would stay with me, that he was being honest when he said he cared about me. Wrong, wrong, wrong, and yet here I am, promoting my fair-weather friends from up above. I should have wished for a meat cleaver. That I could have used.

"I'm going to make things right with him." She ignores my exhortation, grabbing the bottle of wine from my hands and drinking from its neck. "I've never told anyone before what I'm going to tell you."

"Wait," I say. "Don't." If she tells me her secrets, I'll have to tell her mine, and I want to pretend I don't have any secrets.

"It's not for you, it's for me." I turn on my side, this time looking at the lake.

"Diana," Louisa starts, impatient. "Listen to—"

Car lights flood the bank. We both turn, startled.

"Louisa!" A man's voice. Familiar. I hear a door slam; the lights stay on. "Louisa, you've got some friends looking for you." I can see in the shadows; it's Carlos. "Some guys. They're at Millie's. I figured you'd be here." Carlos peers through the haze of the car lights. "That you, Diana?"

"Yes," I say. I notice my diction has blurred. "Yes" has become "yesss."

"No driving, right?" he asks.

"No, I'm letting Louisa chauffeur me around."

"Good enough," he says. "You want me to bring them here?" Carlos asks Louisa.

"I'm coming." Louisa has already, in the space of a second, jumped to her motorcycle and put on her helmet. The sober penitent from five minutes ago has disappeared. Illuminated by the pickup truck's lights, Louisa's face burns red, energy as visible as lava.

"There's three of them. Great guys. I promised them they all could have their own cycle," she says. "I'll take them to Rosie's, then come back." She turns to me. "C'mon, I can't wait for you to meet them."

But I don't move.

"Diana!" Louisa sits on her cycle.

"I'm not coming," I say.

"Oh, for God's sake," she starts. "What do you need, an invitation?"

"No," I reply. "Go. I'll be fine."

"You sure?"

"Yes," I say, resolutely.

"Okay," Louisa calls to Carlos. "Let's go."

"See you, Diana," Carlos yells to me.

"Bye," I say.

"You're okay?" Louisa asks me. "Promise?"

"Yes," I say. "I promise."

I watch the thick tires of Carlos's truck turn to the left, and I watch Louisa as she soars out of Big Bog, her cycle jumping in front of Carlos's truck, which speeds up in an attempt to catch her. Their engines are loud, impossibly loud.

But then it is quiet.

I try another wish. "Star light, star bright," I whisper out loud. "First star I see tonight, wish I may, wish I might, have the wish I wish tonight." I open my eyes wide, feeling utterly alert. "I wish for world peace," I giggle. "I wish that the Monster would die a mean and painful deat—" I look up, embarrassed. "Didn't mean that." I close my eyes for a second. "I wish," I say, and then, opening my eyes, I look to the sky, suddenly in tumult. "I wish I could see my mom." I say this louder, and realize I've been suppressing a swell of wrath I can't control. "I wish I could see my mother," I repeat, more furious. "I. Wish. I. Could. Have. My. Family. Back."

And then I double over. Why won't the pain stay away, why can't it leave me alone; why does it go and come back, go and come back? I hurl a wine bottle toward the water—it hits the ground and doesn't break on the soft sand, which infuriates me even more. I stand, I kick at the dirt, I look back at the stars and beg for help—please, please do something, please.

This time, there are no tears. This time, there is only emptiness, and I feel it set in the straight line of my mouth. I am not strong enough for this. I want an earthquake, a hurricane, anything—even a devil, the one with the cloven hoof—Mrs. Leeds's unfortunate thirteenth child—to rush out and stomp on me, break me into little pieces and hurl me to the stars, let me go back with those people I love. Please.

Fritz and Billy

"Diana!" Someone yells as they poke me on the shoulder. I jerk around, half-asleep. I stare at a face I do not recognize, then another, and then another. My shoulder hurts; I have a crick in my neck.

"Sleepyhead!" That voice. That voice I recognize.

"Louisa," I say. I look at my watch. It's almost eleven. She left me hours ago.

"Good sleep, huh?" says a male voice. I look at him. He's tall, red-haired, but I can't see his face. He paces around, looking up at the sky, then out at the trees. "God's country. See," he says to someone else. "Perfect for camping. Here's living proof."

I close my eyes and breathe. Then I push my hair out of my face.

"How'd you get that?" A new voice, a different male. I turn to my right. A short man, balding, peers at me. He's small-shouldered, and he's dressed in jeans and a long-sleeved T-shirt, normal enough, but I can't take my eyes off the Asian-looking coat he wears. The buttons are gold-plated, and the collar is rounded, Mandarin. It is a blinding bright purple. "Doesn't it hurt?" he asks me.

I think he's talking about his coat. "A little," I say.

"You know, Diana," says Louisa, "I thought you couldn't look any worse." In another time, I would be hurt. But Louisa's right. "It's bleeding again. That thing on your forehead," Louisa tells me.

"You look fine to me," says the tall guy. "Liquored up, maybe, but fine." I see he has dark eyes, hooded, with long eyelashes. There is stubble on his skin, and his smile is kind, lined with slightly crooked white teeth.

"Jack?" I ask.

"Fritz," he says. "Sorry to disappoint you."

"And what a mistake," says the other guy. "I've known Jack and I've known Fritz, and let me tell you, Fritz is no Jack."

I stare at this other man. Short Guy has nice eyes, clear and blue, but his chin recedes, and most of all, there's that purple coat.

"I'm Billy," he says. "You've gotta be Diana."

"Yes," I say.

"Nice entrance," he tells me. "I've done some things to meet people before, but I've never crashed into their grandmother."

"Don't listen to him," says Fritz. "The big bad city is enough to send anyone out here, amidst the thickets and brambles."

I'm too bleary to respond to either of them. "What took you so long?" I ask Louisa. I must have fallen asleep here by Big Bog. In one day, I've traveled so far that I've slept outside, under stars, in a New Jersey wilderness I didn't know existed. It's almost inconceivable.

"Jack didn't show," she says. "Asshole."

"I told you," Fritz interjects. "He's coming tomorrow. He's driving down first thing."

"I just can't fucking believe it," she says.

"Did you think I was lying to you?" he asks.

"We just had this argument," Billy says. He turns to me. "She insisted on calling him, because she didn't believe us."

I look at Louisa. I wonder if she's ever been stood up before. I flash back to the Monster chiding me—*"You don't want me to hang out with my friends?"*—after he had rung my doorbell at three in the morning, eight hours after his scheduled arrival.

"He said he'll be here by noon. You're not happy with us?" asks Fritz.

"Whatever," responds Louisa. I look around the perimeter of the bog. Near the treeline are three motorcycles tilted next to one another, which means that three engines roared into this space, and I heard nothing. It has been a long time since I drank this much.

"I see we came just in time," says Fritz, as he holds up an empty bottle in the air. One solitary drop of red liquid falls to the earth. He smiles, and I smile back. Then he goes to his bag and takes out another bottle. He stops and looks at me. "Will you just look at that? Just look at that, will you?" He points toward the water. "The whole state's a development park, and then wham, this, smack in the middle. Unbelievable."

"I still don't believe it," says Billy. "I still can't believe I'm in New Jersey."

Fritz gestures to me with the wine bottle. I take it, remembering the adage that one way not to get a hangover is to stay drunk. I swallow and then I follow Fritz's gaze to the water. I see it again as I did when Louisa and I first arrived: It is exquisite.

"You wouldn't believe how lost we got," Billy says to me.

"I gave you directions," Louisa responds.

"Directions," Fritz shakes his head. "Call me crazy, but I don't think 'turn left at the firehouse and make a right when you see a dirt path' should be considered directions."

"Fritz made us stop," says Billy.

"Yeah, I kind of thought that a cranberry harvest would be a hard thing to find in *Newark*—which is where we would have ended up if Rosie hadn't helped us out."

"The point is, you're here," offers Louisa, who plops herself down next to me. Billy is the only one who remains standing. He walks over to the boundary of the bog. I look over at Fritz, who is inhaling the air as if he's just been released from a submarine. He catches me looking at him and stops, embarrassed.

"Can't get enough, know what I mean?" he asks me.

"Yes," I respond.

"So what has Louisa told you?" Fritz asks. Louisa glances over.

"Nothing," she says.

"Not a thing," I say. "How do you two know each other?" I ask.

"We went to boarding school together," says Fritz.

"We've known each other fifteen, no—" begins Louisa.

"Try twenty," says Fritz.

Billy rejoins us. "How big is this place?" he asks.

"The whole thing?" Louisa questions.

"Yeah," Billy says, turning around, extending his arms wide. "This whole place, the Pine Barrens."

"About a million acres," she says. "Same size as the Grand Canyon."

"Here?" exclaims Billy.

"Yep," answers Louisa. "No one knows. How wild is that, no one knows."

"Well, I know," says Fritz. "And now so does Billy and our new friend, Diana."

"Wait till tomorrow," Louisa says. "Wait till I show you all around tomorrow. It'll blow your minds."

I'm feeling detached right now, which is probably why I turn and examine Louisa. She is attentive, beautiful, and so very sexy. I realize that if I read a million *Cosmopolitan* magazines, if I had a private tutorial with Helen Gurley Brown, I would never, ever, be as effortlessly sexy as Louisa is right this second. This flash of awareness disheartens me, so I tilt my head back and drink some more.

"How's the harvest?" Fritz asks Louisa.

"Gabe says it's the best ever," says Louisa.

"Never enough cranberries," comments Billy. "That's what I always say."

Their banter drifts around me, not mattering. My mother has reappeared. She is exquisite, young—I have never seen her like this. The pictures I remember do not do her justice. She is confident and intelligent and trusting, too trusting. I flinch, because I know this is what my mother was like before life attacked her—real life, with all its attendant vagaries and disappointments and mediocre, jealous people. But right now, I am seeing my mother when she is my age, her big eyes bright blue and flashing with comprehension. She sees me in this glorious wilderness, with these new friends, and she is pleased. The dress she wears is one I have in my closet in New York. I will wear it someday. She—Mom—seems to read my thoughts. She nods. She *nods. Mom, Mom!*

I do not know that I am crying.

"Hey, hey!" says Fritz. "That's a bit much, right? Don't you think?"

I snap open my eyes, about to say *it's because of the accident* but realize that no one, not even Louisa, knows about the accident.

Louisa smiles at me, the light from the end of her cigarette illuminating her face. "I know," says Louisa. "It's a guy, isn't it?"

For a moment, I say nothing.

And then I nod. "A guy."

Louisa jumps to her feet, her cigarette held between two fingers, her mouth spread into a wide grin. "I knew it! *I knew it!*" Louisa exclaims. "No one cries like you do unless it's over a guy."

Six months ago, I would have reacted the same way.

"A guy, let me tell you—no, let me guess. Your love. Your one true love. He says he loves you; alas, he doesn't. I mean, he likes you. What is there not to like? But love? Nope. It isn't you, Diana, it's him. It isn't personal. In fact, he says, it has *nothing to do with you.*" Louisa stops, inhales.

I cannot believe how wrong and right she is at the exact same time.

"What's his name?" asks Billy. I look down to the sand, discomfited.

"I call him the Monster," I murmur.

Louisa throws her head back. "The Monster! *My Melodrama Queen!*"

"Leave her alone," says Fritz.

Billy interjects. "But what's his real name?" he asks. "What's his real name?"

"Uh—" I stammer. His name is too painful; it is like shards of glass carving into me, whittling me on the inside. I cannot say it. I will not say it.

"Now I understand." Louisa folds her legs under her and sits next to me. "Now I understand everything."

I stare back, as if she's discovered my burning secret, and feel like I did when I quit my job. The tree inside of me flowers; it is bursting with flowers, ugly red flowers, with red beads dripping from its branches, wine or cranberries, I don't know which, but it doesn't matter, because I just nod at Louisa and tell her, "You're exactly right."

FIVE

Delusions

I know I am drunk, because I am overwhelmed by a desire to put my head on a pillow. Sand is apparently not suitable, because whenever I attempt to lie on the ground, strong hands keep pulling me up. My stomach churns, an interior elevator carrying bile up to my mouth. I can take it no longer. I run into the woods, shaking, trembling, my mother's voice—*"I was never drunk in my entire life"*—scolding me, my hair tumbling past my shoulders. I heave, I kneel on the ground, hair falling past my shoulders, and then I feel someone pull back my hair.

"Take your time," I hear. "Breathe. It's okay. It's okay." A man.

I retch again and again, my stomach revolts, my bottom jaw trembles.

"Deep breaths, it's all okay, it's fine."

"Sam?" I ask. I know it isn't him, but my mind can't sort this out. I am ready to say the Monster's name, but even now, in the woods, I can't; it is not him, it will not ever be him.

"Here." A man's hand stretches in front of me, holding a handkerchief.

I take it, I wipe my face, sit back on my knees. I push my hair from my face and look to my savior. I see glints of cheekbones through longish hair. I try to focus, but I'm trembling too much.

"Diana!" It is Louisa.

"Diana!" It is Billy.

"I have to go," says the stranger. "Take care of yourself," he tells me.

"C'mon, stay," I murmur, drunkenly. But he has already left. All I know is that he wears jeans and his voice is gentle.

"Diana!" I hear again. I know I should respond, but I don't. Fritz finds me.

"She's here!" he calls. Louisa and Billy emerge from the trail.

"Oh, God," says Louisa. "Should've known. I should have known. This is my fault. I should've known she couldn't handle her liquor."

Fritz helps me up.

"Didja see 'im?" I ask, slurring my words.

"See who?" asks Louisa. "The Monster?"

"Who?" I ask.

"Who are you talking about?" asks Billy.

"The guy," I say. I watch them look at one another. "Wait," I say, and plant my feet in the ground. I want this equation to compute.

"Didja see him?" I ask. They look at me. I repeat, more emphatically, "He was here, he pulled my hair back, I know it," I say.

"No one is out here but us," says Louisa. "I promise. Now let's get you home; maybe he'll show up again in your dreams."

"But—" I persist, even as I allow them to escort me away. I feel something drop to the ground. "Wait," I say. I pick up the vomit-stained handkerchief.

"What about this?" I ask. I feel suddenly sober. "What about this?"

I thrust out the handkerchief. Fritz shrugs.

"Cool," he says. "I'm with you, Diana. Someone gave you that handkerchief, fine by me. But let's get you home."

I walk with them, unevenly, swaying. I picture a pillow; I see my head lying on top of it. I clutch the handkerchief as Billy walks me back through the trail, Louisa and Fritz behind us. My head keeps bobbing up and down, heavy with the density of inebriated thoughts. Fritz holds my arm, Louisa my waist. I am like the animal at the circus; all I do is follow.

The Middle of the Night

I shudder as I wake. I am on a couch. I lift my head for a moment and then place it back down, on a pillow. I wear the same clothes. There is a blanket. I am alone, and I am scared; there are tears. I see my future, a cactus on a desert, a hunchbacked woman with a whisker on her chin, a mean old lady peering through a window into a happy family's Christmas dinner. Barren, wasted organs, reproducing nothing, a fallow life, no family, no lover, no job, no significance. A wilderness thriving with people—old, young, men, women—people who abide me because I've intruded, people who will forget me once I'm gone. The middle of the night is the worst, it has always been the worst; waking up crushed by a wave of loneliness. I wrack my brain for the thought of something hopeful, but instead I feel as if I am pouring water over outstretched palms. My mother would say to be thankful I am healthy, that I have two eyes, two ears, that I have great gifts, that there are people with so much less.

I close my eyes and hope I will sleep.

Foxhole Girl

When I wake again, I am hit with the mental brickbat of memory—and a colossal hangover. I look around where I am sleeping—Rosie and Gabe's couch. Gwen sleeps next to me. I smile. A dog is sleeping next to me, I'm in New Jersey, and I have met new people who have embraced me and helped me to forget.

Until, of course, I remember.

I am in the Pine Barrens of New Jersey, on a couch, with a strange dog.

I sit up. I am filthy. Gwen stirs but does not move, so I step over her. In this living room, amid the dark wood panels and unmatched furniture, I notice old photographs that I did not stop to examine yesterday. When I walk over to them, I see that they are pictures of Rosie and Gabe from many years ago, Rosie smiling with red hair and Gabe with dark hair and proud features; I see the people they are today in these pictures. It triggers the memory of a game I used to play in New York, after the accident. I'd imagine the death of every person I passed on the street. The man on the corner with the striped shirt will die in seven years, six months, three days, after a bout with chemotherapy-treated prostate cancer. The young woman with the dark glasses and blood-red lips will die in exactly forty-six years, three months, and eighteen days, as she lies in her twin bed at an old age home, wishing that her roommate, Chatty Julie, would die first. Everyone will die, myself included, so why do I take my own situation so seriously?

I walk up the first set of stairs. The bathroom is the first door on the right. I glance at my watch: 5:33 a.m. Good. It is early. I push open the bathroom door.

"Louisa?" A man's voice. "I'll be done in a sec."

I panic. I run back down the stairs, jump on the couch, and pull the blanket up over me and close my eyes, pretending to be asleep. But then I feel foolish and unclasp my eyes.

Gwen looks at me, wagging her tail, and I feel like Gwen knows everything. She knows about the deaths and she knows that I lied to Louisa and she knows that I am embarrassed that I interrupted the guy in the bathroom.

Wait a minute. What guy? That wasn't Gabe. Oh, my God. It was Fritz or Billy. Which one? With Louisa? I thought she was waiting for Jack.

I close and open my eyes again. I feel it—stupidity, ignorance, mediocrity—stinging me, blasting me for my inability to see what is clear to *everyone else in the world.* Yes, Louisa is waiting for Jack, and yes, Louisa would sleep with someone else, and yes, it is only me, Diana Moore, the Smiling Idiot, who doesn't catch on to these nuances of human behavior. Louisa is sophisticated, Louisa is mercurial, Louisa is captivating. I, on the other hand, am oblivious, pedestrian, idiotic. I pull the covers over my face. I want to disappear.

The house is silent except for Gwen's panting. The room is dark, but now I can see everything as if it's lit in floodlights. I am painfully awake. I picture myself as Louisa sees me, as everyone sees me, and I'm dismayed.

I can see her, the Smiling Idiot, as she stands with her ponderous legs apart, waving her bulbous hand, wearing her stupid grin, nodding "yes" and "I agree" and "I'm sorry" like a fool.

And I can see that underneath her straddled legs is a foxhole, almost completely concealed. Inside is another person, a woman, crouched on the ground, against the dirt wall, weary, bony, her arms crossed around her knees, tears streaking her face.

This is Foxhole Girl—the other me, the true me—the one who is intelligent, who is insightful, who is, on rare occasions, intriguing. This is the person hidden by the Smiling Idiot. This is the person who has given up.

I huddle under the blanket. I close my eyes, turn my head both ways, shudder. The house is still quiet.

I pull the blanket back from my face. Gwen thumps her tail more emphatically. I force myself to breathe deeply. I tell myself that I am allowed to give up, that anyone in my position would give up, that once I get my car back, I'm going to drive far away and hide somewhere and live completely alone, maybe in a city, maybe in the country, eating, drinking, running, sleeping, all by myself, until the day (thirty-six years, five months, and one day from now) that I finally die.

Rosie

"Sweetheart, are you awake?" I shut my eyes so tightly, I am sure that I'm wincing. It is Rosie, calling from the kitchen. She must have heard me climb the steps. I open my eyes.

"I'm coming." It is my best sleepy voice. I stand and go into the kitchen.

"Hello, darling," says Rosie. She moves slowly but gracefully. "I thought I heard someone. Want some coffee?" She holds out a steaming mug. I take it from her. "I bet Louisa tired you all out yesterday, didn't she?"

"We didn't do that much, in all honesty."

"She's a mover and a shaker, that one." Rosie sits next to me. Her hair is white and cut very short, almost to her scalp, her blue-gray eyes shine despite the drooping overhang of skin beneath her eyebrows, her skin is still clear and lightly rose-colored. She is one of those people who at first glance register "old woman," and on second, "She must have been pretty once," and on third, fourth, and fifth, "She is so so lovely."

"I get such a feeling from you, child. Such a feeling."

Terrific. *Feelings.* It is entirely too early in the morning—and I am too hungover—for feelings.

"I don't know what it is; I don't know what it's telling me, but I have to trust it when I have it." She takes a sip from her mug. "You shouldn't feel guilty about yesterday, Sweetheart. Louisa and I were just having fun."

"Fun."

"You look so serious," says Rosie.

"I'm just thinking—"

"Did Millie say something?"

"Millie?"

"Millie's like a water tap that's broken, constant flow of information. Her opinions are part of the landscape here; she runs the whole area, if you ask me, and we aren't the worse for it. Usually she makes a lot of sense."

"I didn't get to talk to her that much." I go to the sink. "Is it okay if I use these?" I grab some paper towels.

"Of course," says Rosie. I take the towels, wet them, and then place them onto my face. I press hard, scouring each corner of my nose, my eyes, my cheeks, my neck.

"Feel good?"

"You have no idea," I say. I keep the water running and then splash it onto my face, over and over again. I drip, but at least my face is finally free of filth. Rosie hands me another paper towel.

"Rosie, listen, I really don't know how to thank you for putting me up here; it was so nice of you," I mumble. "But I really am going to have to leave as soon as my car is fixed. You said it might be ready today, right?"

Rosie gulps down her coffee. "Oh, dear, I was—well, of course. Whatever you want."

"What is it?"

"Oh, it's nothing."

"No, I'm sorry, I was presumptuous. What? You were going to say something."

"Well, listen, Mickey is the best car mechanic around. He used to make those farm machines run on pinecones and honey, I think. A magician. I just—" I take a sip of the coffee. It is strong, too strong, but I enjoy the feeling of caffeine jolting my body, the gears in my mind lining up, beginning to churn. Rosie continues. "Well, since you're bringing it up, I was going to ask if you would do me a favor and keep Louisa kind of busy this afternoon while Gabe and I go to Philadelphia." She drinks more of her coffee. "I know the boys are here, but they may want to go fishing or leave her alone, so I didn't want to ask them."

"Oh," I say, words spilling, "of course. I'm not in that much of a rush. Whatever you want. I won't say a word." I realize in that second that Rosie is a person for whom I would do anything.

"Gabe and I are driving up to talk to those damn doctors one more time, although I have to tell you, even though Gabe won't admit it, they all do the same thing—mash all their words up together and say it nicely, or not, and just tell me pretty much the same thing." She sips her coffee. "I'm going to die."

I stare at Rosie. I suddenly see my mom in her; I see everyone who has died in her.

"This feeling I have about you, I just can't shake it. Are you okay, dear?" Rosie studies me.

"Yes," I say. "I am perfectly okay." She moves about adroitly, no sense of having plucked me out of my jungle of self-obsessions to a place where I am to consider her death.

"Then I wish I could just figure this out. I'm rarely wrong," Rosie tells me. She goes to take my coffee mug. "Do you want any more?" She begins to pour.

"Louisa said the cancer was gone." I need Rosie to explain.

"She did?" Rosie asks. "Well. That's right."

"So you don't have cancer."

"No," she tells me, "I do." She pauses. "It's right that Louisa would say that, think that. She doesn't know it's come back."

"Why haven't you told her?" I stop. "Why are you telling me?" I grip the back of a chair.

"Good question," she tells me, sitting down. "It felt right to tell you. It hasn't felt right to tell her." She sips more of her coffee.

"But," I begin. I sit down.

"What is it, dear?"

"You have cancer," I say.

"Yes," she replies.

"I just—" I hesitate. "I wish you hadn't told me."

"Oh," she says. "Oh." She studies me. "I'm terribly sorry. I can't help myself, just blurt out what comes to my head if it feels right, and it felt right, so I wish—well, are you okay, Diana?"

"No." I am definitely not okay.

"Do you want to talk about it?" It is five-thirty in the morning. This woman is dying, and I know it, but her granddaughter does not. And I haven't even opened that box of my own miseries, a box where the gremlins inside keep pushing at the lid.

"No," I repeat.

"Diana," she says. "Look at me." I do. She is grace personified, but that is immaterial. Inside her is cancer, and outside there is this wondrously kind face, and I do not appreciate this chasm between what is real and what seems real. I do not want to acknowledge it. I wish I didn't know. "Look, Sweetheart, maybe the doctors are wrong."

"Tell Louisa," I say.

"I can't do that," she replies.

"Why not?" I ask.

"Because she will not be able to take it. Because I will not be able to take her response." She says her next words with equanimity. "I expect the next few months will be difficult, and I imagine that if Louisa knew, they would be only more difficult for her and for me." She stops, looks to the ceiling, knits her eyebrows. She puts her coffee mug on the table, then stands. I see the scab from yesterday, again reminding me of a little girl falling from her bike. Rosie pulls out the chair, steps up on it, as agile as a teenager, and reaches to the ceiling and pinches a spider from the corner near the cabinets. She steps down slowly, holding the spider. It is a daddy longlegs, brown, limbs like long eyelashes. She puts it on the table. We both watch it scurry around until it crawls over the edge, disappearing.

"I will tell her, of course, when it is the right time." Rosie sits down across from me, looking as if she's going to tell me something else, something worse. "This coffee is horrible." Her face breaks into a wide, wonderful smile. "Why didn't you tell me?"

I return her smile. "Didn't want to offend you."

"Word to the wise, Diana," Rosie tells me. "You can offend old people. They can take it. It's the young ones you should be careful about." She stands and walks over to the sink, pouring out the remainder of her coffee. "Want me to make some more?"

"No," I say. I've made my own decision. "I want to go for a run."

"God's country, Diana. You do what you want."

I put my mug in the sink. I notice a vodka bottle near the sink, opened, the lid on its side.

"Diana?" I turn back.

"Yes?"

"Well, just, now don't get overly worried, Sweetheart, just be careful when you're running near the fields. Actually, I think you should stay on the roads, okay?"

"I hadn't thought about going anywhere else."

"It's just that, well, if you're planning to run near the fields, at this time of morning, just be careful of the men. They're all lovely people, but you have to be careful, you know." She sips. "They may have guns."

Guns? Did she say *guns*?

"It's just that you're a stranger, to these people anyway, and it's the harvest season, and everyone's a hunter around here anyway, and with the whole celebration going on tonight—so just make sure you're in the open, and everything will be fine."

"Should I not go?"

"No, of course you should. It's a lovely morning. I just wanted to cover my bases."

"Is the celebration that big an event?"

"It's a tremendous amount of fun; I really think you'll enjoy yourself if you stay. There's all kinds of food, and if the night is clear, I don't think you'll find a better place to spend an autumn evening. Everyone comes—you'll see, there will be an excitement today in the air; you can smell it, I really think so. We rely down here on our crops, you know, on nature, so maybe it's our way of being respectful to the gods." She says "gods" with a slight twinkle in her eye, and I wonder if she's teasing me.

"Well, you don't have to decide now," Rosie finishes. "Have a good run, Diana. That's what you call it? A run? In my day, we ran, well, that can't be interesting to you, I don't think. Just go straight either way. There's only one road."

I go back into the living room. My bag is there, and I change quickly. I push aside the news of Rosie's cancer and ignore the relentless thrum of my hangover. Instead I think about how I've always liked running in strange places. There is no precedent; everything is new. I realize that this may be the first time since I got here—except for the scant seconds of appreciating the lake right before the accident—that I will be alone and able to grasp the beauty of what I'm seeing.

Of course, I can't help thinking, there is an equal possibility that as soon as I am running I will start to cry, and I will make a wrong turn, and a disgruntled cranberry-celebration attendee will promptly shoot me in the chest. I imagine this, too, as I lace my sneakers, the heavy wet sand steeped in my blood, as I fall back, for the last time, onto the earth.

Red Lakes and a Fisherman

6:16 a.m. It is still dark. I take my first steps. I am running on a wide road, paved, and it is completely quiet. I run on one side, well within the borders of the sandy shoulder and the actual car lanes. I look ahead; the ground is flat for as far as I can see, the road empty but for the deep blue in-between the hood of the pine trees. The air is cold but not uncomfortably so; I feel my legs relax into a groove and my arms move in their familiar pattern, and I remember what a solace running is for me.

I run by an ancient cemetery on my right. I can see the dark stone of knee-high monuments, etchings so worn they're indecipherable. Grass rises in uneven bursts of green against the hundred or so graves, life bursting through the ground like the pine trees.

My thoughts are unfocused, so I surprise myself when I turn onto a sandy road on my left, the kind of trail Louisa drove me on yesterday en route to Big Bog. The voice in my head screams: DO NOT GO IN THERE! GUNS! But I keep running. This is unlike me; I always do what I am told. And Rosie was so explicit: *"Dear, stay on the main road, and you'll be fine."* But my feet turn, they move onto this trail, a trail with no end in sight, trees on every side, the white sand sinking slightly under my steps. Beneath my feet, the path is cluttered with forest litter: branches, leaves, sand, bark. Above me, the sky lightens, the deep black turning royal blue, turning cerulean. I don't know where I am; I'm traveling further and further away from what is known to me, and I don't care. Instead I concentrate on a clearing up ahead; it is not far ahead of me. I am exploring, it is getting closer, I am an adventurer, it is here.

I stop, and I gasp. Not because of running, but because of what I see.

Enormous and sublime. I can't take it all in—it is the Grand Canyon or the Taj Mahal, but it is all natural (okay, so is the Grand Canyon, but that is dry rock, a painting by God, but one that doesn't—in contrast to what I see right this second in the Pine Barrens—*move*). Ahead of me is a vast clearing in the middle of the trees, about the size of a small town, where smaller, oblong lakes are intercut by crisscrossing roads, where the water shimmers under a brightening blue sky, and the green of the pine trees glows from the rising sun. The water is blue-green, but there is a reddish tint in some places. It is stunning, it is quiet; I have never seen anything like this. The area stretches far into the distance, I have no idea how far, and then, encompassing everything, are the pine trees that I have come to recognize as my own private security blanket. I want to run into the clearing— I want to jump into these lakes—I want to absorb every detail of this place. I take a step and look closer. I swat a spider from my arm, sweat dripping. I crouch to my knees, gazing at the sight ahead of me. I realize I don't want to enter it any more than I want to enter the scenes of perfect paintings I see in museums. I just want to watch, to take it all in. What I see, this bounty and beauty and God, this must must be God—I have seen nothing like this. I have seen nothing like this.

There's a rustling behind me. I'm startled in the way a sudden sneeze intrudes upon a sermon at church. I take stock of my whereabouts—the trees are too thin, and I am too wide—there is no place for me to go and be unseen. I stay crouched and turn around. I see denim-covered legs, male legs (don't ask me how I know, I just do), scurrying through the woods. I don't believe he has seen me but—wildly, oddly—I sprint off, following him. Who is this person? What is he doing in the woods? I should be scared, but instead I am bold. I follow the noise, and soon I see a chainlink fence. I slow down.

I see him. A tall guy, lanky, muscular, scampering over the chainlink fence as if he's a hurdler at the Olympics. From the way he hovers on top of the fence, his hair covers his face, most of it, but I see the color, brown-gold, and see that it is straight and hangs haphazardly from his scalp. He throws both legs on the other side of the fence, hangs for a moment at the top. His hair flops back behind his face, and I see he is handsome, sports-guy handsome, not perfect—there looks to be a scar of some sort near his right cheek—but ohmygoodness very attractive. He looks straight at me. He smiles, not opening his lips. A smirk? A smile? Which is it? Welcoming? Not?

And then he winks.

I gulp. I'm tempted to turn around and make certain he is looking at me, like one of those old Richard Pryor movies, but even I know there can be no one else in these woods. Instead, I stand, gripping the thin trunk of a tree and look back at him. He drops to the ground, and picks up a fishing rod. He nods at me, smiles again—this time with teeth—and saunters off. I remain stuck to the tree.

Moments pass before I retreat back to my familiar state of mind: grieving, self-absorbed, and, most significantly, lost. The man is gone. I walk slowly through the woods. Little animals pass in front of me, birds fly overhead; I hear nothing that makes me think I am going to find civilization any time soon.

Yet I trudge along. And soon, without thought, I pick up the pace, breaking into a comfortable stride. I find myself grinning, which surprises me. And then I laugh, a gate swinging open in my mind, a trail leading to a place where a handsome man winks at me and I feel enlivened, pulled toward him in the most fundamental—and for me, of late, unfamiliar—of ways. But maybe this is what it is all about? The little glimpses of an exquisite, natural sight, a lake tinted red, a man on a chainlink fence? The fleeting but euphoric moments with the Monster, the hours and days spent with a mother and father and brother who loved you and felt you were significant—perhaps this is life, and this is what we need to take with us when we are alone, when we are despondent, when we are walking through a woods, lost.

I notice a sandy path in front of me, and I take it. In minutes I am back on the main road, and except for a short detour when I realize quickly that I've gone in the wrong direction, I head back to Rosie's. I smile the entire way.

The Harvest

Louisa slouches against the house, waiting for me.

"Rosie said you went running. You must have gone, what—five, six miles? I used to run, but I was better at lacrosse; running hurts my knees. Do you take calcium?"

"No," I say, as Louisa jolts me out of my chainlink fence–guy reverie. I've been transported from my grief, truly transported, and I feel myself shudder as I come back to earth, where Rosie has recurrent cancer and my family is dead.

"Come on," she says. "I want to take you somewhere."

I don't want to go anywhere, I whine silently. *I want to fantasize about the chainlink fence–guy.*

"You're going to thank me." She hands me a motorcycle helmet. I take it grudgingly. It is futile for me to argue with Louisa.

Ten minutes later, though, I'm feeling the same euphoria as yesterday, soaring through the woods on the back of a green Kawasaki. The Pine Barrens are good for me—they're rejuvenative and exhilarating and new, new new new—and I'm going to be the better for it. I'm going to change this instant: I'm going to go on with my life and accept my family's deaths just like the Kennedys; I'm going to stop living in my head and open up to people, people like my new friend, Louisa, especially people like Louisa, people who are consummately open, always ready to speak and engage and just do. I resolve to become like her, today. This second. The next time I see a sight like the one I did this morning, I'm jumping in the water. The next time I see my future husband on a chain-link fence and he winks, I'm hurtling over the fence like I'm Jackie Joyner-Kersee.

Louisa brakes in a clearing not unlike the one near Big Bog, only there is no water hole in front of us. She parks her bike against one of the ubiquitous trees and motions for me to follow.

"Ssssh," she says.

We walk, tiptoe almost, along a path that only Louisa sees. I watch her dart ahead of me; her body is a dazzling instrument that she wields effortlessly. I've seen her eat and drink, but I want to know what magic occurs that causes the same food and liquid I consume to result in wedges and slabs on me, while she becomes more taut, more golden, more lissome. There are no leftovers in Louisa, I think. I, on the other hand, am all leftovers: pot roast and mashed potatoes, that is me.

Louisa whirls around suddenly, a wide, resplendent grin sweeping her face.

"Wait till you see this," she says. She guides me to a clearing much like the one I saw this morning by myself, only this time, there are men wading in the lake, men outside trucks on the crisscrossing dirt roads, men atop gigantic steel blue–painted machines. The water seems only to reach the men's thighs—I realize what a mistake it would have been had I leaped into the lake this morning thinking it bottomless.

"These are the bogs," Louisa says. "They're flooded." Alicia Thomas would drop dead in her tracks if she could see this place; she would dunk her body into the bog as if it were her own personal UTI vaccine.

I check my watch. It is barely eight in the morning on another spectacular October day. In the section closest to us, each man drives a cornflower-blue lawn mower–like machine with a big disc on one end through the bog. The men wear yellow waders and colorful shirts. They move slowly atop their contraptions in a regal procession, one machine in front of another, following a lone wader who thumps the bottom of the bog with a stick, much like an old man with a cane—and then I notice that red beads, berries, red berries amass on the surface of the water, hundreds, thousands of these red berries. These must be cranberries, they are red, brilliant red, and they form a glorious contrast to the blue of the lake and the redgreengold of the trees and the yellow of the waders and the crystallizing cobalt sky. The men are quiet; some birds chirp, and a slight wind blows, and Louisa and I stand next to each other. It is an extraordinary sight—it is the majestic combination of nature with mankind, and it is astonishing in its beauty. As I stare, I realize I'm unprepared to process this kind of sight. All I can think is that I wish my eyes were bigger, I wish my mind were bigger, I wish there were a way to keep this in my memory—because as I watch, I already know that there will be a moment, an hour, a day, when I will be away from here, and this will be just one more memory, one more sight, one more addition to the slush pile accumulating in my brain next to *People* magazine covers and random quotes and routine dinners; I want to carve this into my head so I will not lose it, so it will be there for me always.

Louisa whispers. "I told you," she says. "Incredible, right?"

"What is this?" I whisper back, afraid to ruin the sight with the turbulence of spoken words.

"The harvest." Louisa speaks these two words with reverence. "The men collect the berries into that dump truck." She points to a gray-green truck on the side of the bog, with what looks to be a steamship-like paddle wheel hanging from the side. "They'll push the berries onto that conveyor belt with the paddles, which drops them in the dump truck, and then the truck will go down the road about two miles to the Ocean Spray processing plant."

"Ocean Spray, in New Jersey?" I say, disbelieving.

"Ocean Spray, in New Jersey," she repeats.

"I had no idea," I say softly. I picture Foxhole Girl peeking out of her hollow in the ground, looking around, afraid but enlivened.

"There's Carlos," Louisa points, and I see Carlos's Afro waving in the distance, only half-constrained by a red bandana he's tied to his head. "He and two brothers run the place. They're like the chosen ones, really, because they could have gone anywhere, but they live here with their families, and they get to be outside all the time, working amidst all of this." Louisa gestures around again, her arms wide, and I nod, understanding.

"This is—this is," I stop, my brain brimming with an impression I'm compelled to describe. "You hear about farms, and you think about rows of corn and men driving tractors, but this kind of thing, with these *colors*, it's just mind-boggling."

My words crest on a wave of appreciation for nature that I wouldn't expect I had—and I fleetingly wonder whether my whole life has been arranged so that I end up at this particular spot, with this particular woman, at this particular moment.

"I know," Louisa tells me. "I feel like that every time I come here. A true example of nature's bounty, right here, an hour and a half from New York City." She leans back onto the tree. "I've been begging my friends to come for years, can't believe they've finally made it." She stops, a frown crossing her face. "Most of them."

"He'll come," I say, remembering how angry she was last night about the guy named Jack.

"Whatever." She shrugs and steps away from the tree. "He's probably enacting some kind of revenge," she says as she begins to lead me around a trail that circles the bogs. I look through the trees to the bogs—the men are extending what looks to be a vast yellow fire hose around the clot of cranberries brimming on the surface of the water. I see Carlos's bandana wave in the wind; he stands closest to the truck.

"Listen." Louisa turns to me. "Tonight's going to be a big night for me," she says. "I was thinking last night that maybe God placed you here on purpose." I raise my eyebrows. She's reading my mind again. "I've decided to tell Jack the truth," she says. "It's been seven years." Louisa's eyes are a shining brown, deep-set, longlashed. "I really hurt him," she says to me. "He probably thinks I'm his monster."

"Seven years is a long time," I say, in what I hope is an appeasing tone. "He's probably over it by now." Louisa's reaction is to give me a look that says (a) either you're trying to be funny and it isn't working, or (b) c'mon, look at me, how could anyone get over *me*?

"How long has it been since you and the Monster broke up?" she asks, only semi-snidely.

Blood pulses through to my cheeks. "March," I say.

"That's not so—"

"March—three years ago," I interrupt.

She laughs. "You're kidding me."

"Nope," I say.

"What happened?"

"I don't want to talk about it."

She persists. "So why is he a Monster?"

"He isn't a Monster," I say, annoyed. "Only to me. Everyone else likes him quite a lot." I pause, frowning. "Especially his girlfriend."

"He left you for someone."

"No," I say, "not exactly." Louisa stares at me, waiting. I look down to the ground and surrender in silence. It will probably be quicker just to tell her what she wants to know.

"He was supposed to come over to my apartment, but instead he picked up a girl from a Knicks game when he was drunk and spent the night with her. I thought he was dead."

"She's the girlfriend?"

"No." I shake my head as I speak. "It's been three years, remember? That was just a one-night stand to get rid of me." I speak harshly, as if I'm throwing spikes into the ground. Whenever I remember this time of my life, even during the last five months, after the tragedy, I'm compelled to punish myself, to make sure I understand the truth of the event. No halfway, therapized "it has nothing to do with you" arguments. I refuse to delude myself with theories to make myself feel better. He didn't want to be with me; he found a way out.

"Diana?" interrupts Louisa.

"What?" I ask.

"I'm sure it had nothing to do with you," she says. I want to kick her. "Really," she says. "My thing with Jack—it had nothing to do with him. It was all about me." She stops walking. "Can you keep a secret?"

I nod. I've become the Queen of Secret Keeping here in this wilderness.

"Jack and I dated in college and a couple years afterward. I got pregnant, had an abortion, and we broke up."

I focus on the white sand beneath my sneakers. I don't know if I'm ready for this. I'm in grief mode, not good-friend mode. Serves me right for not telling her about the accident, I think. But I can do this. I remember how.

"That must have been traumatic," I say.

Louisa takes out her cigarettes and lights one. "It's a rotten operation. You can't forget for one second—even ten years later—what you're there to do, and it's just there in your face, when all you want to do is get out of there and pretend it never happened. Jack was so amazing. He was there the whole time; I was crying, sobbing. The nurse said she'd never seen someone cry as much as I did. Jack cried, tears streaming down his face; I think the doctor cried too. What a mess, the whole day, the whole week. I was a disaster." Louisa inhales.

I can't help it—I stop listening, distracted. Louisa's like an actress on the stage, and while I appreciate drama, my thoughts have catapulted back to my family. I think of myself on the dais at the funeral; I think of myself sobbing in my bedroom. My self-absorption has no bounds, and I'm ashamed by this, but I'm also helpless to its dominion over me.

"Diana!" I turn. "Listen to me! This is important!"

"What?" I ask, instantly apologetic. "I'm sorry."

"I had fallen in love with somebody," she tells me.

"I got that."

"No," she answers. "You don't."

"We're talking about Jack, right?"

"No. We're talking about Alexander." She looks at me, gauging my reaction, which I hope she can tell is *Oh please don't tell me any more.*

"I'll spare you the details. I fell for Alexander, but he didn't have any money, and Jack didn't know anything about Alexander anyway, so I just told Jack it was his baby, and he paid for the abortion." She grabs my elbow. "You can't tell anyone this, ever."

"I won't," I answer truthfully.

"Go ahead," she says. "I deserve it. I'm an awful person." Louisa speaks more softly now, not quite a whisper, but low, the voice of the contrite. "I'm an awful person."

"No," I say. "You were young."

"Not that young," she says. "And I crushed Jack. Just crushed him. I was going to tell him, but he was so devastated when I ended things, I couldn't finish it off. He'd have killed himself, I think."

I feel little pricks of memory—my Mom, shaking her head over Louisa's revelation, disbelieving that anyone could have acted as Louisa had. Go to church, she would be telling her, ask God for forgiveness.

"I think he wants to get back with me," Louisa says. "We've been e-mailing each other like crazy, and I'm sure that's why he's coming down here. In fact, that's probably why he's late. He's nervous. You'll see. He won't seem nervous—he'll be on top of the world, that's how he acts—but inside, I'll just know. His voice will get all gravelly, and he'll wish I didn't affect him. But I will." She takes a deep breath. "That's why I have to tell him. Before we get back together for good. I can't keep a secret like that from him forever."

She resumes walking. I follow her. I focus on clearing my brain, on filling it with minutiae, the leaves, the cranberries, the bark on the trees.

"Well?" She turns to me. I stop. "Aren't you going to say anything?"

"No." I shake my head. "I don't have anything to say."

Louisa scowls. "So you're judging me."

"Stop it, Louisa." I'm suddenly exhausted. "Don't you judge me. I haven't said a word."

"But you think I'm an awful person."

"No," I say. "It's got to be more complicated than that."

We've arrived back at the trail where we began. Louisa's Kawasaki stands just as we left it. Out in the bogs, the men move around the water as regally as before. It is extraordinarily beautiful, but I do not delight in the sight as I did before our walk around the bogs. Instead I feel apart from it, a tourist gazing at the Tower of London, seeing nothing but bricks.

"You won't tell anyone?" she asks me just before we get onto the motorcycle.

"No." I shake my head, thinking about Galileo's test, when he dropped a coin and a paperweight from the sky. What has the most gravity? Who am I to decide that Louisa's story doesn't bear the same weight as my own tragedy?

"I won't say anything about the Monster either," she tells me. I almost smile as I climb on the motorcycle behind her. The Monster is a million miles away right now. Instead, it's my family and how they're gone forever, and I feel that familiar numbness again. I think of the vision of Foxhole Girl peeking out of the ground, and I think of the Smiling Idiot stomping down hard on top of her head, reminding her that all human connections are perilous, that they all bring extreme and untenable pain, and that the best, most efficient way to avoid it is to stay deep within her foxhole. She may miss sights like a flooded cranberry bog—she may not ever ride on a motorcycle deep in the New Jersey Pine Barrens—but she will stay invulnerable to the vagaries of human behavior and the inevitability of a loved one's death.

Dwarf Pines

Louisa and I don't speak the entire way back to Rosie's, and when she parks the cycle, I jump off, remove my helmet and bound up the stairs. I glance at my watch—I have done so much, and it is only ten o'clock.

Rosie's at the stove, cooking eggs. Gabe is at the table, slicing sausage.

"Did you have a good time, Diana?" Rosie asks me. "Did Louisa take you to the harvest?"

"Yes," I say. "It was stunning."

"Let me do it," says Louisa as she drops her jaw and opens her eyes wide, imitating me. "Louisa, this is *incredible*." Her voice is sharp, as it was at Millie's. "Diana's not from around here, you know."

"Sweetheart," Gabe says, looking at Louisa. "You're not from here either." He cuts another piece of sausage with his fork.

I see red creep up Louisa's neck, her face. She's blushing. I can't believe it.

"People here are particular about their backgrounds," says Rosie, sitting down next to Gabe. "So many misconceptions, so many people claim-ing one thing, pretending another, doing whatever—I say it's all hogwash, but you can't stop people from saying stuff they don't know. Human nature, it is. Everyone wants to put people into a little sprocket."

"Sprocket?" I ask.

"Whatever." Rosie doesn't miss a beat. "Here's my favorite story, Diana." She pauses for a moment while she takes a sip of coffee. "A book about the Pine Barrens was written a while back, and they talked about these dwarf pines. Dwarf pines are pine trees that never grow past your waistline because of the fires."

"Fire's the worst thing that can happen here," offers Gabe.

"So what the author meant, what he wrote," Rosie continues, "was about these forests of dwarf pine trees; Louisa will take you there later, if you want. A wild thing to behold, for sure. But these people from New York City and Philadelphia, all over the place, they'd come down in buses, busloads of people who want to look at the dwarf pines. They'd think that dwarf pines are *people* not trees, that there are dwarf Pineys. So this guy, the old mayor, actually, tells the drivers of the buses, yeah, you go on up here, take a right there, then the next left—he sends them on a wild goose chase in the middle of the pines and says, just wait. Wait, and at night, the dwarves will come out. Be very quiet, he says, or else they'll run away. And don't look 'em in the eye, because they say that if you look a pine dwarf in the eye, your children will be cursed, and all their future generations will be dwarves too." Rosie stops to drink. "Now these people, they think they're above all the legend stuff—they pretend they don't really *believe* that these dwarves will be able to curse future generations, but they absolutely believe that these dwarves exist. You should have seen the people, camping out, waiting for the dwarves to appear. Finally, the mayor comes out and says, oh, are you all waiting for people? I'm sorry, I told you the wrong place. Then he'd direct them to the forest of dwarf pine trees, laughing his head off. He'd come over here late at night, and he'd say, if only those people would *read* the damn book, they'd know what they're talking about." Rosie laughs out loud, and I smile, charmed. But Louisa is distracted. She stands and moves to the window by the sink.

"Mickey says the car will be ready tomorrow," Gabe announces. I realize he's talking to me.

"Tomorrow?" I repeat. Gabe nods.

"What's tomorrow?" asks Billy, who has just walked into the kitchen from outside. Fritz follows him. I look at Billy, the morning light behind him. Thinning blond hair, a head shaped like a block of concrete. "Time to start drinking again?" He grins.

"No." I try to sound curt.

"Have some breakfast, dear," says Rosie. "And if you want anything, just ask." Rosie sets out a fresh plate of eggs, bacon, and sausage.

"I'm moving here." Billy holds up a piece of bacon like it's a trophy. "Or else you can come with me. What about it, Gabe, think I can steal Rosie for a while?"

"No," replies Gabe, not even lifting his eyes from his food.

"Okay, then," Billy persists. "What about you, Diana? Do you cook?" Louisa grins, which I catch across the table. I frown. Nothing is less appealing than flirtation from an unappealing source. I shake my head.

"Diana was just saying she wants to go home," says Louisa. I turn, startled.

"Really?" says Fritz. "But today is going to be epic. One day there won't be any Pine Barrens, and you're going to think, Wow, I should have stayed that day; now it's just one big shopping mall and lots of people who eat Cheez Doodles."

"I didn't say that." I glare at Louisa. "What is with you?" Something is off; the tenor of our relationship has changed perceptibly, but I don't know what caused it.

"Oh, relax," she admonishes me. "Have you ever met anyone so sensitive?"

"Where's Jack?" asks Billy.

"He's not here yet," says Louisa. I see her face harden and wonder if I've become a liability because she's revealed her history with Jack.

"So what's the plan?" Fritz asks.

Louisa looks up at the clock. She finishes her cigarette, presses it against an old tile, then looks up, weary. But then a smile breaks over her face as if someone banged a chisel on the top of her head and this new Louisa cracked through.

"Wait till you see what I have in store for you." Her grin is expansive, genuine, it seems, but it's a genuineness with wings. I think she needs to be the tour guide extraordinaire so that her friends and family don't think she is desperately awaiting Jack. "Right, Diana?"

"It's amazing," I say as I put down my coffee cup. "But I can't go anywhere until I take a shower."

"I was going to say something," says Billy. He holds his nose for effect.

"I put a towel out for you, dear," says Rosie.

I bolt from the kitchen, up the stairs to the bathroom, glad to be away from Louisa. She's uneasy, and it's affecting me. But in moments, I'm under the strong shower, and as I scrub my scalp, my shoulders, my legs, I push from my head any memory that upsets me; I want my brain clean, too.

As I dress—pulling on a pair of Louisa's jeans, (which are, of course, too tight)—I see a telephone on a table in-between twin beds. Guilt invades my psyche as I see Wiley furious in New York while I buzz about the Pine Barrens, pretending I'm Diana the Lovelorn instead of Diana the Wacko who missed her (supposedly life-saving) appointment with Dr.

Depression. I peek out into the upstairs hallway; it is quiet. I go back into the room, pick up the phone, and call Wiley.

As the phone rings, I think about how Wiley would know better than anyone how I could convince myself that she didn't care, that no one cared. I would infuriate her yet again, only this time it would be worse, because she would be terrified for me as well. She doesn't deserve this—she is one of those people whose innate grace squelches others' baser instincts, including mine. For a moment, I put Wiley next to Louisa in a line-up in my head. Both beautiful on the outside, I unwrap them to find that inside Wiley is a trove of gold, while inside Louisa is a locked, windowed cabinet, swaths of bright colors flashing through the glass, the source of such luster concealed.

Wiley's voicemail answers. When I hear the beep, I speak. "Wiley, it's me. I'll be back soon, I'm in New Jersey, I'm fine and I'm safe, so don't worry. And don't be mad; I mean, I understand if you are, but I'll be back soon so you can yell at me in person. I think I'll be back soon, and sorry, I am sorry." I replace the receiver and think that at least I've done something right, that the flow of lies has, temporarily, abated.

"Who's Wiley?" Louisa has crept up behind me. "And what are you sorry about?"

I'm shocked. "You were *listening*?"

"You were talking right here; it didn't seem private, and I had to get some supplies." She speaks casually as she leans against the doorjamb. "So what are you sorry about?"

"I don't want to talk about it." Louisa barges into the room, comfortable with the fact that she's eavesdropped. It's like she's a weather system unto herself, blowing in and twirling out whenever she feels like it. And like someone confronted with a hurricane, all I want to do is closet myself into a storm cellar, far away from the turbulence. But of course, I can't—Louisa's too determined to hurl me into the storm.

"You don't speak to the Monster anymore, do you?" she continues.

"What?"

"The Monster. When was the last time you spoke to him?" She talks about him as if he's a person instead of the preternaturally handsome mass who haunts my brain, George Clooney gone the Blob. I don't answer her.

"'Cause I think it would be a stupid thing to do," Louisa continues. "C'mon. They're waiting."

She heads into one of the rooms on the second floor but then stops, turns around. "You're very pretty, Diana," she says, with a strange, almost somber expression. "I thought so but couldn't tell under the dirt." She leaves.

I sink onto the bed. I've been told before that I am attractive (big blue eyes, even features, good skin). But I have not figured out how to reconcile my presumed attractiveness with my barren life. Since the Monster, it's been easy to hide behind a teenage girl's (or a social Xray's) version of the events. The Monster dumped me; ergo, I am not pretty. But that is the Smiling Idiot talking. During those few times when I pondered what happened (as well as during those few moments when realization burst upon me like a hailstorm), I knew I was not rejected because of how I looked.

The problem is I do not know why the Monster rejected me. L was not the reason, at least not initially. (L is only the barometer for how far he has come without me.) "I can't love anyone," he had told me. His words had felt like a poison-filled balloon, expanding through the room until it busted and drenched me. I said nothing for a moment and then responded, "Aren't we a great pair? You can't love anyone, and I don't believe anyone will ever love me." He had taken his hands away from his face and said, after a minute, looking straight at me, "How could they not?" And then I remember wanting to kick him, throw a glass into his face so it would shatter and make him feel—if that was true, if "how could they not" be true, then *what was the matter with him? He* could not. *He* was having a little problem with could not.

But then I saw he was just doing his best, wrapping up adult changes-of-heart with mere words, words that no matter how carefully strung together could never explain the force of changeable love to an unwilling listener. I acted like a child then—I wasn't getting my way, and I hadn't done anything wrong, dammit!—and I still do, when I wallow under my insecurity blanket and say it's about attractiveness. In moments like this, moments of clarity, I see it's just life again, throwing curveballs. I think back to the funeral, when I fell apart on the altar, and I think of me wracked with tears, and I wish again I had the pride of the British or the power of a Louisa. Louisa would never behave as I do—she's an adult who grabs the world, not a child who skulks away in its corners.

"What are you doing? They're waiting." Louisa steps into the room, and I turn from the window to look at her. "Diana, what is with you?"

I look out the window.

"Listen," she begins. I hear her breathe behind me. "I know I'm being a bitch. I'm sorry, I get like that sometimes; I can't help it. Truce, okay? I'll be nice. Promise. I'll even keep Billy off of you." She walks over to me; I feel her fingers touch my shoulder. I turn to face her.

"I'm all right," I say.

"Yeah, you're all right," she assesses me. "Whatever you say, sensitive one." She covers her mouth. "Sorry. I can't help it."

"I know," I say.

Jack

Within ten minutes, Fritz, Billy and I stand outside and listen to Louisa as she informs us about our imminent tour of the Pine Barrens.

First, we're going to visit the old blueberry shed, where Louisa worked in the summer, where she had her first kiss, where she smoked her first cigarette, and where she put cellophane on top of pints of blueberries as a "packer." Rosie used to run the shed, Louisa says, and she'd say things like "Do it my way or hit the highway" and "B Cup, B Cup!" (the size, apparently, of the desired mound of blueberries at the top of the pint before the cellophane is stretched over it).

After we see the shed, we are to go to the unharvested bogs of cranberries. Then we'll go to the harvested bogs. Then we may or may not see a rattlesnake, and we may or may not see the Jersey Devil, or at least the place where the Jersey Devil is supposed to live. We will go and look for exotic orchids, which bloom deep in the Pine Barrens. We will try to fit in a canoe ride. We will definitely go to a bar somewhere nearby that has a deer head on the wall and great french fries. We might drive by the home of the boy with whom she shared her first kiss. We will see the hole in the packing shed where her younger brother drove the forklift through the concrete wall. (Rosie fired him three times on that one day.) We may go back to Millie's. We may drive to the shore. We may go back to Big Bog. We may just go for a motorcycle ride. We may take a nap outside, underneath the October sky and the shade of the magnificent multicolored foliage.

While Louisa talks, Rosie and Gabe leave for their "car ride." (I watch Rosie lie to Louisa without even a second of hesitation.) Gabe walks Rosie to their car, the two of them holding hands, Gabe as tender as a schoolboy with a crush. Meanwhile, Billy commandeers me over to his motorcycle.

"She'll come with me," he says. "Fritz on that one, and, Louisa, you lead the way. Okay with you?" He smiles at me as if he's irresistible. "I'm a very good driver," he says. I see that Fritz and Louisa are already on their cycles, with helmets. I get on behind Billy as a sense of complete absurdity overcomes me. How did I get here? I have to get away.

But instead I latch my arms around Billy's waist. (I can be a very obedient person.) Our convoy begins. But after only a few minutes, Billy slows down. We're following Fritz and Louisa, so I don't know what is happening. But then I see. In front of us, not far from Rosie's driveway, a man stands, tall, wearing a flannel shirt and jeans. He has yellow-brown hair, not too long, not too short. A man with a scar running on his right cheek through to his ear. He holds a fish and a fishing rod.

It is him. He found me. *He found me.* Thank you, God. Thank you, Mom. Thank you, Dad. Thank you, Be—

"Jack!" Louisa cannot jump from her motorcycle fast enough. We pull alongside Fritz. I watch as Louisa runs to Jack, throwing her helmet on the ground and flinging her arms around his neck.

"Louisa," he says as he pulls her close.

Everyone else removes their helmet. I do not. I do not want to; no one can make me. (Truth is, no one cares.) Billy turns slightly to his left, telling me something.

"What?" I ask.

"Let the games begin." Billy grins, an eager spectator to the dramas played out by our most perfect counterparts.

I look at the couple embracing through my black-tinted visor, conscious of myself as a woman in too-tight jeans with a bowling-ball head. The fisherman was Jack. The fisherman—my future husband—is Louisa's.

I remember the way I laughed as I ran through the woods this morning after Jack winked at me, and I feel foolish—the Smiling Idiot who had grinned like an imbecile just as she does with all men, until reality came carrying a fishing rod, visiting Louisa.

I'm sick of this. I do not want to be in a place where I am subject to the same prick and ooze of attraction and insecurity and compulsion that destroys me in New York. I look around. The sky's bright, the trees are green, there are no trucks, blah blah blah. I want out.

Fish

"Hey, buddy." Billy shakes Jack's hand. " 'Bout time you made it. I was beginning to wonder."

"Well, I took my time," said Jack. "Gotta check out new situations by yourself; it's better that way."

"Excepting certain situations," says Fritz. "Like alligator pits."

"Yeah, well, there's only rattlesnakes here, right, Louisa?" asks Jack.

"Animals or humans?" I watch her flutter around Jack and want to choke her. It isn't fair. He was my fantasy, and now she's stolen him from me.

(But he's hers, I remind myself. Their history. Their past. I know it all, and I want to wrench it out of my head and toss it to the wind.)

"Louisa was counting the minutes," Fritz says.

"I was not!" Louisa casts her voice out angrily, like a harpoon.

"Oh, come on, tell him the truth," Fritz continues. "Unless there was some other reason for checking your watch every two minutes."

"It was broken," she answers. "And I was worried."

"You haven't seen me in seven years. Today's the day you're worried?" Jack's insouciance is palpable, and Louisa treads carefully.

But she has noticed the fishing rod. "When did you get here?"

"Well," he begins, "I sort of got here yesterday. But you know me, when I go to a new place I like to do a little reconnaissance."

"Yesterday?" Fritz grins. "Man, oh man. Someone—" he points in an exaggerated gesture toward Louisa, "is going to be mighty angry." Louisa's face pulses in tiny motions, attempting to compose an expression that adequately evokes her frustration yet maintains her exuberance.

"It's dangerous out here." Louisa attempts the it's-only-for-your-safety approach, which, frankly, disappoints me. I want to see Louisa at her peak, as she manipulates and bewitches with one swing of her slender arms.

"Dangerous? Which—the raccoons or the squirrels?" Jack is laughing—kindly—but laughing nonetheless.

"The people are hunters, *hunters,* may I remind you." Even the most harmless laughter can elicit frustration. I see it in Louisa. "They kill things they don't know."

"You're all still alive." Jack grins, and underneath my visor, I grin back at him, fighting the urge to leap like Snoopy and do a dance.

"They do—they hunt; they hunt for the kill." Louisa stops. "They even hunt for swans."

"And just yesterday I sent my check to the NRA."

"Don't tease me," Louisa pouts.

Jack puts his arm around her. "I was careful. I didn't see anyone, with or without guns."

I shut my eyes and silently inhale my disappointment. It seems that I am the only one who remembers our silent communication in the woods.

"Who's this?" Jack asks, pointing to me, Helmet Head. Louisa walks over, knocks on the hard plastic encasing my skull. She turns to Jack.

"This is our new friend, Diana." Louisa says. "Diana, come out come out wherever you are." She knocks on the helmet again. I undo the strap under my chin and take off the helmet, putting it to my side. I can just imagine how I look.

"Hi," I say. I stick out my hand.

"Hi," he says. He doesn't recognize me. He has never seen me before. He is not for me, of course he isn't for me, he's too beautiful for that, he's too cool for that, he doesn't want that role. That role belongs to Falstaff, or Rosencrantz, or Guildenstern. Not Jack.

"Good to meet you," Jack says.

"Good to meet you," I respond. I open my mouth. Then I shut it.

"Are you okay?" asks Billy.

"Yes. Fine." I speak in clipped, curt syllables. *Do not call attention to me,* I want to yell.

"Why didn't you call?" Louisa now speaks gently. Jack is here, next to her. There is no need for her to be angry. "Rosie cooked a breakfast fit for an army, and we already did so much this morning; at least, Diana and I did. And yesterday, we went to Big Bog—I'll take you there later today. Don't you have any stuff? Where's your stuff? Just the fishing pole?"

"My car's back on the street. Didn't seem to be any parking rules," Jack says.

"There aren't any, and even if there were, Gabe's the police. But the fish. What are we going to do with the fish?" Louisa queries him as if we're deciding child labor laws in Thailand. *Oh Prime Minister, what ever will we do about the children?*

"I was hoping we could cook it," Jack replies.

"I can gut it," says Fritz. "Did it in Alaska all the time. What do you have there, a perch?"

"I think it's bass," Jack responds.

"It's too small to be a bass," says Billy.

"I hope it's perch; I hate bass," contributes Louisa. "You sure it isn't trout?"

Basses, perches, instruments, porches. *Talk, Diana, say something, say anything.*

"I like fish," I say, at the precise moment when no one speaks. And then I turn crimson. Oh my God where is my helmet, I want my helmet on, I should never be allowed to take it off, there should be a law against taking my helmet off, I am going to wear it all the time from now on, I will die with my helmet attached.

"Good for you," says Louisa. "We like fish too."

I watch Louisa escort Jack across the street to Rosie's. They fit together as if a cabinetmaker had carved them out of one piece of wood, two people with taut arms and legs and lankiness and beauty. I belong somewhere else; I really have to get out of here.

"Diana!" Fritz calls to me from about twenty feet away from where I stand. He extends his arms wide, a big smile on his face. I notice again the gentle darkness of his eyes, a nose with a bump, wide shoulders. "C'mon, smile! Look where we are." He twirls around suddenly, as if to envelope the area within his embrace. "Just when the wilderness inside gets too much," he says, "there's this."

I take a step backward, staring at him. He smiles, and I wonder what his emotional antennae have picked up. How does he know about my wilderness inside?

"Nature Boy acting crazy." Billy sits back on his motorcycle. "Ignore him, Diana."

"Ignore me at your peril," Fritz answers.

"He's got a point." Jack has returned. I jerk my head back, see him near me, next to me. "Ignore Fritz, and you could end up just like him." He points to Billy.

"Everyone's a comedian," Billy responds.

"Hey!" Louisa's jumped on her cycle. "C'mon!" Jack walks over to her.

"What?" Billy asks. "No helmet?"

"It's okay," Jack says. "I like seeing things."

Reluctantly I sit behind Billy. Fritz starts his cycle. Louisa starts hers. Louisa says something to Fritz. Billy puts on his helmet. I pick up mine, but right before I place it over my head, I look up. Jack stares at me. I want to look behind me; there may actually be someone behind me, Gisele Bünchen perhaps. So I look. No one. When I turn back around, Jack is still staring.

"Ready?" asks Louisa. Billy cranks the grip. Fritz gives a thumbs-up sign. And then, just as Jack turns to Louisa to respond, he looks at me and winks.

"Ready," says Jack. I fumble with my helmet as I hurry to smash it over my head. I must move quickly now—I am never able to hide anything, not grief, nor glee. And right now—even though I know he's Louisa's—I am full of glee, grinning and glowing and gleeful.

He *winked*.

The Blueberry Queen

As I hold onto Billy's waist and we fly down the blacktopped road, I realize for the first time in a long while that I'm pulled toward a man, and I'm stuck. Jack slipped into my psyche just when I suspected my radar was permanently broken. Yet it is unsurprising to me that the man I found is the emotional property of Louisa, my captivating, capricious, gorgeous new friend. The surprise would have been if the opposite had happened—if, for some reason, Jack had been attracted to me.

Billy turns sharply, and I clutch his waist tighter. We stop moments later, in front of a white concrete building that stretches deep along an expanse of orange sand.

"That felt good," Billy tells me. "Hold on as tight as you want, Lady Di." He holds out his hand to help me off the cycle. We're in summer camp, and he's announcing to the rest of the boys that I'm his girl.

Louisa has jumped up on a two-foot-high ledge, with Jack close behind her. "C'mon," she calls to us. Jack follows her up onto the ledge, into the shed. I extract myself from Fritz and Billy and leap up to where Jack and Louisa already stand.

Inside, the walls are gray concrete blocks. Birds flit about in the wooden rafters; the place is swept clean even though it's clear that it hasn't been in use for a while. Alongside one wall in the back, stretching for at least the size of a football field, is a wooden bench—rather, a wooden bench-like structure that stands about five feet tall on one side and slopes down to about four on the other. Louisa walks us around. There is an elevated, traintrack–like belt of silver rollers parallel to the highest side of the structure.

"This used to be where we packed blueberries," Louisa announces, waving her hands to different sections of the building. "This is where the trucks would come in from the fields," she says, pointing to one of the garage doors. "The pickers would handpick twelve pints in the fields during the day, and the shedboys would take the berries from the truck and then stack them here," she motions to underneath the roller belt, "and then all of us would be in this assembly line where we'd pull each pint out of the flat and then stretch out the cellophane on top of it and place this square thing on top of the blueberries to hold the cellophane down, stretch the rubber band on top, and then put it in one of the cardboard boxes on our side. We'd get twenty-two cents for twelve pints." She tells us this breathlessly, and in my head I translate:

I worked hard, I am different from all of you because of this experience.

"Bet you never did this," Louisa says to Fritz. I can see her in elementary school, revealing her flowered underwear; Louisa is the class showoff.

"Nope," Fritz answers. "But I did work on an oil rig in Alaska one summer."

"I love blueberries," says Billy. "I would have eaten them all day."

"I hate them," says Louisa.

"Really?" Jack steps closer to Louisa. "But you're the Blueberry Queen, right?"

Louisa looks to the floor, hair falling in front of her face. Then she throws her head back with a flourish, rejoining us.

"What?" Billy doesn't know what's going on either. "How come I don't know this?"

"Because you don't pay attention?" Fritz tells Billy. "Don't you remember from college?"

"Remember what?" I ask. Louisa turns to me with a teeth-baring, wide-stretching smile.

"Okay. You asked for it," she says. "Time for another secret, Diana." She pauses. "You are looking at the 1982 New Jersey Blueberry Queen."

It is an almost reverential silence. *Blueberry Queen?*

I would not have expected Louisa to be Blueberry Queen. That is a gentle title, a sweet one, one at odds with the Louisa I have met. But over where she sits, I see Louisa grin like the teenager she must have been, and I think I spy a glimpse of that innocent girl, the one who won a beauty contest.

"It was a beauty contest, right?" I ask, because I suddenly see a bunch of young girls dressed up as blueberries, like a Fruit of the Loom commercial.

"C'mon, Diana," exclaims Fritz. "Look at her. Of course it was a beauty contest. Tell that story," Fritz urges Louisa. "Tell them that story."

"Which one?" Jack asks.

"Don't know if you've heard it," says Louisa, smiling. Fritz has given her permission to proceed with the telling of Louisa Story 314-A: Blueberry Queen, Sections 5.2–5.7, and she's elated.

"I had to go to Ocean City, New Jersey, to stand and pose near all kinds of blueberry-themed products." Jars of blueberry jam and blueberry-spotted aprons flash in my mind. "I was tired, so I went off to the side to sit. This guy came up to me; he looked harmless, so I told him I was hungry. He said why didn't I just eat the blueberries, given my title and all. I told him the truth—that I hated blueberries and that I really just liked McDonald's." Louisa pauses. "And then I find out he was a reporter for the *Atlantic City Press*. The next day, all the people in New Jersey read that the Blueberry Queen hated blueberries and wanted to go to McDonald's. Caused quite a furor, let me assure you."

"Right up there with Monica Lewinsky." Fritz laughs.

"How come I didn't know this?" Billy asks petulantly.

"It wasn't a secret," Louisa tells him. "In the scheme of things, it's just not important." Louisa's gaze sweeps the room. "Come on. Time to meet Carlos."

As I follow Louisa out of the shed, I think of how, if I were Blueberry Queen, I'd have eaten all the blueberries I could find and then some, I'd be the best Blueberry Queen New Jersey ever had; I'd tell anyone who'd listen how great they tasted and how necessary they were for good health. I'd wear the tiara and the banner and the gown, and I'd wave from convertibles and hand out pints of fresh blueberries with a smile—"A way to a better life, I'm sure!"

But then someone, Lola Lolita maybe, would step up to the podium and whisper in my ear. I'd grow red and try to stop the tears from flowing. "You're not a Beauty Queen," she would remind me. "Get off of the stage."

Tug of War

Billy and I are second in the caravan, behind Louisa and Jack, and in front of Fritz. The road is empty, and we fly along as I close my eyes, think of the wind, and try to push away the visions of caskets, the inexorability of loss.

When I open my eyes, I see that Billy and I are alone.

"Hey!" I yell, but Billy keeps going. He's driven into the woods, down a sand trail. "Hey!" I want to remove my hands from his waist, but I can't; I'll fall off. I pull one hand away and hit him on the shoulder. He turns his head, but I can't hear anything through the helmet.

Scenarios rattle through my head. Billy's crazy. Billy's a rapist. Billy's a kidnapper. When he stops the cycle one moment later, I breathe a little easier. I see a blue tent.

"We call it home," Billy says as he parks the cycle. "Hope I didn't scare you. I wanted to pick up a camera."

"Oh," I say. Billy walks to the tent and ducks inside. One second later he steps through the plastic, zippered door and leers. "Want to come in?"

"No," I mumble, unsure if I can maintain the necessary blend of amusement and disdain that will keep him at bay.

"Just kidding," he says. He goes inside the tent but in a second peeks out. "Not really." He reenters the tent.

"Diana?" When Billy steps out of the tent, he holds a fancy camera with an entire separate bag of flashes and film. "How do you think we could carry this?"

It's a professional camera, all lenses and levers and flashes. I look over at the bike to confirm there is no basket, no carrying case. "If you go slowly, I can strap it on my back," I tell him. Billy walks over to me.

"It's heavy." He hands me the bag with the accessories.

"I can take it," I say, as I swing the heavy part of the bag so it rests on my back.

"What about this?" He holds out the camera.

"That looks expensive."

Billy shrugs. "I dunno," he responds. "It's Fritz's." He raises the camera up to his eye. "Smile," he tells me. I don't. I don't like pictures. "Aw, come on," he cajoles. "Don't tell me you're shy."

"I am," I say.

"Don't be," he says. "Not around me." The last three words float from him softly. I must have changed my expression because I hear the camera click. Billy lowers it from his eye. "I got it," he says. "I'll send it to you."

"Thanks," I tell him. I look to the trail. "Are you going to know your way back?"

"In a rush?"

"I don't want to be lost."

"Don't worry," Billy assures me. "I was a Boy Scout."

"Terrific," I say nervously, because now Billy smiles at me, and I sense the tenor of this encounter has changed. "I was a Girl Scout," I tell him, hoping an abundance of words will blunt whatever impulse he's feeling. "Until I got kicked out. I don't remember why. We never camped. A Girl Scout troop that never camped, make sense of that."

"Diana." Billy's maintained the soft voice. He believes he's seductive. He touches my hand. "I think the Monster is a very stupid man."

I yank my hand away. "He's actually very smart."

"Impossible," retorts Billy. "To give you up?"

"You don't know me," I say. "I'm crazy." He smiles. "Can we go?" I plead.

"Diana, we're all adults here," he says in a low voice. Like a clumsy schoolgirl, I pick up my foot and look at the bottom of my shoe. "What is it?" Billy asks me. "I'm too short, aren't I? That's the problem. Or the hair. C'mon, I can take it. Tell me."

What I do tell him is, "This is ridiculous. We've just met."

"We're not getting any younger," he tells me.

"Billy." A well of resolve foments inside me. "Let's go."

"Okay, okay," he mutters, but I think he's grinning. I hope he's grinning. I don't need him to be passive-aggressive today—I can already see Louisa's face when we arrive together, and I'm pained that Jack will believe the same thing. (Coincident with the last thought is that, once again, I've created a fantasy relationship with a man based on nonexistent gestures. It's another way for me to stay alone, my therapist used to tell me, but I never believed her until it was too late.)

"If you change your mind . . ." Billy begins.

"Doubtful," I cut him off, strapping the camera around my back.

"Can't blame a guy for trying," he says as he pulls on his helmet. I actually think you *can* blame a guy for trying, but I don't say anything. Billy starts the cycle, and we speed away. At the mouth of the trail, right before we turn onto the highway, we abruptly stop. Fritz—face flushed, helmet off, red hair splashing against the backdrop of the blue sky—waits for us.

"So that's where you wandered to," he says, looking at me.

"Your cameras," I tell him. Fritz stretches over me, sees the camera and equipment. He glowers at Billy.

"Anything breaks, you're paying," replies Fritz after a moment.

"Fair enough," responds Billy, unaffected

"Okay." Fritz motions toward me. "My turn." He moves forward on the seat so I can fit behind him on his cycle.

"Aw, c'mon," Billy protests. This is a superficial tug of war, as if we're pulling on cotton candy, but I enjoy it nonetheless.

"You choose," Fritz tells me.

"Sorry, Billy," I say, grinning. I'm skating, I'm skating on the ice and it isn't breaking. Billy accepts defeat graciously.

"I'm a much better driver," he says.

"Get on, Diana," Fritz commands me as we both ignore Billy. "Let's go find our compatriots."

I do as Fritz requests and am relieved I don't have to speak. In fact, I smile. This is what it means to be relaxed, to accept the bouquets of human interchange with appropriate but not overweening gratitude. I have about five seconds before I lapse back into hypercritical mode, in which my every move is challenged by my own internal funhouse mirror, so I tell myself, *Enjoy this, accept it, and move on, Diana, move on.*

A Fight

Louisa and Jack wait for us at the entrance to yet another trail through the Pines. I ignore Louisa's officious look.

"A little detour?" Jack asks.

"Where are we going?" I ask, avoiding all questions.

We head back into the forest. This time we stop after we've gone about ten minutes down another white sand path. We are presented with a vista that stretches for miles and encompasses wide swaths of sunken moats, big circular green-and-red mottled moats, surrounded by crisscrossing orange-red sand roads. In the distance, I see a truck with two people standing alongside of it. They begin to walk along the sandy road. One of them steps down, inside the moat, and they continue to walk, side by side. From our perspective, it looks like a giant is walking next to a child.

Fritz pulls the camera from my back as we approach the edge of the moats. He snaps a picture. "Land's sake," he says, and steps down on top of the bog. Jack follows. The rest of us, Louisa, Billy, and me, stay where we are. Fritz reaches down and pulls at the ground. Vines come up, root-like vines, tangled and festooned with small green leaves. And then I see him pull cranberries off the vine, holding them up for us to see.

"Christ," Fritz says. "It's like a carpet of cranberries." Jack walks in a different direction but also kneels down to examine the vines.

"How deep does this go?" Fritz calls to Louisa.

"I don't know, about five feet, maybe?" she answers.

"Can't be five feet," I say.

"How would you know?" asks Louisa.

"Because this morning the guys in the bog weren't seven feet tall, and the water was at their thighs, their waists, at its highest."

"You saw the harvest?" Billy asks me.

"I told you. Louisa took me this morning," I say. "You've got to see it. They fill these areas." I motion to the ground, "with water and use some machine to make the berries come off the vine and float up. That's right; right, Louisa?" Louisa glares at me. I shrug. I'm tired of her moods. I step down into the bog, joining Fritz and Jack. Billy follows, but Louisa doesn't.

"I'm going to grab Carlos; he'll tell you everything," she says and saunters off, lighting a cigarette as she walks.

"I've seen pictures of this," Fritz tells us, "pictures of women at the turn of the century sitting on these bogs and scooping with a shovel. Their gowns are turned to the side, and they use this weird rake-like shovel to scoop out the berries. Don't know where they put them though, maybe in their skirts?"

"I've got a cranberry scoop," Jack says.

"You do not," says Billy and turns to me. "Jack's got this thing for trying to be more ascetic than the rest of us."

"I think you mean esoteric," says Jack.

"The bottom line is you don't have a cranberry scoop," responds Billy.

"I got it at a thrift store in New York about five years ago, had no idea what it was. It looks like a shovel with spikes. Seemed pretty wild, bought it for fifty bucks."

"Christ, who cares?" says Fritz. "I mean, would you look at this? Hundreds of years ago people thought this was just swampland."

"No, hundreds of years ago people thought this was the place to hide from the colonists," Billy says.

"Someone's been reading too many history books," teases Fritz.

"The Revolutionary War colonists. New Jersey hid a bunch of Hessians— Hessians and Tories. The Hessians, remember, the ones Washington trounced on the Delaware? They all hid here." Billy's proud of himself for knowing this information. I turn and look around at the line of pine trees and believe that if I were a Hessian or a Tory I'd hide in the Pine Barrens. (I *am* hiding in the Pine Barrens, I remind myself. And I am just a Gemini.)

I walk over to a different section of the bog, away from the men. I look down at the vines upon which I stand, and then I kneel and pick up some cranberries. I put one to my mouth; it is pink and small and hard. I deposit it slowly into my mouth, and I suck on it so that I can feel how solid it is; then I bite, and the sourness spurts out and my mouth springs open and I spit the cranberry halves back into my hand.

"Any good?" asks Jack, from behind me. I clench my fist, hiding my spit-out cranberries.

"It's bitter," I say, keeping my head down to hide from him the blood rushing into my cheeks.

"Just think how much sugar they have to add to make the juice taste good."

"Right," I say, head still down. Please, God, I'm a smart woman, I know words, I've read books; he's just a guy, he's just a person, I can speak to him. "Hmm," I say, and during the subsequent silence, I consider various ways to kill myself.

"Diana?" Jack asks. "Is there something you're looking at, or do I scare you?"

I look up and see him with the sun shining behind him. His eyes are light brown and his face is oval-shaped and tan. The scar runs high on his right cheek over to his ear. "What happened?" I ask, as I point to my right cheek.

"Oh." He's startled, and I want to cover my face again, hide my abject stupidity for bringing this up. "A dog. It was my fault. He was in some sort of stomach pain, whimpering, so I picked him up, and I aggravated whatever he had, so he bit my face and ear." Jack turns so I can see his ear. It's slightly mangled at the top. "Me and Evander Holyfield," he says, smiling. "I forget about it now. But really, the sweetest dog in the world. Totally my fault."

"It looks fine," I say.

"Gives me character, right? Please don't say that."

"Okay," I answer. "But it does." We smile at each other, and my heart feels like someone just lit it on fire.

"Been here long?" he asks.

"No," I answer. "Maybe you heard about it. I crashed my car yesterday when I hit Rosie on her motorcycle."

"I did hear." Jack looks off in the distance, toward where Louisa stands next to Carlos. "But don't be too hard on yourself. Rosie's fine, and Louisa's had her own mishaps behind the wheel. One time, Louisa crashed my car because she refused to let the person behind her pass. Road rage, she told me—totaled the car."

They have a history. A long history of crashed cars.

"But she was okay?"

"Obviously." Jack smirks. "Don't let her fool you. The inside of that woman is pure steel; nothing can hurt her." I watch Jack as he speaks, and hear a wistful but distinct edge to his voice. Jack must be made of softer stuff than Louisa, or rather, he must think he is made of softer stuff, the pile of melted wax after a lit flame. But he's here, so it can't be over between them. She invited him, she waited for him, he came.

"Where did you come from?" I ask.

"New York," he says.

"Oh," I say. "Me too." I want to say more, but I notice that in the bog adjacent to where Jack and I talk, Louisa is watching us, hands on her hips. I can almost see her face. I feel a pang of anxiety, as if I'm betraying her, but then I think, the hell with it. She's been a bitch to me since we returned from the harvest this morning.

"You run every day?" Jack can't see Louisa. When I turn, I recall Louisa's story and wonder what's going to happen to him, to them.

"Not every day." I answer. "Do you run?"

"Nope," he says. "Soccer ruined my knees." I should have known. Soccer. I've always had a weakness for soccer players. Some women like men with money. Me, I just need a soccer ball.

"Hey—" says Billy. "Jack, hold up. Don't you think one woman's enough for you; do you have to monopolize both members of the fairer sex?" I groan, inwardly.

"Hey!" Louisa comes back along the road, dragging Carlos. She avoids my gaze. I see that her smile is wide, as it was in the kitchen when she tried to convince all of us that she wasn't desperate for Jack's arrival. "This is Carlos. He runs the place," she says to the men, pointedly ignoring me.

"Glad you could make it," Carlos says. (He's in the middle of work, and he's glad a bunch of aging prepsters are interrupting him? Carlos is a liar.) "So what do you want to know?" Carlos asks all of us.

"Well, just about—" Billy stammers.

"You get to work out here every day?" asks Fritz. "That's living. I mean, that's honest living, the way it should be."

"It's work—don't get any ideas—but yes, it's great," says Carlos. When he smiles, all the creases in his face expand or contract, and it's clear he smiles quite a lot. "The winter's tough; we have to be out here all night to make sure the bogs don't freeze over—"

"Freeze?" asks Jack.

"We leave the water in the bogs throughout the winter, but it has to stay wet, it can't freeze; the water's got to keep flowing underneath," says Carlos. He turns and points to a place far in the distance. "The river's over there, the stream we feed from. There's also an aquifer underneath us, some of the purest water in the world, right under your feet." He turns back to us. "Right now, we're flooding one bog at a time, but after the harvest we just leave the dams open to keep the water going through the whole time. Can't risk freezing the vines."

I look at Fritz and picture him pitching a tent, somewhere in the woods, and living off the wilderness, reveling in how epic and addictive it is.

"What are the—are there any dangers here?" Billy asks.

"Nah. It's quiet here, usually. Sometimes kids from nearby will come out and drink in the woods. It's fire, really, that's the most dangerous. You can see the remnants of what's happened before. In the summer, once a fire's started, there's nothing you can do. The firemen do all they can, and the state government steps in, but it's devastating what it does to all the wildlife, all the forests you see. Even a cigarette can make it blow up. See, everything's so dry here, everything's so porous—I mean, look at the sand in the Pines. That's why the water's so pure; it seeps right through the sand and into the aquifer underneath us."

"So this one isn't flooded yet?" asks Jack.

"No," says Carlos, and in perfect comic delivery, continues, "that's why it's dry." We all smile. "We start over there." He points to where the truck is, "and the water works over the land by gradations. See, each of these bogs is slightly lower than the one next to it. The water flows from one bog to the next when it's ready for harvest. All these roads—" he gestures around. "They also double as dams; see in the middle there—" In the center of the road nearest us, we see a wooden plank, rectangular, a miniature drawbridge. "When the bog's ready, we just lift up the dam, and the water comes in."

"By hand?" Jack questions.

"Yeah, one of the few things left over." Carlos looks to the ground for a second, flicks a spider off his wrist. "We used to have, I don't know, a hundred, hundred and fifty employees? Now we're down to about twenty during harvest. There's machines for everything nowadays. We just gotta adapt, and it goes faster, better. The great thing, though, is that no matter what, no matter how many machines, we'll still be outside, grabbing the berries off the vine. That never goes away." A sudden movement distracts Carlos.

In the adjacent bog, a large white bird nips at the vines, jaggedly, frenetically, its neck pulsing as it bites at the cranberries.

"Goddammit," says Carlos. He races over, leaps onto the bog, and pushes the bird.

"Oh my," I exclaim, for the bird has pulled its neck from the vines. It is a swan.

"Get out of here, c'mon, shoo!" Carlos prods the swan, which stares back at him defiantly. "C'mon. Go! Go!"

We watch, stupefied.

"Now this," says Jack, "this is something."

"Ladies and gentlemen," says Fritz. "Man versus beast, check your local cable stations."

"I told you swans come down here," says Louisa. "Aren't they beautiful?"

They are; it is. In the strangest of tableaux, the swan's beak reaches Carlos's neck, its soft, white, dirigible-shaped bulk squatting on legs the width of wine-glass stems. Carlos has resorted to kicking the swan, who has retorted by snipping at Carlos, its neck bending near Carlos's ear.

"Oh, Christ," we hear Carlos mutter. He shoves the swan away from him, and finally the swan, like a deposed king, raises its neck, looks around disdainfully and then lifts itself off the ground and soars away.

"I gotta radio over to the Lanzas," Carlos says as he climbs back toward us. "Those damn birds will be at their bogs in a second."

"Do you really kill them?" I ask. The question bolts from my mouth before my brain can clamp down its doors. A long time ago, I swore off commenting out loud about things I knew nothing about. But here I am, wearing my bonnet of righteousness.

Carlos stares at me. No one speaks. I wish I had my motorcycle helmet.

"Diana," Carlos continues, "those birds look beautiful, they're gorgeous, I'd be the first one to tell you. But they're nasty, spiteful creatures. They fly in here, they cause thousands of dollars worth of damage; but it doesn't matter, they can do what they please." Carlos takes a breath; he is sweating from his exertion with the swan. He holds out his arm. It bleeds from the swan attack.

"I don't have the answer," he says. "Some people have told me it's only money, but I don't think they'd say that if it was their cash going down the tubes. You've heard this before: Don't believe everything you read or see on television. Now if you'll all excuse me, I've got to run. I'll see you tonight at the celebration, right?" He waves goodbye to us while Louisa runs and kisses him on the cheek before he trots away, a walkie-talkie pressed against his mouth.

I look back toward the bog where the swan bit Carlos; it is possible to see the ripped-up vines where the swan gnawed away the years of growth.

"Hey, Louisa," Billy calls over from where he stands. "Is there going to be a Cranberry Queen crowned tonight at the celebration?" She smiles. I watch Jack look at her, and I feel resentment and jealousy boil up inside me.

"No," she answers. "They stopped it a while back. People took the spark from it; it made them feel dumb and reddeckish, as if you were supposed to chew on a cornstalk and wear a red checked halter top."

"A travesty," says Fritz.

"Let me be clear." Jack grins. "I would love to see Louisa chewing on a cornstalk wearing a red halter."

I turn away, positive my jealousy is visible. I walk to the side of the bog by myself. In the space between the bog and the dirt road, there is a swampy, watery stretch, narrow enough to step over. I hadn't noticed it before, but now I kneel down because I think I've heard a splash.

"What're you doing?" asks Fritz.

"Did you hear something?" asks Louisa.

"Yes," I say. "I thought I did."

Suddenly Jack crouches next to me. I hold my breath, he is so close. Then he puts his hand in the murky water and pulls out something wriggling, long, skinny, wet, flailing. Oh my God. He's holding a snake.

"I thought I read about these," he says. There is a weird rattle on the end of the snake. There is a weird RATTLE on the end of the snake. This is a *rattlesnake*.

"Scared, Diana?" Louisa walks up beside Jack. She takes the snake from him, holds it by its neck, close to its broad, flat head. It is long and yellowish, with black crossbands over its skin. As she holds it in front of her, I notice her arms are relaxed, no different than if she were holding a kitten.

The snake's mouth opens and shuts, and each time the jaws widen, a skinny ugly tongue peeks at me. The rattle is black and about six inches long, and the snake swings its tail back and forth. It is the noise that unnerves me most.

"A timber rattlesnake," says Fritz as he walks over. "They're not always lethal." He gets right up in its face. "Hey there, fella," he says. He touches the body of the snake. Billy joins Fritz.

"They're not lethal?" he asks.

"Not always," says Fritz.

"But sometimes," Louisa declares, looking straight at me. "Here," Louisa pushes the snake toward me. "Want to touch?"

I shake my head. I've never seen a snake this close, and I never want to see one again. The rattle swings, the sound thrums in my ear, a swarm of locusts concentrated in these six scant inches.

I wrap my hands across my chest. I have begun to breathe quickly, too quickly, I cannot catch my breath, I'm choking.

"Diana." Jack puts his hand on my shoulder. "It's okay. Really. Calm down. Take a deep breath."

I recognize the voice. The guy from the woods. When I was drunk. The handkerchief. I look up at him, breathing more slowly. He grins. "Take a deep breath, come on."

"It's you. It was you."

I am looking at Jack so I don't see what happens next, except that there is a snake, the snake, the rattlesnake, the timber rattlesnake is on my shoulder, its tongue near my ear, I hear it, only for a second, and I swing my arm at it, hard, adrenaline pushing me; I swing at the arm holding the snake near my neck, and the snake flies up in the air, I see it fall a foot from where I stand, I whip around, on fire.

"Louisa!" It's Jack's voice. Then Fritz's, then Billy's.

"I'm sorry," Louisa says. "I must have tripped."

I examine her, silhouetted this time by the afternoon sun. She is beautiful, and she is vicious.

"What is the matter with you?" I feel as if an invisible gnome is pouring 100-proof hatred down a hole in the back of my neck.

"It's just a snake," she says.

The events of the day unfurl fast, an anchor rope uncoiling itself down to the bottom of the sea. She had seen me talking to Jack; she had seen Jack talking to me. It is sometimes that simple.

"Don't, just don't." Louisa throws back her head. "I see what you're doing. Diana the martyr, where's your tears? Don't make me look bad, don't fucking do it."

"I don't have to do a thing," I blurt out. "As usual, you do it all yourself."

Volcanic, destructive. The cap blows, the finger's off the dike, she explodes.

"You come here, you come here, you hit my grandmother with a car, you impose on my family, my friends, you cry and cry and cry, and you cry—and we're supposed to feel sorry for you because a guy dumped you at a Knicks game?"

"Do you even get what you did?" I'm trembling. "Do you have any idea what you just did?"

She ignores me. "Her boyfriend." Louisa is an aqueduct of rushing hate now, all of it directed toward drowning me. "Her boyfriend. The Monster. The love of her life." She turns to the men. "He dumped her at a Knicks game. 'I thought he was dead,' she told me. Dead? No. He was fucking someone else. He said he was coming over, and then he went out and fucked someone else. Reality. He's not a monster. He's a human being who got tired of you and your righteousness and your pathetic insecurity, and I bet right now he is so fucking happy he doesn't have to think about you." A beat. "Wait," she begins anew. "I forgot. He isn't thinking of you. That's the best part.

"It's been *three* years. Three years. Not one, not two, but three years. Three years so we can all feel sorry for her, so everyone she knows can feel so sorry for Diana the victim. Grow the fuck up."

"Louisa." Jack steps to her. She's lit up inside, never prettier. "Let's go for a walk." She whirls around at him, pushes him away.

"Get away from me!" She's a top still spinning, verbal spikes attacking anyone who draws near.

"Go on Diana, tell everyone what you want to say." This is Louisa's version of hanging from the rock, twenty thousand feet above ground. "Tell us what you know."

I'm crying now, a mess of conflicted feelings, grief and helplessness and confusion. Part of me wants to uncurl her fingers from the rock and flick her off; I could tell Jack what Louisa told me in the woods, but I can't, I know that, I don't want to, and it makes no difference to me anyway, *my parents are dead,* I keep seeing the snake, and I feel punched, punched by Louisa, by the Monster, by the Smiling Idiot, by me.

"Speak up, Diana, I can't hear you."

"I, I—" The fact is I can't speak. Words crush one another as they fight to push through the all-too-thin funnel in my brain: JEALOUSY and PETTY and INANE and HEINOUS MONSTROUS SPITEFUL. My breathing pattern shifts to overdrive; the gusts are jagged and short and perilous.

I surrender completely, wholeheartedly. I leap out of the bog and run, more random, pointed thoughts like arrows darting through my skull.

"Hey!" calls Jack. "What'ya—hey! Hold up!"

"Diana!" shouts someone, maybe Fritz, maybe Billy. But I am running, I run as fast as I can out of this bog, toward the motorcycles. I can figure out how to start the cycle; I watched Louisa and Fritz and Billy and old Evel Knievel shows, how hard can it be? My strides are long and hard and quick, I know how to run, this is something I know how to do. I reach the cycles. I can hear people running, but I have a sufficient head start. The keys are in the ignition. I hold onto the handlebars; I have one foot on the ground, the other I use to jump on the kick start. I turn the handlebars to rev the engine, I turn to the left, I turn onto the sand path, I hear the motor catch and I inject more gas to the engine, and then I move. Finally I move. I am in the air, my hair is blowing and I leave this place; I drive down the path, and I say goodbye to everyone mentally and tear down the barren road toward something else, anything else, a place where I can find familiarity and comfort and pursue happiness, like the long-ago colonists or Hessians or Carlos or anyone who lives. I want that, I want to pursue happiness, and that is what I am doing, pursuing.

SIX

The Cemetery

I can't see. I have no helmet, my hair is in my face, my eyes tear—I wear no sunglasses and the wind forces my eyeballs back into my head. Soon I will crash into something and die and it will all be over.

A car passes me. I see the driver whip his head around when I zoom past him in a crooked path.

Have I stolen this motorcycle? If I stay on this road, I will hit Philadelphia, and then I can keep going; motorcycles can go forever on one tank of gas, I have no money, Louisa is such a bitch, Rosie must be at the doctor's right now—someone somewhere else on the globe is fleeing fraudulent friends just as I am, in Italy or Greece or Japan or Mali, he or she is my true compatriot, and my world should be dedicated to finding him or her. I decide this is what I will do. I will drive to China.

A car passes me again, a Saab; I think it is the same one from before. Another person lost. I want to tell the driver, You just keep on going, drive right on out of here, cranberries or no cranberries. I'm kind of sick of Ocean Spray, you know?

I go faster, I feel the tears stream backward onto my cheeks, I'm gasping, choking, I pull to the side. I stay there for a moment, the engine roaring in my ears; I turn the key and shut off the machine. It is silent. I look around. The cemetery I ran by this morning is across the road.

I race to it, not caring that I hear the motorcycle clatter to the ground behind me. I run to the cemetery and like an insane person I have a fit, a tantrum, a moment of hysteria where I don't know where I am or what I do, only that when I look up, I'm on the ground in front of a charcoal-gray gravestone, the name GLADYS ALLOWAY barely visible. *"Beloved wife, mother, grandmother"* is etched underneath her name.

I lean back on the gravestone. I stare ahead, eyes suddenly dry. I tried. I tried and lost. The vivid moments of the past two days are gone. I'm giving up. I am no match for Louisa. I picture Foxhole Girl in the bottom of her pit. It's dark, clammy, and she's lying on her back, eyes closed. She's dead.

SEVEN

A Truce

"Diana!" I hear my name above the sound of an engine. I have not moved. It may be only five minutes from when I leapt from the bog. Or an hour. I have sat here, against Gladys Alloway's tombstone, staring ahead, my mind effectively blank.

"DIANA!" The noise of the engine disappears. The sounds behind it are gentle, indecipherable. But then, loudly, disturbing everything, "DIANA!" She's seen the fallen motorcycle. And now I see her, her head above the gravestones, walking toward me.

We just look at one another. I meet her stare head-on. Inside, I feel deadened, implacable.

"I saw red," she says. "I'm sorry." I don't avert my eyes. "I'm sorry, Diana. What do you want me to do? I fucked up."

Words aren't supposed to matter; they are not supposed to batter you like punches or stab you like knives. "I didn't sleep here last night," said the Monster. "There was an accident," said Uncle John. "Grow the fuck up," said Louisa.

Maybe it is just me who feels words like gunshots. Maybe everyone else knows they don't matter at all.

I check my watch. It's three o'clock. Rosie will not return until five. Rosie. Guilt creeps on the blacktop and over the grass like a three-toed sloth. It is lashing out to brush me with its tar-heavy lips; this is not the way I was supposed to keep Louisa busy.

"Come on, Diana. Everyone is furious with me. Jack just lit into me like I've never heard. I don't know what happened. I'm screwing everything up." She stops. "I am, not you. I'm sorry."

I still say nothing, even though I know she's sincere, even though I know she wants everything to go back to normal.

"Say something, say something for God's sake, Diana; this isn't fair— you're the nice one, forgive me. I don't have a pound of flesh, or I'd give it to you. What do you want me to say, what can I do?"

I drift away during the last part of Louisa's plea. I hear her getting angry, frustrated, which I almost think is funny, because it's like me most of the time, a little child not getting her way. Instead of responding, I stare at the horizon, the road merging with the trees far off in the distance.

"Diana, c'mon, don't make me beg. I shouldn't have said all of that. I don't know what I'm talking about, I wasn't there. When I get mad I can't focus, I just spew." She pauses. "I'm a Scorpio. Maybe that's it. We're all about stinging people."

Louisa's put me in the untenable position of being righteous or weak-willed. Even now I'm remarkably clear-headed, and it makes me rage inside. Why can't I have Louisa's mind for a moment, a place where it's all furious bursts of energy, all day, all the time? It's a perfect setup—she goes too far, she apologizes, she says it's because of stress or astrology or a bad genetic pool; she's charming and contrite, and on cue I say it's okay, everything's okay, and she's grateful for a second before she forgets everything she said, and then we're best friends heading to the seventy-seventh annual cranberry celebration.

But I am nothing if not predictable.

"It's okay," I say finally, because the silence is too much, because I've already capitulated, because I cannot compete at this game, because I'm tired.

"Christ," she says, as she flops to the ground next to me. "A fucking cemetery." She pauses. "I should have known. You cry and you hyperventilate and you make me feel guilty, and now you're sitting dazed in a cemetery. You should apologize to me."

"I'm sorry I threw a snake at you. Whoops." I pause. "Oh, right. That was you, not me." I'm not used to being sardonic. It feels good.

"I should have told you about the rattlesnakes. We have snapping turtles too, and green bullfrogs, which are, apparently, quite rare if you talk to the environmentalists. They cut property values in half down here because of the Pine Barrens bullfrog. Or tree frog. Or something like that. I personally don't care enough about frogs to think that's fair, but what do I know?"

"People shouldn't mess up the natural ecology."

"People shouldn't hit old women on motorcycles."

Neither of us speak for a moment.

"So do you want to talk?" Louisa asks.

"No," I answer.

Louisa studies me for a second, and I can see her plunge into the waters of personal intrusion even though I asked her not to. "I was married once, you know."

(I look around the cemetery. I suppose it's as good a place as any for another Louisa-Diana heart-to-heart.)

I'm not surprised Louisa's been married. She is my age, mid-thirties, and beautiful. Most people are by this time married or divorced; I am the exception, the outlier on the bell curve.

"I didn't know."

"He was great, handsome, smart, and it was fun, party party party and then the biggest party of all, the wedding, in Italy, even Rosie and Gabe came over; Mom had everything just right, and Dad went around saying, 'He's a good guy, a terrific young man' when everyone knew he despised him. I knew when we married it was all wrong, but how do you stop the train once it starts?"

"You say, 'I don't want to get married.'"

"You've never been married?"

"Nope."

"Then you don't know."

"Okay," I say.

"No."

"No what?"

"No, you can't say 'okay' to everything."

"Why?"

"Because you can't."

I remember a line from *Angels in America*: *"It's no fun picking on you, Louis; you're so guilty, it's like throwing darts at a glob of Jell-o—there's no satisfying hits, just quivering, the darts just blop in and vanish."* But unlike Louis, I'm not guilty. I just don't care.

"After my divorce, I could have just curled up and done nothing. But you've got to get on with your life. I'm sure you've heard that."

"Yes." Louisa likes hearing herself speak, especially when she thinks she is being selfless. Because she is still trying to make amends right now, this could go on forever.

"I could have done nothing, but Rosie and Gabe and my friends, they all came through. But it all came down to me. I had to decide for myself to stand up and shake myself off."

I think of Polonius and wish I could effect a law that restricts people from blanket statements meant to inspire someone else when instead what they do is smother whatever flake of boldness remains in an otherwise vanquished spirit. But I don't want to listen anymore to Louisa's sermon. I want to talk about me, just *me*. I want to talk, I want to be heard, I want to hurl words from my mouth and have someone catch them, Steve Carlton to Tim McCarver. And I have a theory I want to test, my own little garden of white flags, my own little surrender plot.

"Louisa," I say. "I want to tell you something. I have my own theory." I hear the resolute tone in my voice, and I'm pleased.

"I do not have to stand and shake myself off. I do not have to. I don't want to. It is not a given. Everyone does not have to listen to 'nothing ventured, nothing gained.' My theory: Nothing ventured, nothing lost. I'm sorry about your divorce. You want to apologize to me, heartfelt, you're sorry, that's fine. But I don't have to forgive you. I don't have to do anything. I don't have to try to do anything. If I want to wallow in the mud of the Monster—or whatever it is—until the day I die, I can." (I realize as I say it that "whatever it is" may be the biggest understatement of the day.)

Louisa appraises me, but I feel strong, pleased that I've come up with this philosophy. It's new, innovative really, and particularly—

"That's ridiculous," Louisa says finally, smirking. "You know, you should be an actress. You are so fucking dramatic."

"Says the 1982 Blueberry Queen."

"Says the 1982 Blueberry Queen."

We sit next to each other, our backs on a tombstone. On the road, cars rush by, more than I've seen since I've arrived.

"The celebration's tonight," Louisa announces.

"I know," I say.

"You wouldn't believe how mad Jack was. Nothing like reminding him what a bitch I can be." Louisa stretches out her legs, touches her toes.

"He was mad?" I feel the insecurity seep through my implacable self, and I wish I could sop it up, make it disappear. But I want even more for Jack to have told Louisa they'll never be together, ever.

"Furious," she says. "But then he calmed down. He understands me, he told me. Actually." I see a smile begin in the corners of her mouth, and I want to cover my ears. "He said it was probably his fault, because he stayed away for so long."

Despite my new theory of staying on life's sidelines, I hear a silent death knell to whatever I had hoped would happen with Jack. Equilibrium, common sense, that's all well and good, but Louisa's imbalance is captivating. I decide in my next life I'm coming back as a crazy person. I'm so tired of them getting all the attention.

Which reminds me of something. "Hey," I say. "Were you with anyone last night?"

"Why?"

"Because." I debate for a split second whether I should invent a reason but decide it is too much work. "Because I went to use the bathroom, and a guy was in there."

Louisa hesitates only for a second. "Fritz," she says.

"Fritz?" I repeat.

"It had nothing to do with Jack," Louisa replies.

"Right." I know she's telling the truth, and I envy her ability to consider only her own emotions regarding matters of the heart. "I'd just have never put you two together."

"Sometimes, when we drink too much, it wasn't the first time, not a big deal. We had, may I remind you, just taken *someone* home, *someone* very drunk, not mentioning any names, *Diana,* and then he asked to use the bathroom and I said yes, and then I walked in on him as he was washing his face, and he is really cute, you've got to admit, and there was a tiny speck of dirt on the back of his neck, so I had to, as a good friend, clean him off, which I did, with my lips. . . ."

Louisa grins. So do I. I used to do things like that, back, back so long ago my memory has rewritten the script and the youthful me is a character from another play. My mind bolts to a scene where youthful me was on a roof during an electrical storm and youthful he was framed by all these pulsing extraordinary colors, eyes burning into each other's. . . . But I don't know her, the one beaming, hair wild in the wind. She looks happy and pretty, but I don't know who she is.

I return to the conversation. "But you just said Jack—"

"I told you, Jack has nothing to do with it."

"But—"

"It was just sex."

"Right."

"C'mon, don't tell me you've never done that."

"I didn't say that."

"It just happened. There's no reason to dwell on it. It was fun, and now it's over, and Jack's here, and Fritz is fine with it."

I believe her. I watched Fritz with her all day and didn't pick up any strange vibes. Maybe, just as I seem impervious to sexual vibes from any man myself, I can no longer discern them between others.

"Diana!" Louisa breaks into my reverie. "Earth to Diana, where were you?"

"Nothing," I say. "Just absorbing the grandeur of this place."

This is believable, because it is just at that time of day, twilight, when the sun sets, the bright blue of the sky bleeds into a sweeping block of blue-white, the air crispens, and the sensation of the atmosphere is one of complacency and contentment.

At that precise moment, Louisa pitches another, albeit smaller grenade.

"You know, some really successful women have bad luck with men. Really. A ton of really terrific women, all of them members of the walking wounded."

Every woman has her emotional trigger. Mine, for whatever reason, is being a "member of a club" of frustrated, desperate, clawing women lamenting the loss of their own personal monster. I am not one of them. I am different. (Which, I know, is what every one of those aforementioned desperate clawing women feel, but for me it's true.)

"Louisa." I stop walking. "Do not, I repeat, do not bring him up again." Even when she thinks she's being understanding, she errs. One minute, she's carefully polishing a diamond, the next minute, she's throwing it into a swamp.

"Sorry," she tells me. "That came out wrong. Don't be angry."

"I'm not."

"You are, but get over it. You can't be angry at the celebration." Louisa checks her watch. "It isn't like I threw a snake at you this time."

I shake my head. She's all momentum, pressing forward, oblivious to consequence and self-examination. Not, I reflect, a bad way to be.

"Truce, right?" she asks me as we walk from the cemetery.

"Okay," I say. "Okay."

Sam

Louisa and I walk our motorcycles the rest of the way to Rosie's house. I see Gabe's car in the driveway. At least I've kept my promise to Rosie. I park my bike behind Louisa's; she is, as usual, a million times faster than I. She's already inside the house.

I climb the stairs and push open the screen door. "Hey, Ros—"

I see him. Sam.

"Hey, Diana," says Louisa. "You've got a visitor."

Sam is well dressed, his dark hair groomed, his eyes intent. Did he tell her? I examine Louisa. She smiles at me. Oh, my. She thinks Sam is the Monster.

"You two just met?" I say slowly.

"I'm not allowed to talk about him, remember?" Louisa pauses, lights a cigarette.

"Uh, that's not," I stammer, "that's not *him.*"

"Him who?" asks Sam pleasantly. Louisa winks at me as if to say she's got this under control.

"Oh, you know, Diana just kept referring to you in the third person; she was very discreet, actually. But now the mystery's solved, and I know Diana wouldn't want me to say anything, but I for one am glad you made the effort to come down here and find her." She inhales. I look at Sam. He looks at me. I think T.S. Eliot: *In a minute there is time for decisions and revisions which a minute will reverse.*

"Well," announces Louisa. "I'm going to leave you two alone to talk."

"Where's Rosie?" I ask. Louisa shrugs.

"She's resting," says Sam.

"You've been here for a while?" I ask.

"Not that long. Rosie was kind enough to invite me inside after I introduced myself."

Louisa has not left the room. "Good to meet you, Sam. Glad I finally know your real name."

I want to throw Louisa a life preserver, a pride preserver, but I don't know what words to use. I can't tell her about the accident. Not yet.

"So I'll go now," Louisa announces for the second time. "If you need anything, just holler." I hear her walk through the living room up the stairs. I look at Sam.

"So. You found me," I say.

"I found you."

"How?"

"Caller ID. I talked with your friend Wiley and convinced her I should be the one to come here."

"How'd you know Wiley?"

"Through your Aunt Margaret." I nod. Nothing surprises me right now.

"Listen, I haven't said anything to anyone about, about—"

"I know."

I grab a glass of water.

"Who's *him?*" Sam asks me.

"It's a long story," I answer.

"I've got time," he tells me.

"I don't."

"Seems to me you have buckets, trainloads of time."

"Seems to me you don't know what you're talking about."

"Can we go somewhere to talk?" he asks me. I pick up my glass and head toward the door.

"Sure," I answer. "Follow me."

Futures

I lead Sam outside, to Rosie and Gabe's backyard. There is an old picnic table, wooden, with matching benches. Sam and I sit across from each other.

"So." I'm remarkably calm. "Sam. Tell me. Who are you?"

He has carried his mug of tea outside with him and now lifts it to his mouth, closing his eyes while he sips.

"I have to admit I'm disappointed you don't remember me. I'm Sam. Sam Joyce. Your dad's friend from law school. I was at your house all the time when you were little."

Sam. I do remember. He was from Los Angeles, and he had told me that he knew David Cassidy. At the time, I had the thickest glasses ever for a little girl and used to skulk around with the latest Agatha Christie clutched to my chest.

"I remember. Now I remember." I slump against the bench. A memory: Sam in the living room, my mother bringing him escarole soup. He ate it with a spoon in the beginning, but he liked it so much he soon turned the bowl over and slurped the rest out like a man drinking his last liquid. Mom had acted as if this breach of dinner etiquette disturbed her, but I could tell she was secretly pleased. Sam was my dad's best friend in law school, his best man at my parents' wedding. He was from Los Angeles but had lived on the East Coast for a while, before he met George and moved to San Francisco. Dad and he had remained in contact, through e-mail and visits he and Mom would take to Sam and George's home in Marin County—but for some reason, I hadn't seen him for about fifteen years.

I think back to the movie theater, when I had briefly sat next to him and thought for a moment he was auditioning for the role of my Older but Kinder Handsome Boyfriend. Lucky I didn't jump on his lap and start kissing him—nothing like embarrassing yourself with a gay older man who was one of your parents' best friends.

"Want to go and get a drink?" he asks. I look at my watch. It is six o'clock at night. Sam obviously thinks he's in a place where right around that bend will be some Keith McNally kind of café, serving thick slices of bread and red wine. There will be a guest list, and we will have to wait at the bar.

"Yeah. Why don't we just go to that four-star restaurant that the Pine Barrens has at every corner?"

Sam takes a drink from his tea. "You're thirty-three, right?"

"Yes," I nod. "How do you remember so much about me?"

"You left quite an impression on me when I was—well, when I was actually a bit younger than you are now."

"Why don't you just punch me?" I ask, as I realize that Sam, the Sam in my head, the Sam who was much much older than I, was younger than I am now.

"You don't look a day over thirty-two," he says. We pause.

"It's been . . . it's been a hard time for me," I say.

For at least two minutes, neither of us speaks. I drink from my water glass; Sam drinks from his mug of tea. The sky darkens, it is now that deep royal-blue color used in Technicolor movies like *The King and I*.

"What do you want to do?" Sam asks me.

"I've never seen a cranberry celebration before, should be kind of interesting, although I have to confess, I really don't like fresh cranberries. They're very bitter."

"Diana, listen. I—what do you think you want to do? With your time, with your life?" Sam ignores me, and this irritates me.

"Rosie says there's a bonfire and that a ton of people come from all over the place, celebrating the harvest; it's like a pagan ritual."

"Your behavior." Sam doesn't miss a beat. "You've worried many people. Even that little man from your job, what's his name, Darius, is concerned."

"You talked to him?"

"I have a proposition for you," Sam says. He takes another drink. "I want you to come work for me."

"I don't want to work. How 'bout that?" I say.

"So what are you going to do?" He persists.

"I don't know. Maybe I'll go trekking to Nepal. That's what bereaved people do, I think. Maybe I'll become a Buddhist. I have no idea what I'm going to do. I don't know anything. I don't even know—I know nothing."

"There has to be something. Eventually you'll have to do something."

"I may just throw myself off a building."

"Well that would be doing something."

"I don't have to do anything."

"Yes. You do."

"No, you're wrong. You know something, Sam, I don't have to do anything. And don't think," I begin again, urged on by Sam's silence, "that you can change me or change what I want to do. I am so tired of people telling me what they think should happen to me. I don't even know you. I don't have to listen to you." I stop. "What do you even do?"

"Interested?" Sam asks.

"In a very benign, noninterested way," I say. "I'm just making conversation."

"You were a much nicer child," he says. I grin. I like this New Me. I think this is what car dealers would call a successful test drive, only the model is me.

"No. I was a much *quieter* child. Now I'm just an embittered adult. I'm a spinster, did you know that?"

"Yes, actually." *What?* Oh. I get it. He's playing the reverse-psychology game, as one does with little kids who say they're going to scream for hours unless they get their Pokémon cards and their mother says, Go ahead, scream.

I am not, I think, *technically,* a spinster; don't you have to be fifty?

"Maybe I'll become a lesbian."

"You can't become a lesbian."

"Yes I can."

"Okay, you can." Sam swallows, moves his shoulders up and down, looks at me, resigned. He really is a handsome man, big, impressive, well dressed, smart. "Diana, this is pointless. I'm not going to spar with you; it makes no sense, and I know that anything I say you'll twist around."

"You've been talking to Wiley."

"I am a very rich man. I'm retired. I want to start something; I'm only sixty-three and George died two years ago. I don't know what it is I want to do, but when I went to the funeral and I saw you, all grown up, I thought that maybe, a crazy thought, but just maybe, we could do something together. I don't have any children; we were going to adopt, but then George died."

"AIDS?" I ask.

"Heart attack," he says. He stops and gives me a steely gaze, just like I've seen formidable men do in business meetings in the movies, Peter Finch in *Network* or Michael Douglas in *Wall Street.* "One minute, he was playing tennis with me, the next he was on the ground, gasping. He died about an hour later."

"When?"

"March."

"I'm sorry," I say, but I'm not, not really. He lost George, his lover of many years, when I've lost everything, parents, brother, and don't have any person to rely upon—who will sleep next to me, who will be home at night and tell me I'm going to be okay, all right, that with time and faith and opti-mism and wisdom and with him, whoever *he* is, I'll be okay. I don't have that. I think that if I had shared my life with someone and if he then died, at least I'd remember that for a while I was normal, that what I was going through was part of life's cycle. Sam had George for a large part of his life, he had had partnership; he had been normal.

But sudden orphanhood at thirty-three? Not normal. Abnormal. Totally off the charts abnormal.

"The fact is, Diana," he says, "I'm looking for a new—a new path too. I didn't expect—I didn't think—" Sam takes a breath. He too looks around the landscape, and I see for the first time how effortlessly Sam fits in anywhere. He is the human equivalent of a wrinkle-free garment; throw it into a bag, pull it out, and it looks perfect. He isn't too handsome, he isn't too big, he isn't too small, he isn't obtrusive. But he's formidable and compelling.

"I've had a difficult—a challenging—" Sam can't find the words, and I sense how strange a predicament this is for him; I remember my father speaking of Sam's oratory skills in an almost reverential manner. *That man, that man speaks like a silk ribbon, he is effortlessly eloquent, you should spend some time with him, Diana, if you ever get the chance, that man could charm anyone. Hell, he even charmed your mother.*

Sam hesitates still. "Diana." This time he is going to force himself to speak. "You do, one does, the best one can. You do what you can, you wake up and you're still here, and you think, goddamn it, that horse's ass down the street is going to get the better of me—"

"I told you—"

"Let me finish. Get the better of me because he's a stupid sullen bigot, a man with the brainpower of a pea, a person who carps at his television, is mean to his wife, is stingy to his children, who votes against politicians because of some perceived spite to him, who has done nothing for his brief time on earth—I mean to say, Diana, that giving up is just not an option. It is not an option. I am not that man yelling at his television set. I am not going to sit at home every night growing inward. I—"

"Sam, Sam," I say. Suddenly I feel old, very old, and very broken. "I am not a guy. You are telling me guy things. Man things. Maybe there are some women who would care about this stuff. I don't. I don't care if someone, even a fat man in San Francisco who beats his wife 'gets the better of me.' I understand if that's what's motivating you, but it isn't what drives me."

"I'm saying this all wrong. I have a hunch, I know, your father and mother would want this; they would be supportive. They would want me to be involved. I've been acting peculiarly, I know. I kept telling myself to just approach you, tell you my story, but each time I saw you I couldn't do it. Then today I said to myself that I had to speak with you no matter what—if it meant interrupting your time here, intruding onto your new friendships, I didn't care. Your father was my best friend. I'm alone now." He stops, runs his hand through his hair. "Life's a short trip, Diana; you've seen that at a tragically early age and—"

"Life's a short trip, I'll remember that." I can't help responding bitterly, but Sam is verging so closely into New Age, Self Help, Twelve Step territory that I want to push him off the cliff. And that is exactly what happens, even as I realize I want to pull him back up.

"Listen." He stands, pulls out a business card. He hands it to me.

"I'm failing here, which is not a sensation I'm comfortable with. You're a healthy, smart woman. I don't need to be concerned. I just had assumed you would consider my proposal, at least use it as a jumping-off point for further conversations, for further discussion. If that is, or is ever, I should say, of interest, please call." Sam has regained his composure. He's the successful business guy again, the one who tried to do something out of the ordinary in honor of his dead friend, his dead lover, his dead life.

"You're leaving?" I should be incapable of people surprising me, but these days, it seems that every day someone does something unpredictable. He's been haunting me for days, for months, and now he's just leaving?

Sam shakes my hand, which I've extended automatically, almost unknowingly.

"Good to see you, Diana, and good to talk to you. Best of luck on your adventure, best of luck to you."

The answer to my question is yes. Yes. He would leave me, he does leave me, he is gone. I remain at the picnic table, looking at the new paint on the house across the street, the intersecting main roads, and the pine trees that huddle in groups of three and four in this main part of town.

EIGHT

The Preparation

Louisa looks stunning. Maybe it's because I've never seen her dressed up, maybe because Jack is here, maybe because Rosie makes a fuss over her, I don't know, but I'm seriously doubting that I want to accompany her anywhere. Yet we're best friends now, it seems; she even pulls my elbow close to hers in that way that Upper East Side old-while-they're-still-young women do with their mothers.

As I was drying my hair, Rosie had entered the room. She didn't talk much, only to thank me for not telling Louisa where she had gone that afternoon. I asked her if the doctors were helpful, and she had nodded; *yes dear,* she said, and *it's all just words anyway.* When she left the room, she said I *understand a friend visited you today,* to which I answered yes, and Rosie just nodded again and left.

So now I'm downstairs with Gwen the dog. Gabe is on the porch. Louisa is in the bathroom, redoing her lips. I walk to the porch.

"Hey, Gabe," I say.

"Hey," he answers.

"It go all right today?" I ask.

"Did you talk to Rosie?" he answers.

"Sort of. She didn't say much."

"Huh," Gabe responds. He smokes a cigar, staring at Millie's store.

"Right," I talk to myself. "But she's going to be okay, for a while?"

Gabe puffs at his cigar. He turns to look at me. I see I am a stranger to him, he has no reason to reply to me at all. He blows out smoke. His elbows lean back into the armrests.

"I don't want to talk," he says.

"Okay," I respond quickly. "Right. Sorry." I go back into the house and sit on the couch. Gwen is there, sitting with her head raised, and I pet the soft hair between her ears. The news about Rosie is bad, I know. She is going to die.

I lean down and grab Gwen's face. She looks at me resignedly, and I have the feeling that Gwen has read my mind and is sorry that I am so pathetic.

Louisa emerges from the bathroom, all angles and white teeth and long hair and effortless charm.

"Why the face?" she asks.

"Nothing," I say. "Just thinking."

"I thought he was cute. You didn't tell me he was so old."

"I told you a hundred times that was not the Monster. That was my father's best friend from law school."

"Sure," she says. "My dad's best friend from law school follows me around too."

"I wouldn't doubt it. But it isn't like that."

"Then what was it?"

"He had a business proposition."

"Oh." She looks into another mirror, flashes her teeth, and smiles. "Billy will be very sad."

She grins, and it's all I can do to keep my mouth shut. Any reply would be useless, for Louisa is one of those people who arranges her friends together like gameboard pieces, and if it doesn't work out, she just rearranges them. I've come to realize that it isn't that Louisa doesn't feel, it's just that her feelings are like the water in a children's swimming pool, fluid, moving, and six inches deep.

"You look terrific," she says, and I roll my eyes. People like her should never be allowed to compliment people like me—there should be a rulebook somewhere that she has to follow. "Come on. The boys are supposed to be at Millie's." She grabs my arm. We are now at the roller-skating rink waiting for the boys in braces to ask us to skate doubles. "I'm nervous."

"Why?" I ask.

"Jack," she says. "I haven't felt like this for a while." She takes a deep breath. "He said he had something he's been wanting to tell me." Her grin is childlike, expectant—I see the girl right before she's crowned Blueberry Queen. I recall Jack looking at Louisa this afternoon. They look so perfect together—it's right for them to reunite. They can pose in commercials together, like Bruce Willis and Demi Moore before they split up.

"You know, Diana," Louisa says, "Fritz and Billy are single." We walk out the door down the approximately seventeen steps to Millie's. "I think Billy likes you," she says as we reach the building.

"Please," I say, with as much gravity as I can muster, "I'm the only other girl. Of course he likes me. For tonight."

"No, I think it's real," Louisa persists. I put my hand on the screen door, preventing us from entering.

"Stop this. Now."

"Okay, okay, no need to get so testy," she says, and we open the door. The only person I see is Jack.

"Hey," he says, to both of us, but I of course think it's directed only to me, which means that I am suddenly flummoxed.

"Hey, handsome," says Louisa. She goes over to him, bestows a kiss on the cheek.

"There you are," says Fritz. He looks at his watch. "Glad to see you haven't changed."

"We're late?" I ask.

"Only by an hour," he answers.

"Never be anywhere early," says Louisa. "I have run it through my mind several times, and I can find no good reason to be on time to anything."

"The consideration for other people, who are waiting for you, clearly holding no significance," responds Fritz.

"Okay, okay," interjects Jack, "enough turmoil for one day." Does he know where Fritz slept last night? Would he care? "You two okay?" He questions us both. Louisa and I look at each other.

"We have a truce," Louisa says. "Right, Diana?"

I nod. "I hit Rosie with my car, she throws a snake. It's the least I can do."

"Glad to hear it," Jack says.

"Here." Millie stands behind the counter, holding a large paper bag. "Take this." She hands it to Jack.

"What is it?"

"I just put together some food and things; if you left it up to Louisa you'd have wine and not much else, so here's some bread. They'll have food, of course, but you should bring something yourself. And a sheet's in there, to sit on, so you don't have to get yourself all dirty."

"That's Millie," Louisa grins. "What would I do without you?"

"That's why I'm still here, Louisa," she answers. "That's why I'm still here."

"Where's Mason?" Louisa asks.

"He just left," Jack answers. "He's mad at me."

"Only because you're back," Millie tells us. "He's jealous."

"Oh, come on, Millie." Louisa submits the weakest of protests. I want to leave.

Billy emerges from the back. "Finally," he proclaims. "We've only been waiting for about an hour."

"Already scolded, thank you very much," says Louisa.

"You look great," he says.

"Thank you," Louisa answers.

"I meant Diana," Billy replies, and I blush.

"Of course you did." Louisa picks up the ball as if it's been thrown to her, but now she's stymied, because I have been so emphatic in my disinterest in Billy.

"Well, let's get this show on the road," says Fritz.

"Have a good time," voices Millie.

"You're coming, aren't you?" asks Jack.

"I'll be there," she says. "Later."

"Millie won't miss it," Louisa offers. "No one misses this, I'm telling you, not that it's such an enormous event, it's just one of those special times when everyone gets together."

"Well, I'm glad I'm here for it," says Billy.

"Me too," I say.

"A bonfire in the middle of the Pine Barrens," states Fritz. "I thought Carlos said fire's the most dangerous thing around."

"This is carefully controlled," says Louisa. "They've been having this event for years and nothing's ever happened."

I think back to the night Ben said he had proposed to Laura. I had been at home, in Princeton, where I spent many weekends post-heartbreak. Our family was exceptionally close, I think, compared to some of my peers, so when Ben bounded home, aglow with his news, *she said yes, she said yes!* I immediately said congratulations, I'msohappyforyou and just as immediately thought, oh, he's leaving, he's leaving us, he's gone. I recognized that Ben's news was appropriate, that it was his time for walking out of the door called Family and toward the gate labeled Normal Life Cycle. And Laura was terrific, and he was so happy, and I thought, this, this means that our family is normal because Ben is doing this normal thing, and that means that I am normal too because in all families the children get married, and if he's doing it, then I will too, and we will finally, finally, be like the characters in *Our Town*.

But then, because nothing involving me is ever normal, they head down to a perfectly ordinary meeting-of-the-parents, an event that other families have held effortlessly for years and years, and wham, they are dead.

The Celebration

The field where Louisa leads us stretches flat into the distance. It is night now, white stars glittering against the black sky. We have taken three motorcycles here: Jack and Louisa, Billy, and Fritz and me.

In the middle of the field is a blazing bonfire made of wood and leaves, splashing red and orange flames in disparate directions. It is contained and bright and warm. Pickup trucks surround the bonfire, and people mill outside their vehicles wearing fleece jackets and flannel shirts. A band is playing some kind of Latin music—it is a Spanish-style band, and I remember Louisa talking about the number of Puerto Ricans who work on the area farms. There are about fifty, sixty people; a grill is broiling something to one side. I smell steak and roasted onions and beer.

Louisa smiles at all of us as we take in the sight. "See," she says, "nothing to be afraid of."

"We weren't exactly afraid," answers Fritz.

"You know what I mean," she responds.

"C'mon." She grabs Jack's arm. "Let's go get some food."

The two of them leave while I take out the sheet Millie packed for us and lay it on the ground, as other people have done. Fritz and Billy sit beside me. Billy takes out a bottle of wine from the bag and a Swiss Army knife from his pocket. He begins to uncork the wine. I look in the bag—Millie has not forgotten the glasses. I remove clear plastic cups, hand one to Fritz and hold one for Billy. Billy pours the wine. With the music and the chatter of the other people, it is right that none of us is talking. I look up. The pine trees stand tall around the entire field. This must have been a place for blueberry bushes once, like the bushes I saw when I first drove down here, what seems like months ago, when I left New York and—

"Hey!" It's Carlos. He stands next to a pretty woman with dark hair and green eyes. "This is Alice."

We stand and shake Alice's hand.

"So Louisa's dragged you all down here," she says.

"We wanted to come," Billy tells her.

"I bet. You all want to come down here in the boondocks. All right. You believe what you want to believe." She grins, I like her, and the idea that she and Carlos have found each other gives me that quick sensation of hope yet again; maybe it's there for me, too.

"Sorry about the swan today," Carlos says sheepishly.

"Hey, man," answers Fritz, "no problem. How's your arm?" Carlos extends it, pulling back his shirt from the wrist. Ugly welts remain, mottled and blue.

"I hate those damn things." This from Alice. "Goddamned environmentalist groups come down here and say we can't do this, we can't do that, we can't sell our land, we've gotta save a bullfrog, and then a swan goes and wrecks the vines and everyone's hard work, and the deer trample

200

over everything, and I want to say, Did you pay for this land? Did you do anything to keep it as good as it is? Then shut the hell up why don't you, I want to say, go back to where you're from and stop telling us what to do. They'll be sorry if they ever have to deal with *me*." Alice is tiny, about five feet tall. Her eyes jump out at you when she's excited. "I say shoot all of 'em; I tell Carlos all the time if it was me—"

"I think you've said quite enough," laughs Carlos. "She wouldn't hurt a fly is the truth of it."

"If I saw that swan right now, I'm telling you, I'd get your gun and—"

"Right," Carlos interrupts. "They get the picture, Sweetheart."

"I hate swans," says Fritz.

"Me too," I join in, grinning.

"We'll kill them all," Billy adds.

"You kids haven't eaten yet?" asks Carlos.

Kids. He called us kids. We're probably only a couple years younger than he.

"I think Louisa's getting us some—" I start, but then I look over to where Carlos points. She and Jack are not, in fact, getting us food. They're dancing.

"Someone's been taking lessons," says Fritz. "Looks like our friends have gone a little Marc Anthony on us."

Near the band, backlit by the fire, Jack and Louisa dance to a salsa tune, and I can't even get jealous. They are so in unison, they look so graceful and sensual, that I just want to watch, like a little girl at her first grown-up party. Other couples dance too, all adeptly, all delighting under the stars and near the fire. This is extraordinary, this must be why I am here, this is what it means to be present and accounted for.

"Want to try it?" asks Billy. I recoil. Dance? When I dance, it is a disaster, all elbows and large feet and fear-of-being-wrong.

"No." I say this so emphatically that I scare him. "I mean, I can't dance. Not at all."

"Right," he says, looking hurt. "Okay." I look over at Fritz, who shrugs.

"I'm getting some food," Fritz announces, impervious to my exchange with Billy.

"I'll go with you," Billy tells him. He looks back at me. "Want anything?"

"No," I say as I sit back to watch.

When I was younger, I used to wear glasses, and every time I put them on, I believed I was invisible. Now, at this second, in this field, even with my contact lenses, I feel that same serene sense of invisibility, a freedom to stare and gawk and absorb whatever I want—the man over there with the water-balloon–like belly and mug of beer; the older bald man and his rotund wife spinning and twirling around in perfect rhythm; the little kids jumping on the back of the pickup truck; the dogs barking the fire crackling the music the smell the talk.

I lean back on my arms. I take a deep breath. It is something, I think. It is me beginning to take a step, me as a giantess, extending a leg over a miniature world of despair, reaching for whatever exists on the other side.

"Hey," I hear. Someone's whispering. I turn. It is Jack. I look back toward the music. Louisa dances with Billy.

"C'mon," he says. He holds out his arm. My thoughts slam up against each other like a five-car pileup on the Garden State Parkway.

"But . . ." I say.

"Sssh," he whispers, grinning, the same smile that made me want to leap off my motorcycle earlier in the day. He can see me, I think, I am not wearing my glasses, so take his hand, *take his hand,* and, not looking anywhere but straight at him, I do.

Puppets

I ride behind Jack, on a motorcycle, on an empty road, my hands around his waist, my chin near his shoulder. We go fast, the engine churns, my heart beats, the wind against us and the sky dark, sewn with needlepoints of stars, the deep dark green of the trees hovering over us, the blacktopped road; I am holding onto him, I am holding onto him.

I cannot regulate my thoughts. A ride, what does it mean, what about Louisa, where are we going, can he feel my heart, what is he thinking what is he *thinking*?

At the same time another voice, maybe Foxhole Girl, another couple steps up the ladder, says, *Breathe, Diana, breathe, remember this moment, this time, this is one of those times you must remember, hold it, carve it into your psyche. This you must remember.*

So I try to give Foxhole Girl her due. I concentrate on my fingers, grasped together at Jack's waist, I focus on the wind against my shoulders and my face, I think of the night and fear and speed and excitement. I close my eyes. Magnificent, I think. Magnificent.

Jack slows down. I hold on as he turns onto one of those sandy paths, a trail barely illuminated by the lights of the motorcycle. We ride more slowly here, ducking under errant branches, slow enough to sense the tires spinning against the sand.

And then we reach it, his destination. The unflooded cranberry bogs of this afternoon, the "carpet of cranberries" we trampled upon hours earlier. Jack stops the bike and waits. I unlatch my hands and step off. He leans the bike against a tree.

"Jack?" I say.

"Not yet," he answers. He's pulling at something from the motorcycle. I don't know what to do, I'm completely perplexed, so I turn around and take in the sight. It is dark, but the terrain is visible in the shadows. I walk toward the edge of the nearest bog. This is my night, I think. God and the Fates and Furies have pulled and twitched me this way and that in order that I end up here, in this place, with this man named Jack. I cannot be here out of whimsy or happenstance. It is too big. This is my brother from up above tugging at one string, my dad swirling another, and my mother guiding the last one, the one most hesitant, the girl from the foxhole, who is slowly crawling out of her refuge in the ground, forcing herself out here, tonight, to live.

Spiders

"Got it," Jack says as he turns around toward me.

"What?" I ask, thrilled he's begun a conversation about the tangible.

"The fundamentals," he answers. He pulls out from the bag two items: a corkscrew and a bottle of wine. "Millie packed for me too."

"You know her?" I question.

"I met Millie and Mason years ago, spent a bit of time with her the last time I was here."

"Right," I say. Jack comes alongside me, passes me, steps onto the bog. I follow him. He kneels down, grabs some berries from the vine.

"Incredible, isn't it? Look at this place." He sits on the tangled vines, thick and dense and matted vines woven with berries and leaves. His elbows rest on his kneetops. "I mean, it's just mind-blowing," he says. My feet are stuck.

"What're you doing?" he asks. I like that the tone of his voice is completely normal, as if this is not an extraordinary circumstance, me with him, now, while Louisa must be fuming over at the celebration. "Diana?" Jack asks again, interrupting my thoughts.

"I'm coming," I answer. I step over onto the bog, following him. I stand awkwardly near where he sits.

"You're just going to stand there?" He asks. "You're blocking my view." It's a *joke,* Diana; sit down, I tell myself, bend your knees. Stop making everything so traumatic. Sit.

I sit next to him.

"Louisa's going to be mad," I say, slam-dunking the winning ball in the tournament of what-not-to-say in important moments of one's life.

"I'm sure," he says seriously. "She will definitely be mad." Jack scratches with the side of the corkscrew the metallized material protecting the cork on the bottle. He rips a line down the center and pulls it off like a waiter at Le Cirque. He sniffs the mouth of the wine bottle.

"Very nice," he says as he holds the bottle by the neck, whirling the bottom. "No wine glasses. We have to improvise." He takes a sip. "Ah," he swallows. "Perfect." He hands me the bottle. I take it, sip from it. I taste the wine as it sinks down my throat.

"Lovely," I say. "No expense spared, I suppose?"

Jack squints to see the label. "Millie's finest."

I grab it from him. "Millie doesn't make wine." I look at the label—it's from California.

"She does, but she only gives it to her most special friends."

"Like Louisa?" I ask.

"Why do you keep bringing her up?" *Why do I keep bringing her up?*

"I don't know," I say. But I do. Because she's the reason I'm here, because she's supposed to be with him, because this is not the way it should happen.

While I think this, Foxhole Girl speaks up and tells me maybe, just maybe, this is a good time to concentrate on myself.

"Louisa will be fine, I promise," Jack tells me. He looks at me, and I wonder what he thinks. I tell myself to be gentle, to be confident. Only the most self-loathing woman in the world would believe that a man would take a woman here, in full view of nature's glory, under God's most brilliant sky, and *not* think she is, at minimum, compelling. I am not that self-loathing. I am confident.

"I'm engaged," Jack says.

The word cuts the night, slicing the air and my heart cleanly.

"Excuse me?" I ask.

"Engaged. I'm engaged to a woman named Eliza." Where is that swan, where is the mean nasty vicious swan and why can't it swoop in right now and bite him in his vocal chords so he'll stop saying the word 'engaged'?

"Diana?" Jack calls. "You're okay, aren't you?"

"Oh, yeah," I answer. I am so happy it is dark. "I'm very okay." I drink from the wine bottle. I know it's wrong, but I can't help thinking how this is going to make Louisa livid.

"I didn't expect that."

"No, can't see why you would; I've been flirting with you all day." I can tell he's smiling. I don't think this is funny at all.

"Yes," I say. "You have been." Petulance, I am pure petulance.

"Yeah, I think I surprised everyone."

"Who else knows?"

"Fritz. And Rosie. I told her this afternoon, when you were out gabbing with Louisa."

"Rosie didn't tell Louisa?"

"Rosie would never do that. She understands."

"But it's her granddaughter, who's sort of—"

"Sort of what?"

"Nothing."

"What?"

"Nothing. I spoke out of—it isn't my business, never mind, don't ask me."

"Listen." Jack's voice deepens just a little; this is his serious voice. "Louisa's had a little fantasy about me since her marriage ended, just like she did when her last relationship ended, and the one before that, and probably the one before that; I've lost count."

"So you *would* be with her if she didn't keep calling you up after."

"What?"

"You know what I'm saying."

"No, I don't."

"Come on. You and she are a couple, then she leaves you for someone, and then she calls you back, and the first time you're hopeful, and the second time you think it's true love winning out, and the third and fourth time you realize that your feelings for her will never be matched by her feelings for you, so you go on with your life and find the woman you're going to marry, who is, by the way, where? Why isn't she here?" I'm suddenly indignant. Where are the *male* engagement rings?

"You're insane," Jack tells me. "I came here to tell her myself; I thought that was the right thing to do. But I haven't had a chance, with her as tour guide for the past twenty-four hours." He stops, looks around and then back at me. "What about you?"

"What about me what?"

"You're the mystery woman. Nobody can figure you out. Well, Rosie can, but she's not talking."

"Rosie doesn't know anything."

"You are so wrong. Rosie knows things that haven't happened yet."

"She said she had a feeling about me."

"Whatever it is, she knows."

"If she does, it's only because this guy told her stuff today."

"The guy in the Saab?"

"Nothing is a secret in this place."

"I wouldn't say that." Jack extends his hand toward my face, my cheek. *Oh my God.* He touches it, I hold my breath—and then he swats something off it.

"Spider," he says.

"Agh!" I jump up. "I hate spiders."

"Well, it's good it's dark then. Carlos told me there's hundreds of spiders on every inch of this place."

I'm still standing.

"Sit down." He tugs at my pant leg. "You didn't even know it was there till I touched you."

I sit back down. The spiders have gone; they have sensed my anxiety and they have fled. I hope.

"Why'd you take me here?" Now that I've discovered Jack's engaged, my suit of armor is off and I'm confident, flippant Diana, the woman with whom he should have fallen in love.

Jack doesn't say anything for a long while. When he does speak, he says, "Smell that air."

I inhale. And then I repeat, "Why'd you take me here?"

"Feel that breeze," he says.

"Not funny," I answer. "And I hate it when people ignore me."

"I don't know, Diana, I took you here because when I came back to where we were all sitting, you looked so pretty and so sad at the same time I just wanted to talk to you." He stops. "And I didn't think that was the best place for it. Good enough reason?"

I usually commit one of two errors: the talking-to-death-in-fledgling-relationships blunder or the stay-mute-at-all-costs faux pas for which I am legendary. This time, I'm somewhere in the middle, which ordinarily would be a major triumph. But it isn't, because Jack and I don't have a relationship. I would never be so presumptuous to construct a relationship with an engaged man, with an engaged man who has taken me to an unflooded cranberry bog.

That is, I don't think I would be so presumptuous.

Still, Jack sounds irritated that I forced him to explain what was just instinctual to him, and I pushed him there. Brilliant.

"It's an okay reason," I tell him.

"Okay?"

"There are better ones."

"Like?"

"Like . . ." I think for a moment. "Like I waited all day to whisk you away onto this field so we could sit under the stars; or like I knew from the moment I saw you, as I dangled over the chainlink fence, that I would carry you off with me to this unflooded cranberry bog." I pause dramatically. "Those would be better."

"Those would be lies."

"Well, thank you very much Prince Charming. I'm now going to move over here so the spiders can eat me in peace." I move over, an inch. Jack laughs and hands me the wine bottle. I drink from it, and as I do, Jack lies down, his back on the vines, his head resting on his bent elbows, staring at the sky.

I pull at the ground, inadvertently coming up with a two-foot stretch of a cranberry vine. I hold it, twirl it. Berries are still attached under tiny green leaves. I extend it toward Jack; I scratch him with it on his nose.

"Hey." He sits up, takes the vine from me. "If you tear up the place, I'm going to have to tell Carlos." He grins. "Or worse. Alice."

I smile. So does he—and as we do, the moment tiptoes over from friendly to charged. Eyes locked, I am quiet. We look at each other. I hear a voice saying *he's engaged, Diana,* but I know it's the Smiling Idiot talking, and I let Foxhole Girl kick her.

Jack takes the vine he's holding and puts the two ends together, making a circle. His eyes light up, and I see him grinning.

"What?" I ask, softly.

Jack reaches over and lightly puts this circle, this crown, onto my head.

"There," he says. "I hereby name you this year's Cranberry Queen." He reaches over and with his hand touches my face. I wait, *it must be a spider,* but he just touches my cheek, traces the side of my face, by my eyes, by my lips.

My hand rises, I take the hand that is tracing my face. We just look at each other, holding each other's fingers. And then he leans in, and we kiss.

Later

I do not know how long we kiss.

But that is all we do, and it is, all of it, wonderful, and later, Jack lies back down on the bog and looks up at the stars.

"What d'ya think, Diana, what d'ya think?" Jack speaks so softly it is like a murmur from the soft earth.

"About what?"

"Anything. Us. Existence. Farming. Motorcycles. Anything."

I have an urge to lie next to him, alongside him, imitating him, hands locked behind my head, staring up to the sky. For a moment, I remain, staring straight ahead, into the forest of pine trees. I think, It is only tonight, Diana, it is your memory, it is all yours.

I lie next to him.

The stars stare back at us, streaming against the sky in jumbled, sparkling patterns, an extraordinary sight. I think of us, how we look from the sky, two humans, outstretched, in the middle of a field, surrounded by trees. It would be a sight to behold, I think.

"My parents and brother were killed by a drunk driver four months and twelve days ago." I whisper this in a voice so delicate I do not recognize it as my own. I am not even sure I said it out loud.

Jack turns on his side, his head resting on his elbow.

"What did you say?"

I don't move. I remain staring up at the stars.

"My parents and my only brother were killed by a drunk driver exactly one hundred and thirty-three days ago."

"Diana," Jack says, reaching out to touch me. I move, sharply, and his hand hits my face.

"Ow!" I exclaim. I overreact because I don't know how to deal with what's about to happen. I know that outwardly I am just a body lying on the ground, and I know that inwardly I have burst into flames and it is all I can do to stop from running into the woods.

"Diana," Jack says more softly, and his voice matters, it makes me fall back slightly, back on my elbow. We face each other, lying on our sides. "Are you serious?" he asks me.

"No, I made it up; that's the kind of thing people just make up." This is how I respond to people when they are kind.

"Oh my God," he says. "That's—that's just monumental."

I want to say something like, You have no idea, or Good thing it can't happen again. But now I can't speak. Now I cry.

I sit up. I'm sobbing into my knees, I shake, it is the same frenzy I felt in my apartment, alone, wracked by pain and grief. I have cracked; it is a never-ending fall of despair.

Only now, here, under the stars, Jack holds me. Jack, this stranger, Louisa's Jack, someone else's fiancé, holds me. It makes all the difference.

And later, minutes, hours later, we hear them. Sirens.

Sewing

At first it is faint. My sobs have abated, I am just being held by Jack, as I hold his arms, which are stretched around me. I know he is engaged, I know he has promised to live for the rest of time with another woman, but for now, nothing else matters but this second.

But the noise grows. An external clanging, a scream growing louder, sirens.

We hear birds and animals move about the forest. The sirens blast through our serenity.

"Fire," says Jack. "It's gotta be the bonfire."

I wipe my eyes. Tomorrow I will have balloons on my face, puffy, fleshy, pouchy balloons smothering my eyes.

"Diana," he says. "We have to go back."

I look down to the bog. He's right. But as soon as I stand up, our moment is gone. I know it, and I don't want it to happen. The god or goddess who sews our lives has stopped only for this brief moment, and as soon as we stand, the needle will start up again, going in and out of our respective fabrics (his, no doubt, is a life as comfortable and content as broken-in Levi's; mine is probably a patchwork quilt with an empty hole in the middle where children should be).

I do not want to stand. But Jack has already stood up; he is tall against me, my head is at his knee.

"Diana," he repeats.

It is over. Over and ended, the door slams shut.

I stand. We both walk out of the bog toward the motorcycle at the same pace, not touching. It is over.

NINE

The First Time

As we ride, we hear the sirens, the screams, the cacophony of mayhem.

They've been having this event for years, and nothing's ever happened.

When we reach the area of the celebration, we see the fire trucks surrounding the bonfire. Hoses are pouring water, blasting the malevolent blaze with what seems to be all the water in the Pine Barrens. I look around. Soot covers many people as they huddle together near their pickup trucks. The fire has been prevented, so far, from reaching the perimeter of neighboring pine trees, but I can see the path it would take if given the chance. So can the firemen, and they are in its way.

"Hey—" Fritz spots us; he is covered in black ash.

"What happened?" asks Jack.

"A piece of wood from near the top pushed in, and a clump of burning wood fell over there." Fritz gestures with his hand. "I guess there were some remnants of blueberry bushes or something, and it all went up like a rocket. Luckily it just rained last week," Fritz continues, "so it's not as bad as it looks. It was dicey for a couple of minutes, but they think it's going to be contained."

I watch. The firemen are relentless in their effort to quench this blaze; the others don't seem to know what to do, so they pace, they huddle, they stare out at the flames, or turn away and look to the trees.

And then I see Rosie and Gabe. Gabe has his arm around Rosie; she wears a wool sweater over her housecoat. I run to them.

"Rosie," I call, "Rosie." She turns. I cannot interpret her expression. Gabe just stares at the fire.

"Diana." Rosie utters my name very faintly. "Diana, why didn't you tell us?"

Behind me, the fire burns. I feel it, I know it is there, illuminating this.

"Sam told me everything. Told us, me and Gabe." Rosie flinches; the sparks from the bonfire spray from behind us, one has just flicked by her face. "It isn't his fault—I forced him to tell me, I had such a suspicion. He's still here, you know."

I am not surprised that this has happened, that my secret has been revealed to Rosie. "I didn't know—I didn't know how to say it." I say this slowly, realizing it is true. "Are *you* okay?" I ask her.

"That's a dumb question." Gabe turns abruptly and answers me. "Look at all this, and you go ask a dumb question about Rosie. The whole place could be gone in a second." Gabe shakes his head as if he's never contemplated a more absurd creature than myself.

At that second, the fire goes dark, for one moment before it lights up again. Only when it does, it's diminished; the firemen have stopped the flames from creeping down the field.

"Why don't you go back to the house, Diana," Rosie suggests. "Louisa's waiting for you. And maybe Sam. I think the fire's under control, don't you think, honey?" She pulls at Gabe.

"I want to watch it a bit more," he says.

"Fair enough," she says.

"We'll talk later," Rosie tells me. I nod. In a different section of my brain that isn't saturated with Jack and fires, I recall that I have heard no verdict about Rosie's condition. But now is not the time. I turn and walk toward Fritz and Jack.

They are both transfixed by the fire. When I arrive, a slight smile crosses Jack's face. He pulls something out of my hair, a small section of vine with one tiny slice of cranberry caught in a tangled tress.

"Been rollicking around the bogs, have we?" asks Fritz. I blush and look down; although the force of the fire has diminished, there is still enough light from it to illuminate my reddening cheeks.

"Never you mind," says Jack.

"I don't mind," answers Fritz. "Live and let live, all the same to me."

"I'm going back to the house," I say.

"Now?" asks Jack.

"Yeah," I say. "Okay if I take the bike?"

"Sure," Jack answers. "Fritz's got me, right?"

Fritz says yeah, sure, but he's mesmerized by the fire again.

"Are you sure you're okay to go yourself?" asks Jack.

"Yeah," I tell him. "I'm sure."

As I walk away from the bonfire, past the pickup trucks, past the collection of fire engines, past the food thrown haphazardly on the ground, I inhale the air, the stench of the watered-down bonfire, the crisp October wind, the untainted part of the atmosphere that is as pristine as it was yesterday and will be tomorrow. Then after I've walked far enough away, I stop and turn back. I don't just focus on the fire; instead I cast my gaze way in the distance, above the fire, through the smoke, to the pine trees, to the dark sky, to the expanse that lies behind.

Rosie says it isn't about me. Jack says I'm the Cranberry Queen. It is time to go home.

My Drive

It is only about eight or so miles from the bonfire to Rosie's house.

As I drive by myself, I remember I arrived just yesterday.

I remember that it has been one hundred thirty-three days, maybe now one hundred thirty-four days, since I have talked to my mother. One hundred forty-six days since I've seen my mother and father. One hundred fifty-two since I've seen Ben.

I remember the Monster telling me that he had cheated on me. I remember Peter and me laughing at Darius behind his back at work. I remember going to Tavern on Jane with Wiley, and I remember a lonely night where I ate a slice of vanilla cake with buttercream icing for dinner. I recall, memories flying faster now, more of them, time-irrespective, memories of Mom telling me to be quiet in church, of Dad explaining what it means to be a Democrat, of Ben warning me away from his lascivious friends, of my grandmother, of roads I ran, of food I ate, a bowl of spaghetti, a plate of pancakes, a day at the river, a car, a bike, a blade of grass, a blue jay, a rose.

A crown of cranberries, a motorcycle, and a bonfire.

I pull into Rosie's driveway. The light is on in the kitchen. I alight from the bike and walk it to the garage. I take a deep breath, walk up the steps, and open the door.

Late Night

"Well," she says. "Look what the cat dragged in."

Sam and Louisa sit at the kitchen table, playing cards.

"I'm winning. I've won the last seven games. If you ask me, he's cheating, but that's his prerogative if he wants to cheat, it's still a loss. What do you owe me?" Louisa's on overdrive. I look at Sam. He shrugs.

"I think I'm down about a million two."

"Well, at least you admit it. Some men, just sore losers, if you ask me."

I take a seat at the table. Louisa deals the hand, omitting me. I don't say anything.

"Big night, huh, Diana? I know you live in the city and all, but this has to rank up there in the all-time wild escapades of Diana from Princeton. Think of the stories you can tell." She deals frantically now. In a different time, I would be sure she was having a cocaine rush.

"Louisa," I say, putting my hand on top of hers. "We have to talk."

"Oh, there she is, she's so dramatic, don't you think, Sam; did you ever notice that about Diana? We have to talk," Louisa mimics me, as if I sound like Richard Nixon. "We barely know each other. What do we have to talk about? There, Sam, there's your cards." She picks up hers.

"I don't know what you're thinking—actually, I may know, but that isn't it." Louisa puts two cards down, draws two from the deck, ignoring me.

What I do is unlike me. I pick up the deck and throw the cards on the floor.

"Oh, now you're active, now you're venturing forth," she taunts me. "Ruin a good card game, why don't you, or am I not allowed to play with any of your boys?"

I shake my head. Sam stays silent. Louisa gets up from her chair and begins picking up the cards.

"Wait," I say. She stops, looks up at me.

"I don't want to talk to you."

"Four months ago, my mother, father and brother were killed in a car accident."

The silence is prick-up-your-ears loud. Sam looks at the table. Louisa stands slowly. I continue.

"I've gone a bit crazy." My voice is dispassionate.

The kitchen light hits Louisa's cheekbones as she turns slightly to her left, then her right.

"Sam's my dad's—"

"Best friend. He told me," interrupts Louisa, "but he didn't tell me he was dead." Her voice mirrors mine, detached, unemotional. She sits down.

"I should have told you earlier, but you had concocted that story and that was sort of true too, but I didn't want to talk about it anymore, the deaths, that's why I left New York, that's why I was driving that day, that's why I wasn't paying attention." I stop. "That's it. That's my story."

Louisa folds her hands together on the table. Sam watches me, watches her. I move to the counter and rest against it. We can hear each other breathe.

"That's it," Louisa echoes. "That's your story." She stands up again, slowly, moves toward me. "That's your story," she repeats again. Sam backs up in his chair, alert.

"Your family was killed."

"Yes."

"And your brother."

"Yes."

"And you thought it was okay to come down here, you thought it was okay to come here, to my home, to my family, and lie, and fucking lie, and lie every day every fucking second. You thought this was okay, you—why, why didn't you tell me?" She hurls words at me as if she's heaving a bucket of boiling water at my face. "I can't believe you. I cannot fucking believe you. You make me feel like shit, you throw up some moral superiority to me out in the fields, you come here, you lie to us, to Rosie, who's fucking sick, Gabe, my family, my friends, who the fuck are you? Who do you think you are?"

"Louisa," begins Sam.

"Shut up," she says.

"I was going to tell you," I say. "But then—"

"Then you figured you could make me look stupid, you could make us all look stupid."

"Right, that's all I was thinking about, how to make you look stupid. That's all. Because I didn't have anything else on my mind, only you, always, always you." I'm livid too. "You set it up Louisa, not me. 'It's a guy,' you said. 'My Melodrama Queen,' you said. I didn't have to tell you the truth, I don't even know you. You have no idea what it means. Listen to me. My family is dead. *My family is dead.* I didn't have to tell you anything."

In Louisa's mind, the mechanism for absorption has cranked up. The cogs are moving, the wheels turning, she is taking my tragedy, mixing it with her life experience, spicing it up with the events of the past two days, pushing it through the dark chamber of her intelligence, all the cogs and wheels turning in her narrowing gyre, until she produces a sliver of comprehension, much like the jeweler who must cut through a block of black glistening rock for the one appreciable diamond.

"This is true?" she asks Sam. Sam nods. She's depleted. So am I. For a long while, none of us speak. Then Louisa walks over to the table, grabs the back of a chair.

"Where's Jack?" she asks, her tone even.

"Back at the bonfire," I answer, "with Fritz." I'm similarly composed. "Where's Billy?" I ask.

"He took someone to the hospital with Mr. Adamchak," she answers. "Apparently he volunteers as one of those guys in the ambulances, what do you call them—"

"EMTs," offers Sam.

"EMTs," continues Louisa. "He'll be back at some point, I guess." Her voice trails off. I look at Sam.

"What are you still doing here?" I ask.

"I had gone, actually, fairly far from here, but then I turned around and drove back. I didn't like the way we left it this afternoon."

"Me either," I say.

"You should go with Sam," Louisa says. The awful moment has passed. "Sounds like a great career opportunity." She stops for a second. "Listen to me, like I would know a great career opportunity if it hit me in the face." She gets up and takes a glass out of the cabinet. She turns on the faucet and fills the glass. She returns to her seat.

"Your parents and brother died?" she asks me.

"Yes," I answer.

"I don't know what to say to that," she tells me. "I really don't know what to say."

"No one does," I reply. I feel suddenly, under this bright light in the wee hours of the morning, displaced. It is as if I'm an actor on a stage, reciting words from a script about a woman whose family has died. It is not me, not Diana.

The screen door slams. Jack and Fritz enter. Louisa looks at them.

"I know everything," she says.

"Diana told you?" Jack asks. He looks at me strangely.

"Yes," Louisa says. "She just did."

"Well, I was going to get to it sooner or later. Eliza's a great girl, you'll like her."

Silence. We've gone from tragedy to comedy in less than ten words.

"Eliza? Who's Eliza?" Louisa's capacity for emotional absorption is about full.

"You don't know?" Jack repeats.

"Who are you talking about?" Louisa senses danger.

"I thought Diana told you." Jack looks at me for help.

"She told me about her family." Louisa stares at Jack.

"Oh." Jack holds onto the counter.

"What about her family?" asks Fritz. "What's she talking about?" He looks at me. I can see he's confused, but my own brain is ceasing to operate. I cannot help him.

"You all figure this out," I announce. "Sam, will you come talk to me?" Sam stands, nods to everyone, then follows me into the living room.

"Sam," I begin, but he cuts me off.

"Take your time," he tells me. "You don't have to tell me anything

227

right now. Whenever, if ever, you want to do something, call; I just want you to promise me you'll call."

"My dad thought you were very special," I say. I don't think he ever told him that; Dad wasn't one to express his feelings. "Mom did too," I continue. "I think they'd, well, we'll see. I'll figure it out, I think." I pause. "I hope."

"Me too," says Sam. He looks around the room. Gwen is there, as if she has not left since this morning.

I realize I am exhausted.

"You can sleep on the couch," I say. "That's where I was last night." I begin to walk up the stairs.

"There's room for you?" he asks.

"I'm the first one up here, aren't I?" I respond as I trudge up the steps.

I reach the landing and go to the first room on the left. The twin beds are neatly made up. I think for a moment I should go downstairs, I should make sure Louisa and Jack and Fritz and Sam are okay, that Rosie and Gabe are home safely, that Billy hasn't been hired by a South Jersey ambulance squad.

But instead I lie down on the bed nearest me. I close my eyes, and in moments I am asleep, deep black sleep, no magic birds, no fires, no cranberries, no people.

Daylight

By the time I walk downstairs, everyone has already eaten. Plates are stacked in the sink, stained with remnants of scrambled eggs and blots of ketchup. Around the table are Rosie, Gabe, Louisa, Jack, Billy, Fritz, and Sam. Gwen smacks her tail against the kitchen floor.

"Hi," I say, dreading the inquisition I'm about to receive.

"Morning, dear," says Rosie. "Coffee?"

"I got it," I say, and go to the cabinet. I've prepared my lines: I don't want to talk about it. It's hard, but I'm dealing with it and it'll be okay. Everyone says so. They'll chuckle at my attempt to be noble, and they'll all stammer condolences.

"You're kidding," I hear Billy say, my back turned, "over a bullfrog?"

"We couldn't sell the land, because the state said we had to protect a bullfrog, tree frog, whatever they called it." Rosie charms the table. There's a story being told. Not mine.

"It must be a special kind of frog," offers Jack.

"As opposed to the ordinary warts-giving kind," says Fritz.

"Frogs don't give warts," says Louisa. "That's just a silly old wives' tale. Like that other stuff, like you can't go swimming for an hour after you eat. You can, it's been proven."

I stand there listening, ignored again.

"Hey," says Jack. "Want to sit down?" There are no chairs. Jack stands.

"No," I say. "I'm okay."

"Here, dear," says Rosie, getting up and going to the stove. "We saved some eggs for you." She retrieves a plate from the cupboard and spoons the remaining eggs onto it. "Your car's ready, by the way. Mickey called this morning."

I wonder if I am to leave right this second, find Mickey the Mechanic, and go. But instead Rosie hands me the plate of eggs. I take it, look to the table. Fritz goes into the living room, returns with an extra chair.

"Here," he says. "We'll all squeeze." Everyone moves over so I can join them at the table. Now, now is when I'll get the third degree.

"Diana." Louisa looks at me. I grow tense. This isn't about to happen. "Do you think you can get me a free account with your company?"

"Yeah, sure," I answer, after a beat. "No problem."

"Good company," says Sam. "I know the founders from years back. Wonderful people, the kind who can't help making a million from any of their enterprises."

"I almost worked there," says Fritz. "But there was an issue."

"What's that?" asks Rosie.

"They had this thing about vacations."

"What?" I ask. "It's pretty normal, two weeks, three weeks after a while."

"I don't call that normal," Fritz answers. "Doesn't make sense to me to go to an office every day in your life when the entire world is just outside the door." He drinks some coffee. "Life's too short."

I glance around the table to see if anyone's looking at my reaction to Fritz's words. No one is. I frown. Shouldn't they notice?

"Well." Billy stands. "It's time I better be starting off."

I see packed bags on the floor, near the door.

"I may want to come back and take pictures next year, if that's okay," Billy says. "Maybe do a story or something."

"We'll ask Carlos, Sweetheart," says Rosie.

"They hate reporters," says Gabe.

"Yeah, well, lots of people do," Billy replies. He looks back to Rosie. "Thank you so much, for everything. I had a great time."

"Anytime, dear," says Rosie. "Anytime."

Fritz pushes back his chair. "I guess that's my cue." He stands too. "Although I'm thinking about staying."

"You'd fit right in," says Louisa.

"I don't know," says Jack. "Remember the Unabomber? Fritz might end up with the bullfrogs, no running water, and a long red beard."

"The wilderness," says Fritz. "Don't be scared of the wilderness."

Everyone at the table stands. I wonder if Jack is leaving now, will he say goodbye, how will he say goodbye. He could have forgotten about last night, he could have decided it just didn't matter, he could've—

"Keep your chin up," Billy says. It's the first anyone has said about my situation, and I'm surprised how grateful I am.

"Thanks," I say. Billy steps out of the doorway; the screen door slams behind him.

"Where's your car?" asks Jack.

"We left it at the firehouse, near where we had our tent," Fritz answers. Jack extends his hand. Fritz shakes it.

"Good to see you, man," says Fritz. "And congrats on the whole marriage thing. Can't wait to meet Mrs. Jack." I look at Louisa, ignoring the
bulldozer trampling over my own heart. But she doesn't meet my eye.
Instead she hugs Fritz.

"You could stay, you know," she says.

"Tempting, but I can't," he answers. "But I'll be back."

"I'll be counting the minutes," responds Louisa. They hug, and then a
quick kiss, on the lips. When they release one another from their embrace,
Fritz approaches me.

"Good luck, Diana," he says. I kiss him lightly on the cheek. "Keep in
touch."

I nod. Fritz then hugs Rosie, shakes Gabe's hand, and then he too is gone.

"Diana, dear," says Rosie. "You think you might help me hang these
clothes? It's a beautiful day, and I just love clothes dried in the wind, don't
you?"

"Not necessarily New York wind," I say.

"What she meant was—" from Louisa.

"It's pure down here," says Gabe. "Everything's pure down here."

I look from Gabe to Rosie. Gabe looks at Rosie while he speaks. Love
and the reality of cancer collide in his expression—these two are like the
thickest sailboat rope, used for years in races and jaunts and long trips,
rope that is finally, after decades of use, breaking.

I pick up the clothes hamper by Rosie's feet. Rosie walks out before
me. I follow, holding the door open with my foot, pushing against it with
the hamper. I walk to the backyard, where Rosie stands, next to a long
clothesline, holding a bag of clothespins.

I put the hamper on the ground and stretch out a towel. Rosie takes it,
clips one end to the rope with a pin, then motions for me to pick up
another towel.

"I always like to put things of matching size together," says Rosie. "That's how my mom used to do it. That's how she taught me."

Side by side, we hang the damp clothes on the clothesline. A breeze wafts past; the hanging fabrics barely move. Another towel. All of them white. A washcloth. A sock. A T-shirt.

"Thank you so much, Rosie," I say. Rosie turns to me, her hands holding a wet shirt of Gabe's.

"Don't," she answers. "Please don't." She hangs the shirt, clipping it at the shoulders. It looks strange, a big blue flannel shirt alongside white towels.

"My mother taught me to hang clothes, not sort them," Rosie says. "I've ruined more clothes than Carter's has liver pills."

"My mom used to say that," I say, which is true. I hand Rosie a white undershirt. She clips it to the line. "The doctor's?" I ask.

"Not good," she says.

"Did you tell Louisa?"

"No," Rosie answers. "And please, don't you tell her either."

"I wouldn't. Never."

"She guesses anyway," comments Rosie. "But there's nothing to be gained by going over it one more time. Anything I say she'll use as an excuse to stay here longer, hiding, and I just can't have that."

"I hardly think Louisa is hiding," I say.

"Yes," Rosie answers. "Forgive me, dear, but you must stop doing that."

"Doing what?"

"Doing what you just did. Louisa *is* hiding, you know that very well, yet for some reason you deny it out loud."

"I'm sorry," I start. "But I don't understand."

"Louisa isn't like you," Rosie says. "It's cruel for you to categorize her just because it's easy, especially when you know the truth. It's as if you told someone blind that they really could see. Louisa is hiding; anyone with a brain could see that, and you have a brain." Rosie picks up another undershirt from the basket. I am just standing there now, listening.

"I'm very sorry about your loss," says Rosie. "No one should have to go through that." She clips the shoulders, the thin cotton waving slightly in the wind. "But someone up there has a reason for keeping you on the earth without them, so you must make the best of it." She pins the final sock onto the line. The clothes stream in the wind; the air is pure and fresh, and I realize I want to use that towel, put on that sock.

"You must make the best of it," says Rosie. "Not in one day, not in one week, but over time we all die, we all start to die as soon as we're born." She stands, looking at me, her eyes bright and young.

"Maybe you could come and see me in New York," I say. I don't want to leave. *Don't die,* I plead. *Please don't die.*

"Maybe," answers Rosie. It is impossible what I want from her, and we both know this. "But I have a favor." Rosie puts her hand on my shoulder.

"Anything," I answer.

"Listen before you say yes, dear; you should always hear what you're agreeing to first." Rosie smiles. "Just talk to her, once a year, something like that, make sure she's okay."

"Oh, it'll definitely be more than that," I say, but I wonder if I am telling the truth. I am also struck that she hasn't mentioned looking after me. Don't I need someone checking in on *me?*

"She may behave abominably; she has before."

"Right," I say.

Rosie picks up the empty clothes basket.

"And this way," Rosie says, turning to walk in, "someone will check on *you.*"

Jack Redux

Sam and Jack have left by the time Rosie and I return to the house. Gabe sits on the porch with Louisa.

"They're leaving," Gabe says.

"Oh, dear," says Rosie. "They'll be back, won't they?"

"Sam just drove Jack to get his car," says Louisa. "They wouldn't leave without saying goodbye to Diana."

"Would you quit that?" I ask.

"Quit what?"

"Just don't do that," I say. "They wouldn't leave without saying goodbye to any of us."

"I didn't say they would. I just said they also wouldn't leave without saying goodbye to you. Don't get so huffy."

"I'm going to put this inside," says Rosie.

"Your car's done," says Gabe.

"I know," I say. "Trying to get rid of me?"

Gabe doesn't answer.

"You said you wanted to go," says Louisa.

"Well, I have to," I say.

"You don't have to go," interjects Gabe. I look up at him. He puffs on his cigar. "I was just giving you a hard time," he says. Gabe laughs to himself, the first time I've seen him crack a smile. I laugh too.

"Yeah, well," I say. "It's time."

"Time for what?" The porch door opens. It's Jack. I look at him and imagine our children. Timmy and Lucy. We are good parents.

"Time to go," I say.

"Good time, though," Jack says, "thanks to our gracious hosts." He smiles at Gabe and Louisa.

"I'm so glad you could come," enthuses Louisa. "It's been so long." Jack walks over to her, gives her a bear hug.

"Don't be a stranger," Jack tells Louisa.

"As if I could be," Louisa answers. "When you least expect it, I'll be there. And I'll want dinner, so tell your wife."

"She isn't my wife yet," Jack replies.

"Tell your fiancée," Louisa says. "I want steak. And spinach. And potatoes, lots of potatoes. And vanilla ice cream. And wine. Wait, scratch that. I'll bring the wine." Louisa stops. "No, scratch that too. *Diana* will bring the wine."

"Where am I bringing wine?" I ask.

"To Jack's, when we have that lovely dinner with him and his not-yet-wife." I can't tell if Louisa's being sweet or bitchy.

"You know the number," he says to Louisa.

"And you can be sure I'll use it," she says.

Jack shakes Gabe's hand. "Always a pleasure, sir," he says. Gabe raises an eyebrow.

"Get outta here," he says, but he claps him warmly on the back.

"Take care of her," Jack says. Gabe nods.

"She'll be okay." Gabe says.

"I meant Rosie," Jack continues.

"I know."

Jack turns to go inside. I don't move. I don't know the script that Jack and Gabe and Louisa have read from. The porch door slams behind Jack. Maybe that's it? Maybe I was too obvious in my Timmy and Lucy thoughts? Maybe I'm—

"Hey, Diana," Jack calls from inside. "Want to give me a hand?"

I stand in such a way that I am looking straight at Louisa. We both hear Jack's voice at the same time.

"Go ahead," says Louisa. "Don't worry about me." She looks straight at the road, alongside Gabe. Their faces are in profile, and they are similar. We are all noses and cheeks and brows and chins and—

"Don't you think you better go in now?" asks Louisa.

"Right," I say. "Right."

Volvos

I walk through the kitchen, where Rosie and Sam sit. They seem like old friends, two people who share a long history together, rather than one bereaved houseguest. Neither says a word as I walk by them and go out the door.

Jack's car is behind the house. It is the same exact car I drive, a 1990 Volvo. Only the color is different; his is black.

"What do you want me to carry?" I ask.

Jack looks at me, ever-so-slightly exasperated.

"Are you always so literal?" he asks.

"Oh," I say. "Right. Car's packed already, huh?"

I want to tell him so many things—that he should wait to get married and get to know me and realize what a great person I am and how happy we would be—but then I remember that he already has a woman with whom he's decided these things. Still, I have to tell him something.

"You know, I'm a Gemini." *And an idiot.*

"Is that right?" he answers. I don't know why he isn't talking to me, why isn't he saying something? But he doesn't. He just keeps looking at me. I feel like I should look to the ground, but something keeps me staring straight at him, looking into his eyes. We are in the children's game, the staring contest. Whoever blinks first loses.

Or, I hear Foxhole Girl, he's waiting for me.

"I—" It is my voice. "I think we, I think we have something here." Each word is a concrete block, and I feel lighter as each one drops from my lips. "I know you're engaged, but I just," I stop. The fog that is always in my head clears. *Keep going Diana, keep going. You know what to say.* "I just wanted you to know that we have something and," I stop. I hear the words in my mind, and then I say them out loud. "And that is enough, I think."

Give the girl a medal. She speaks, even if she isn't sure she's telling the truth.

"Strange, how it all works out," Jack says. I nod. I have a sensation that a long goodbye scene may be in the offing, and I realize I want no part of it. There is nothing left to say.

"One day at a time," says Jack. "One day at a time." He is now referring to my grief.

"I'll be okay," I say, and wonder if it is only me who makes pronouncements sound like they are profound truths rather than shifting, changeable assemblages of words.

Jack reaches in, he hugs me, just a couple of seconds, and then he lets go.

"And congratulations," I say, because I feel for some reason I need to be proper and embracing of this woman whom I've never met.

"You don't have to say that," Jack says, getting into his car. "That's another thing. You don't have to bring that here."

I know what he is saying. I keep trying to melt the reality of his life

239

outside the Pine Barrens with the reality we've experienced in the Pine Barrens, and it is not only unfair, it is incongruous.

"I've got the same car, you know," I tell him. "Only mine is green." The words mean nothing now, mere raindrops.

"Bye, Diana," he says.

"Bye, Jack," I say. He winks at me, and he is gone.

A Moment

I sit on the back step for a while after Jack leaves. I try to remember last night, what happened, and the only memory I feel, the only one I can relive, is Jack holding me.

Leave-Taking

Sam pushes out the door, hitting me in the back.

"I'm going with Rosie and Gabe to pick up your car," says Sam. "And then it's up to you whether you want to follow me back to the city."

I nod; I like it that other people are planning my departure.

"I think it's probably good to go back," I say.

The three of them leave, and I remain outside, waiting. And waiting. And waiting. I know they have all left because of Louisa, because we need to talk before I go, but why is it that I have to be the one to go inside?

I do anyway.

I walk through the house. Louisa is on the front porch, where I left her with Gabe minutes earlier.

"Hey," I say.

"Hey," she answers. She holds an unlit cigarette.

"New habit?" I ask.

"Just haven't gotten around to lighting it yet," she says.

"So—I should, I want to give you my address, my e-mail, all that," I say.

"Cool," she replies.

"You okay?" I ask.

"Me?" she replies. "I'm fine. You're the one to worry about."

"No, no, I'm okay. Really."

"Diana, you are the most un-okay person I have ever met."

"Then you must not meet many people."

I think we both almost laugh.

"And the whole Jack thing?" I ask, because I feel guilty.

"The whole Jack thing?" she repeats. "What whole Jack thing?"

"C'mon, Louisa, don't do that." I hate pretenders.

"Don't do what? You're talking in circles today, Diana. There's nothing wrong. I'm sad everyone's leaving, that's all."

"That's not all."

"Diana." Louisa turns to me. "Listen to me. That *is* all."

I know I cannot respond to this, but I do not understand. Louisa is sweeping her mind clean; Jack has been whisked into a little dustpan and thrown into her mental trash can. Now, like women before her and women after her, she is going to pretend she never had any romantic investment in Jack. It is called pride. I think it is absurd.

"Did you get to talk to him at all?"

"You're kidding me, right?"

"Not even about the engagement?"

"I was married, remember?" she tells me, so I can put up a tie on the scoreboard. She was married, he's engaged, they're even, and that is the only thing that matters. "Really Diana, you've got to go on with your life. I'm fine." She lights her cigarette, inhales.

"Great," I say. "I'm glad you're fine."

I sit down next to her, looking straight across the street at Millie's.

"I'm sorry," I begin. "I'm sorry I didn't tell you earlier about the accident."

Louisa inhales before she speaks. "I understand," she says. "I mean— you're right. I have no idea what it's like. I really have no idea." She smiles at me. "Can you believe I'm admitting you're right?"

"You'll change your mind in a second," I say, returning her smile. "Hey. Can I have a cigarette?" I ask.

"No," she says, her smile growing bigger, brighter. "No, you can't. You don't smoke."

"I was going to start."

"No, not on my time you're not."

"You can't tell me what to do. Maybe it's time for me to smoke."

"Maybe it's time for you to jump off a bridge." She inhales one last time, then throws the cigarette on the ground, crushing it under her feet. "But I do know what we should do one last time." She stands, grinning.

"What?" I ask.

"Come on," she says. For the last time, I follow.

Inhaling

Louisa and I drive around on her motorcycle one last time. We drive to Big Bog, we drive to the cranberry fields where Carlos is, we drive to the unflooded bogs where Jack and I were last night.

I close my eyes underneath my helmet. I take a deep breath. There are no secrets anymore, there is nothing left to reveal. There is only Louisa and I, on this motorcycle, in this place of farmland and bogs and pine trees. If we were in a movie scene, this would be the part where a helicopter would film us from above, an aerial view, the two of us just a tiny dot zooming on a miniature and untraveled road, cutting and swerving in between dense swatches of trees, under the blue sky, alive.

TEN

Three Hundred and Twenty-two Days Later

It is April. I am moving to San Francisco in two weeks. Sam says he found a place for me, an apartment that he says is a big improvement to the "rustic" place I have now. (I say that he's a snob and that he doesn't appreciate what it means to live in New York. He tells me it isn't about snobbery; it's about a skylight falling on a person's head. That happened in January after a snowstorm. I needed stitches.)

We've decided to start an atypical investment company: We will give money to people whom we trust, in exchange for an ownership stake and a fair rate of return. We've been told we are remarkably naive, but really, it just doesn't matter. We have enough money, both of us. Plus, we figure more people will want to work with us once they realize we're telling the truth and we're not out to rape their bank accounts or their hard-earned money. I have no idea what I'm doing, but Sam says he's sure I am a good judge of character, and that's eighty-five percent of it. He has the remaining fifteen percent—actual experience and contacts—so he thinks we should be fine, although, as I tell him all the time, "fine" is a shifting concept, one I do not trust.

Wiley and her new husband, Christopher, are coming to visit me in June.

Betsy and Aunt Margaret and Uncle John and Peter think moving to San Francisco is a good idea, albeit a temporary displacement. You're gonna die without the big city, says Betsy. I give you six months, says Peter. Then you'll take Darius's offer and come running back, professing your love for him and his tight pants.

The Monster got married to someone whose name begins with "K." I saw it in the *New York Times* wedding section. We have not spoken in more than three years.

Fritz and I exchange long, funny e-mails. He's currently in Canada, skiing from Ontario to British Columbia. Because he persists in attempting these "epic adventures," I expect every day to get an e-mail stating that he has been killed—by starvation, by freezing to death, or by becoming dinner for a nasty twelve-foot-tall polar bear. But when I examine the pictures he sends me, of stark flat landscapes and multicolored sunrises, of white-toothed wolves and ramshackle rowhouses, I understand.

Billy, according to Fritz, left reporting and writes for a sitcom in Los Angeles.

Jack's wedding is in June. He sent me a Christmas card last year, signed only "Jack" and addressed to "The Cranberry Queen." I have decided I do not like his sense of humor and therefore it is a good thing he is marrying someone else.

Rosie is still alive, but she is in a hospital now, in Philadelphia. I have driven to the Pine Barrens four times since last October. Each time, she is worse. Yet she remains gracious and forthright, and each time I visit she reminds me I promised to check in on Louisa.

I take Gabe to church on Sundays when I visit. We don't talk much, but the last time I was there, he leaned over and clasped my hand before he got out of the car. It is heartbreaking to see him without Rosie, and it is heartbreaking to see him with Rosie. The rope has almost snapped, and I can see that Gabe already feels as if he is alone.

Then, of course, there is Louisa. I have kept my promise to Rosie. We've seen each other several times, in Philadelphia—where she lives now, with her mother and father—and in New York, where we've gone to dinners, Broadway shows, Ellis Island and Bergdorf's. Most of our time together is quite fun, a friendship between opposites that seems to flourish in spite of ourselves. But there have been moments when I wish I had never agreed to Rosie's request—when we've screamed at each other and I've vowed never to see her again. But I can't do that—not to Rosie, nor to her, nor to myself. Sometimes I see the two of us as old ladies, rocking on a chair on somebody's porch, arguing over something neither of us considers important. Other times, I see our friendship as a sealed envelope, intended to be understood but never opened.

Ben and Dad and Mom, always Mom, run around my mind as they have every single day since last June. Mom tells me to change my sheets. Dad tells me I have to start investing wisely but to stay away from technology stocks. He also wants me to get married and does not understand why I am still single. Ben does not understand why I have not made it a priority to attend every single Springsteen concert on the planet. It is not nearly enough, these voices, but it is all I have.

ELEVEN

Today

Rosie died yesterday. By May, the cancer had entered her brain, tumors growing like peaches. She wanted to go home, to go to the Pine Barrens and die in
her bed, so one night, her brain operating on a different channel, she snuck
out of her bed, found the stairs, and climbed to the roof. Pushing open the
door, she thought she found what she wanted, her home. Instead, it was just
a gray-painted roof under a dark May sky in Philadelphia. The problem was
that she had locked herself out. People looked for her everywhere—in the
stairwells, in the rooms—her face was flashed on television and in the newspapers and everyone in the Pine Barrens went on search missions, suspecting
that maybe Rosie had convinced someone to drive her home.

No one knows if it was the cancer or the lack of food and water that
ultimately killed her, but when they finally opened the door to the roof and
found Rosie's body, she was lying on her side, curled up. But she was facing
east, and I like to believe that she was seeing the Pine Barrens instead of
Philadelphia when she drew her last breath.

Louisa thinks she must control every facet of the funeral, that she must be in control no matter what her mother and father and Gabe say; she's the only one who can make the funeral perfect. Her eyes seem vacant, her energy jagged and frenzied. She does not cry, and she does not want my help. She can do this alone.

Tomorrow

It is September.

The postcard was brief. *"Wedding off. Heading west. I'll call. Jack."*

It is almost impossible for me to believe in this speck of hope that has just floated into my life. I see it as one does spots in front of one's eyes, but when I reach out to hold it, there is nothing there.

But it is all about hope. Hope that exists, visible or not, a rung on a ladder in a foxhole, or a night under stars in a cranberry bog, or something else altogether that ignites you, that lifts your thoughts and your energies toward the next minute, the next day.

I hope I have a child.

I hope there is a heaven like I learned in Catholic school so I can see my mother and father and brother again, frolicking amidst farmlands, trading floors, and a Bruce Springsteen concert.

I hope that the money I just persuaded Sam to invest against his better judgment in an independent (gasp) movie won't be lost.

I hope Gabe finds peace and that Louisa finds whatever it is she wants to find and that it isn't hallucinogenic.

And I hope that I retain, even in this tiniest of forms, even if I am hurled up up up in the air, the faith that nature will find me, tap me on my shoulder, and lead me on my way.

Acknowledgments

While the Pine Barrens are very much real, the rest of the book is fiction, and any resemblance to anyone alive or dead is purely coincidental and unintentional.

My family—Mark and Lucy DeMarco, Anthony DeMarco, and Jennifer Applegate, Barbara DeMarco Reiche and Dean Reiche, Mark DeMarco, and Christopher Reiche—is the source of love, humor and support to which I turn every day. (Sometimes twice.)

My grandfather, Anthony R. DeMarco, was killed before I was born by a drunk driver on Route 206 in New Jersey; he is the visionary who purchased thousands of acres of land in the New Jersey Pine Barrens because he wanted to work outdoors. His wife, my adored grandmother, Gladys Alloway DeMarco, was a descendant of a family who began cranberry farming in the Pine Barrens centuries ago. My uncles and aunt—J. Garfield DeMarco, Angelo Falciani, Anna Lynne & Robert Allen Papinchak—have taught me much about the dual powers of creativity and academic discipline. Also deserving thanks are all the people who now and in the past worked on our family farm, including Pat Slavin, Ron Ogle, Don Ogle, Earl Kershner, Marcella Stevenson, Luke DeLeon and the late Cuci Monzo and Bill Scott.

It is a privilege to work with John Leguizamo, the most decent and most talented person I know. Laura Dail is a friend first, agent second, and an inspiration always. My editor, Jonathan Burnham, imparted such significant commentary that the book was reshaped without, I think, losing its intended spirit. I am profoundly grateful for his input. Thank you, also, to Christine Verleny, James Adams, Steve Hutensky, Ira Schreck, Kristin Powers, Farley Chase, Hilary Bass and Kathy Schneider.

Tad Roach, Al Filreis and Shelley Evans are extraordinary teachers who could not know how important it was for me to have their encouragement.

Many people assumed the burden of reading this novel in its early drafts. For this, and their continuous friendship, I thank: Lynda Radosevich, Hillary Lane, Betsy Kramer, Susan Fine, Carrie Cohen, Elise Pettus, Jennifer Dewis, Lindsay Marx, Frank Pugliese, Doug & Eliza Burden, Julie Merberg, Jane Lury and Scott Omelianuk.

In addition to those mentioned above, the following people have been, and continue to be, the support system for which I continually give thanks every day: Meg & Tom MacClarence, Jenny & Burt McHugh, Laura & Stuart Parker, Michelle & Tom Roloff, Stephanie & Peter Ahl, Alison Churchill, Alicia Sams, Diana and Matthew Weymar, Eunice Lee, Ted Madara, Matthew Baird, Winston Goodbody, Eric Hamilton, Alexis Alexanian, Martina Papinchak, Gillian Grisman, Matthew Horvat, Nick Adamchak, Dan & Sally Wigutow, Matthew Bardin & Mo Ogrodnik, Arielle Tepper, Charles & Sean Silver, Leanne & Michael Graeff, Geoffrey Smith, Alexander Fields, Georgina Sanger, Mike & Lisa O'Malley, Mac &

Acknowledgments

Toni MacClarence, Lisa Hintelmann, Dan Goldman, Theresa & Richard Lanza and Bob & Margaret Wallis.

And finally I want to single out three people: Julie Cohen (because she would never forgive me if I didn't), Jamie Levitt (because I know no one more loyal, exuberant and smart), and Liz Baird (because she is my best friend).

ABOUT THIS BOOK

"The butterfly flutters past, its white wings flashing, sprinting toward the lake. I look up and see another one, orange-and-black wings, alighting for an instant on a tuft of green spindly weeds, until it flies away in front of me, until it goes out of sight. I check my watch. I am far away from everything I know. The Fates have (finally) intervened and thrown me here . . ."

It should not take a tragedy to put life in perspective. As *Cranberry Queen* opens, Diana Moore, a thirty-three-year-old single woman living in Manhattan, is despairing over an ex-boyfriend and obsessing about her dot.com job. She is consumed with the prospect of attending a wedding the following day where her ex and his new girlfriend will also be guests and sees this as a defining moment in her life. Diana is right that the day will change her life, but not for the reason she believes. Instead a tragedy occurs that unravels Diana's world and redefines it.

After months spent trying to cope with her grief, Diana tires of the well-intentioned interference of family and friends. She walks out on her life, driving aimlessly through the back roads of New Jersey. She reaches a destination by default when she has a minor car accident, landing in the Pine Barrens in a rural corner of the state. It is here in this oasis of simple living, cranberries, and tradition—and where she tells no one of the tragedy she has endured—that Diana is temporarily free of the confines of her life. Here she can be "someone else, someone new and different. Diana Moore, adventurer."

Embraced by a group of strangers, Diana is asked to stay for the upcoming cranberry harvest and celebration. She meets Rosie, a woman who is dying of cancer yet determined to live life to the fullest; Louisa, Rosie's beautiful and abrasive granddaughter who is hiding out in the Pine Barrens for reasons of her own; Jack, who touches Diana's fragile heart in the most unexpected of ways; and Sam, a mysterious man who gives Diana the chance for a new beginning. In this hidden landscape of intoxicating beauty, and with these newfound friends, Diana is finally able to explore the possibilities of change and renewal.

Cranberry Queen is a poignant and mesmerizing debut novel about life's most complex contradictions—hope and despair, love and loss, life and death. Kathleen DeMarco's vivid prose, laced with sharp wit, a sardonic sense of humor, and compelling candor, brings to life the bittersweet story of a woman's resilience in the most adverse of situations.

QUESTIONS FOR DISCUSSION

1. The first person narrative allows the reader to view the story entirely from Diana's perspective. What do you think of the narrative style? Were you comfortable being inside Diana's head the entire story?

2. At one point in the story, Diana says of her family and friends, "I pretend to everyone that I am okay, the Super Recoverer, and then, at night, I am infuriated that everyone believes me. Are they dumb? Or do they just not care?" (pg. 17).What do you think of this statement? Is Diana being fair to them? Is she justified in having these feelings?

3. A turning point for Diana happens when she hits Rosie with her car, an incident that is eerily reminiscent of what happened to Diana's parents. Why do you think the author chose this occurrence as the catalyst for Diana remaining in the Pine Barrens?

4. In one instance Diana says, "No wonder I have no boyfriend; I say awful things. I think awful things. I'm trying for that gallows humor, and instead I'm churlish and unfunny" (pg. 11). Do you agree with Diana's assessment of herself? Does her self-image change as the story progresses? How does she appear to the people around her?

5. Why does Diana allow Rosie, Louisa, and the others to believe that she is distraught over the breakup with her boyfriend? Why doesn't she tell them the truth?

6. How would you characterize Louisa? At times Louisa is cruel to Diana. Why does Diana remain in the Pine Barrens given

these circumstances? How did you react to Louisa's motivations and behaviors? Did you empathize at all with Louisa?

7. When Sam tracks down Diana in the Pine Barrens, why does she at first rebuff his offer of kindness and support?

8. Do you think the author has effectively portrayed the emotions of someone who has suffered a tragedy? How about the actions of the people around her?

9. During their first encounter in the woods, Diana sees Jack only from a distance and yet she feels an instant attraction to him. What is it about Jack that attracts her to him? Why does Diana reveal the truth about her family to Jack when she hasn't told the others?

10. Diana seeks refuge with her new friends in the Pine Barrens for her own reasons, but how does she in turn help and influence the people that she meets?

AUTHOR INTERVIEW

1. Most of the book takes place in the Pine Barrens in Southern New Jersey. Is this near where you grew up? Did you travel these same back roads and explore the cranberry bogs when you were younger, or just when you researched this book?

I grew up in a terrific small town called Hammonton, NJ, which is smack in the center of the southern portion of the state— equidistant between Philadelphia and Atlantic City. The majority of the book takes place in and near a town called Chatsworth, NJ, which is exactly 28 miles from Hammonton, driving north on Route 206. The reason I know the exact distance is because almost every day during every summer, from 1970 until 1984, my family and I drove to Chatsworth to work on our family's cranberry (and at the time, blueberry) farm. When I was a child, my mother would drive my three siblings and myself to the farm to pick blueberries; beginning at 11, I "packed" blueberries— meaning I put the cellophane and rubber band on top of the fresh-picked pints of blueberries that just came in from the fields. Also, when I was a teenager, I used to spend my lunchtimes cruising about the back roads in the Pine Barrens on a dirt bike with other "packers"—and I still can't remember a moment more blissful. In fact, I haven't been on a motorcycle through the Pine Barrens since I was eighteen— which, alas, is now many years ago—but the memory remains as potent as ever.

2. Have you ever attended a cranberry festival?

While there is a cranberry festival every year in Chatsworth during October (the time of the cranberry harvest), and while I've attended it one time (and was sort of aghast at the 40,000 people crowding this tiny, one-road town), the cranberry celebration in the book was invented— drawing from some of the smaller barbecues we used to have at the farm, as well as some of the bonfire celebrations we had in Hammonton while I was growing up.

3. Aside from the setting, did you draw on aspects of your own life and experiences for the plot and characters in this book?

Whenever I hear this question I want to say "well no, because clearly I'm a happily married grandmother with six children with a background in astrophysics. Diana and Louisa, etc., are completely made up." But as I am a single woman in her thirties living in—yes, a fifth-floor walk up in the West Village—I certainly did draw on my own life experience for many of the novel's plot and characters. I do want to be clear that my mother, father, older brother (and sister, and younger brother) are all alive and well—there is no immediate autobiographical truth to the tragic accident Diana confronts early in the novel. (As I say in the acknowledgments, however, the accident I describe in the novel is the way my grandfather was killed in 1964, before I was born.)

4. Cranberry Queen is a very visual book. Did your work in film influence your writing?

That was sort of inescapable for me—I have written hundreds of treatments for films and television movies and have read probably thousands of movie scripts over the past nine years. The cardinal rule in screenwriting is "show, don't tell," and while a novel is certainly a forum through which I can tell (and do tell, some would say, ad nauseum), I don't think I could write anything in prose form that wouldn't have a strong visual component. It is, for all intents and purposes, my "training."

5. Diana uses humor to help cope with the despair she is feeling. Do you also use humor to deal with tough times?

No. Instead I do what I think any self-respecting adult should do in times of trouble: I beat myself to a pulp with whatever apparatus I have nearby—a hairbrush, a keychain, A HEARTBREAKING WORK OF STAGGERING GENIUS, whatever. All right . . . I suppose, however, that I do sometimes resort to humor, but only if it's very serious. Otherwise Breyer's vanilla ice cream usually does the trick.

6. Do you relate more to Diana or Louisa?

Well . . . there are certainly parts of me in both characters . . . but I suppose Diana is the character who is closer to me, since her inclination is almost always to hide what she's truly thinking and instead say only that which she thinks other people want to hear. Not the most wonderful of traits, I don't think, but it certainly keeps confrontations to a minimum.

7. This book has at its center an extremely emotional issue—not only the loss of someone close to you, but also the loss of three people, an entire immediate family. Was it difficult for you to write about this topic?

Without question, this was the hardest part about writing the novel. I didn't intend on killing everyone on page four—I just knew very quickly that I couldn't sustain an entire novel about Diana's heartbreak. I am extremely close to my entire family—so to have to think about living without them, which is what I had to do to write about Diana post-accident, was not only grim, but torturous.

8. Each chapter contains a number of subheadings. Did you plan to do this from the start, or is it something that evolved during the writing process?

I didn't plan on this at all—what happened is that I would tell myself I had to finish one chapter every morning, so it just helped me psychologically to name each one so I had a definitive goal, i.e. "Finish Foxhole Girl now . . . and then go and eat a cupcake."

9. What is the one "message" you would like people to come away with after reading this book?

I'm not really a "message" person—but I will say that last October, when I turned in the final manuscript, I told my editor excitedly "the book is about hopelessness to hope!" To which he replied, "You're just getting that? Well, they say authors are the last to know . . ." I suppose Diana learns to engage again in life, i.e. to hope once more, but on her own terms. (No "stiff upper lip" for Diana—she willfully falls apart in public, uncaring what others think, until she figures out herself, and with the help of some friends, how to put her toe back in the water again.)

10. Are you working on another novel?

Yes. It's called *Pheasant King* . . . okay, that's a lie. In truth, the next novel will be another character-driven story set today in both LA and NYC, although I wouldn't be surprised if some of the characters end up (if only for a moment) in the Pine Barrens—I'm too attached to the place for it not to reappear!